Goodwood
Holly Throsby

ALLEN&UNWIN
SYDNEY • MELBOURNE • AUCKLAND • LONDON

This edition published in 2018
First published in 2016

Allen & Unwin
83 Alexander Street
Crows Nest NSW 2065
Australia
Phone: (61 2) 8425 0100
Email: info@allenandunwin.com
Web: www.allenandunwin.com

A catalogue record for this
book is available from the
National Library of Australia

ISBN 978 1 76063 334 9

Text design by gogoGingko
Set in Perpetua Std by Bookhouse, Sydney
Printed in Australia by McPherson's Printing Group

10 9 8 7 6 5 4 3 2 1

Holly Throsby is a songwriter, musician and novelist from Sydney, Australia. She has released four critically acclaimed solo albums, a collection of original children's songs, and an album as part of the band, Seeker Lover Keeper. *Goodwood* is Holly's debut novel.

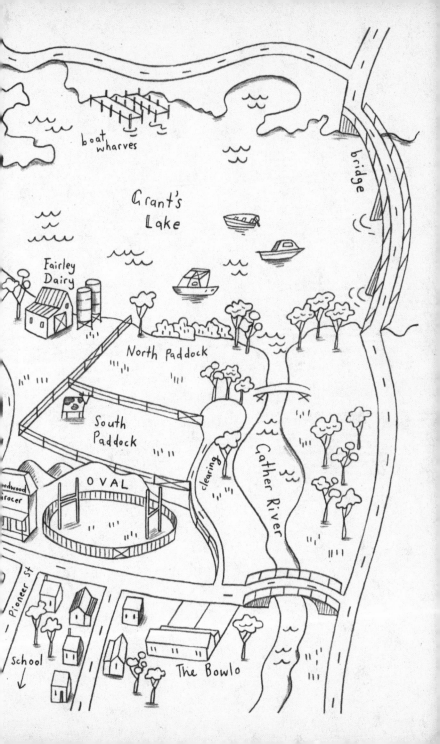

For Alvy

1

Goodwood was a peaceful town before the tragedies. It sat itself quietly between a mountain and a river. After a long stretch of flowing, the river became a lake. The lake was vast and brown and brimming with bream. It was a top spot for fishing and boats cut silver waves across it on the weekend.

As any one of its long-time residents would've said, Goodwood was a glass-half-full kind of town, and weekends were a trusted time. People washed their cars in their driveways of a Saturday. They baked and mowed while their dogs slept in shade. Sundays were dozy and mainly for fishing. And the first one of the month meant a little market in Sweetmans Park where a few dismal stalls sold enormous pumpkins and disappointing jams.

A green metal sign announced the township as you drove in—past the Bowlo, past the oval, under the mountain. *Welcome to Goodwood*, it said, with the sound of the brown river, and the smell of cows and fish. Front doors hung wide open in warm weather. The bar at the Wicko hummed with drinking. Wood-panelled television sets glowed and flickered on living room walls of an evening. Backyard swing sets creaked with children. People died of heart attacks and strokes and cancers and time, lying in their beds at twilight, or sitting in their cushioned reading chairs.

It was generally considered a good thing that Goodwood was home to small, humble lives that didn't bear much mention. Events that were regarded as dramatic were a minor traffic incident or a lack of rain. It was not a place where you'd expect to find corpses. There were no bodies on the forest floor, entwined like vines, hurtled from a harmless existence by rage or madness or spite. Horror did not visit Goodwood. Nor did sorrow—or not in the way we would come to know it so well.

I was born in the city but we only lived there till I was two, which was when Mum moved us to Goodwood to be close to my Nan and Pop. They had a big brown brick house, with a rose garden out the front, and a verandah with cane furniture on it. I liked to lie on Nan's daybed and get a good view of the street, where there were never that many people, but of what people there were, everybody knew everybody, no question.

Mum had a lot of friends. She gardened with company and joined clubs and took minutes. Most mornings in high school I ate brown toast and Mum told me about her CWA class or the latest meeting at the hall. Mum's cousin Mack was Goodwood's own Constable 'Mack' Mackenzie. He sat on our couch commonly and drank Reschs Pilsener. Mum and Mack were very social, which was nice, because they mingled a lot and talked a lot and I liked to hear about people.

Everybody knew everybody, no joke. Including me, including Mum and Mack; and Big Jim and Fitzy next door; and Nance who ran the Grocer; and my Nan and my Pop. A person in Goodwood was forgiven for knowing the intimate business of their neighbours and their neighbours' neighbours, just for the sheer proximity, as well as the chatter, and the simple fact that seeing and hearing is, to some degree, knowing. There was Helen at the newsagent, having one of her panics; or Smithy at the Wicko, having deep feelings; or Coral, from two doors up, who was ancient and dragged her tartan shopping trolley past our house twice a day, the wheels singing like a baby bird.

Everything in my memory was regular and pleasant and unremarkable before the disappearances. That was in 1992, when I was seventeen and the winter had set in, making our breath misty and our curtains drawn.

It wasn't just one person who went missing, it was two. Two very different people. They were there, and then they were gone, as if through a crack in the sky. After that, in a small town like Goodwood, where we had what Nan called

3

'a high density of acquaintanceship', everything stopped. Or at least it felt that way. The normal feeling of things stopped. Hope dwindled like an unstoked fire. And before too long the grief crawled in. A plague of sadness infected our shop fronts. It rested on our awnings and nested in our gardens and gnawed its way through the walls of our houses.

First, it was Rosie White.

She was eighteen years old when she dropped off the face of the earth, one year older than me. Years are long when you're younger, and each one makes a marked difference. Rosie was almost a whole year clear of high school and working at Woody's Takeaway on Cedar Street. She was older and cooler and prouder and free.

My best friend George and I would stand by the drinks fridge, waiting for our hot chips, and try to pretend we weren't intimidated by Rosie. But we were. We loved her; and we wished more than anything that she'd say something— anything—and preferably say it in our direction so we might feel like we belonged; like we might one day be her friends; like we were, in some way, a part of her faraway and much more interesting world.

Mostly, though, Rosie didn't say an awful lot. She half-smiled and kept a look of deep intensity. Then she'd turn to the bain-marie to retrieve a pie and George and I would stand back and silently admire her clothes, which were a spirited combination of the army green racks at the Clarke Disposal

4

Store and the black and flannel racks at the Goodwood Vinnies, where Val Sparks worshipped a porcelain baby Jesus and listened to old pop songs on a silver radio.

Many boys in Goodwood wanted Rosie—encouraged, in part, because she didn't want them. She walked along with her headphones on, as big as earmuffs, and there was always something defiantly unapproachable about her. Of course, her remoteness attracted many a rebellious boy to the grand idea of approaching her, but that never turned out so well. She dismissed their advances summarily, with some form of wry put-down, and it only made them, and us, love her more.

I saw Rosie behind the counter at Woody's every weekday when I went past on my way home from school or took Backflip for a walk along the river. Then, one day in August 1992, she was gone. And in her place were more questions than one town had ever asked about a single subject.

•

A week after the last sighting of Rosie—by her mother, Judy White, who saw her close her bedroom door after saying her goodnights, only to not be there the next day to say her goodmornings—Bart McDonald vanished.

Bart ran Bart's Meats—*Pleased to Meat You!* said the sign on the awning—and was tremendously popular as a member of the Gather Region Council, co-president of the Goodwood Progress Association, and the main provider of the myriad meats required for Goodwood's long tradition of backyard barbeques. Bart was also just a terrific guy. He clinked more beer glasses than any other man in town. He fished the lake with constant enthusiasm. He had a deep hearty laugh and was fluent in good advice. Bart had time for everyone. His face was kind and his skin was weathered, like he'd fished a lot, and drank a lot, and otherwise lived in it thoroughly. If Goodwood had designated one person as the sole recipient of its unalloyed affection, that person would have been Bart McDonald.

On the Sunday, Bart went fishing on Grants Lake and never came home. His boat was found drifting like a cloud. On it were his lures, his bucket, his scaling knife, chopping board, esky and a half-drunk beer, snug in his favourite stubby holder that said *Goodwood's Good For Wood* with a picture of the old sawmill and a cartoon man superimposed on top, winking at a blushing lady.

All that, but no Bart.

In the days after he vanished, Mrs Bart, as everyone called her, even though her name was Flora McDonald, paced the inside of her husband's shop window, the silver trays empty except for the green plastic trimming that made the meat look pastoral.

Mum said maybe Mrs Bart thought the shop was the most obvious place to wait, since ordinarily Bart did seem to be there every minute of the day, six days a week. 'Everyone grieves in their own way,' said Mum. I said I would've waited at home, with the blinds drawn, so no one could have seen me pacing. But Mrs Bart was still there in the evenings, patrolling under unkind fluorescent lights, or staring at the trays where the meat should be, as if desperate for a sirloin.

Divers dived for Bart. George and I stood on the side of the lake where a group from town had gathered and we counted four men in scuba attire. They searched all morning, snacked on the police boat at lunchtime, and then went over the side again, only to come up empty-handed at sundown.

Some people in town thought they should've spent more days searching. It was just the two. But the police who attended, apart from Mack, seemed to hang a big question mark over whether Bart had drowned at all, and there was speculation among the police from Clarke that he'd done a runner. We saw one officer giggling in his flippers. The indignity of laughter in the face of such tragedy was not appreciated by the local huddle. The general consensus among the community—some of us gathered by the lake on the browned grass near the boat wharves, others sitting hopefully in the safety of their houses while Mrs Bart paced and paced—was that Bart had certainly not done a runner. How could he? And how could he leave Pearl?

No. The people of Goodwood knew Bart McDonald. And Bart McDonald did not leave of his own accord.

The Thursday after he vanished, the McDonalds' son Joe arrived from Sydney. On the Friday morning, promptly at nine, he opened up Bart's Meats again, in an attempt at familial support. The fluorescent lights flickered on. Lamb and beef were piled high on the silver trays, and price tags with smiling sheep and cows were inserted among burly Joe's meaty display. Mrs Bart stopped pacing and started sitting, on a stool in the corner behind the counter. She did not serve customers. She just sat, staring out the window, as if Bart might materialise, covered in lakeweed, and wander into the shop asking for a towel.

Coral, from two doors up, said that when she went in on the Friday afternoon, Joe was holding Mrs Bart against his generous chest while she wept, and he appeared teary himself when Coral asked for two lamb cutlets. Suffice to say, buying meat became a sombre affair and some people in town were subdued into reluctant vegetarianism, or drove the forty minutes to the big Woolworths in Clarke.

In the week preceding, when it was just Rosie missing, there were no divers. There was no evidence she was in the lake. There was no evidence she was anywhere. Mack, accompanied by Sergeant Simmons from Clarke, made a formal visit to the White residence, with formal manners, to alert them that a missing persons report had been formally filed.

'It's just a formality,' said Mack. 'She'll show up.'

Judy White, clad in blue denim, sobbed on the front steps. Later, Opal Jones from next door, leaning out her living-room window with both ears cocked, heard Judy wailing somewhere indoors, a sound that continued well into the night.

The day after Rosie vanished, I rerouted my walk to school to take me past the Whites' house, with clouds for breath and my face stinging with cold, hoping for a glimpse of *something*. A clue? A lonesome light on? A suggestive silhouette at Rosie's window?

All I saw was Terry, Rosie's brother, sitting in the passenger seat of Judy's car in the drive, behind a frosted windshield, wearing Rosie's cardigan. He just sat there, covered in pimples, with no destination or driver, for as long as it took me to get to the end of the road, and who knows for how long after.

•

That's how it all started.

First Rosie, and then Bart. Two people from Goodwood— two very different people—inexplicably gone. And the rest of town holding its breath.

After that, a lot of things happened. There was a mess of conjecture, and a great many theories and stoushes. Dozens of beer glasses were set down in misery, precious hopes were forsaken, and blood spilled from the most unlikely. All the while, gallons of brown water ran along the river, filled with fish, and surged under the bridge into the lake.

It was not until later that we finally found some answers, and Goodwood was given the slow and elusive gift of a conclusion. But before going on to everything that happened next, it's best to go back a fraction. It makes sense to start two days before Rosie vanished, which was nine days before Bart did. That was when Goodwood was still peaceful: a modest town under a mountain and beside a river.

That was the day I found the money.

2

Backflip and I were walking along the bank of the river on a Friday afternoon after school while birds sang in the branches overhead. Goodwood was about a half-hour drive inland from the coast, and the Gather River, flowing generally south and then sharply north, was imponded near Goodwood by the lake and eventually relieved itself into the Tasman Sea.

The clearing was half a kilometre from the back fence of the oval. It was a nice walk and Backflip and I made it often. I would go on the pebbles and sand and she would splash along beside me with the water up to her furry belly. She was a Labrador and always wanted to be in the river. The clearing lay ahead as if waiting: an open area with a natural pool that was perfect for swimming, where the bank fanned out, and the river widened like a snake that's eaten a cow.

Everyone from school used the clearing in summer. You could drive a car right up near the tree line and park under a grove of eucalypts, or in the cul-de-sac at the end of the road. If self-confidence allowed, you could sun yourself on the sparse lawn that hugged the bank. The weeping willow had a low-hanging branch that hovered over the water and was popular to sit on. The drooping leaves parted there and allowed a good view back up the bank. After a lot of rain, you could dip your feet in the current, and see all the way back to the goalposts on the oval. Lots of kids, from times past and present, had carved their initials in the trunk.

I had never seen one other person at the clearing in winter. In hot weather there were always kids from school in the deep water, on weekday afternoons and all weekend long, but when it was cold it was ours, mine and Backflip's, and sometimes we'd meet George. It was peaceful and private. Only the cows looked on, when they wandered close enough in the adjacent paddock.

That day, the cold wind chopped at the shining water. Backflip roamed the bank, sniffing, and I climbed up to sit on the branch of the willow, and watch the river run underneath. The birds were loud in the canopy above. I looked up at them, squinting in the dappled light. Just below, where the trunk bent inwards among the branches, something was glinting. It was a bag: white, plastic, poking out just a fraction from a hollowed-out hole in the trunk.

I stood up carefully, holding onto the trunk, and pulled the bag out of the tree-hole. It had a knot tied in the top and something bundled inside in a brown paper bag. I tore the plastic and reached inside the paper, pulling out the contents. There, folded over in a wad and held together with an elastic band, was more money than I'd ever seen. Five hundred dollars. Ten fifty-dollar notes. I counted them, after pulling the band off and spreading them out like a lucky hand of cards.

I looked around the clearing. There was no one. Just Backflip and the birds and the cows. Some ducks near the bank opposite. I sat down on the branch again and stared at the water.

Wow.

How thrilling it was to find a small fortune—and for it to be mine. I began smiling—beaming—on the verge of laughing, sitting in the weeping willow. It was more money than I'd ever had in my life. I was exhilarated as I laughed aloud into the clear day.

But where had it come from and who had hidden it there?

Backflip waded into the water and swam out to the middle where a branch was drifting, half sunken. Her body made little ripples in the water and I looked down at her and then across to the other side of the river. The trees were dense there: thick bush that grew close together and made good spots for hiding. The cold wind that chopped the water was moving through the branches. There was rustling here, and stillness there, and sounds that could be animal or human or wind.

My heart beat faster as I peered over at the dark places in the bush. I knew there was nothing ordinary about finding five hundred dollars hidden in a tree, especially in a place like Goodwood. It was not ordinary and nor did it seem right. I could not imagine there was an innocent explanation. I began to wonder if it was stolen. Everything under the high sun on that cold day seemed suddenly untoward. Then Backflip dragged herself out of the river and shook herself so hard I almost fell right out of the tree. She stood, oblivious, dripping into the dry leaves. A cow snorted loudly behind us in the paddock and broke the air with sound.

If I'm honest with myself, I know the decision I made was not noble. It was not a good deed done to honour the rightful owner of the money. I did what I did out of fear. I folded the wad of bills, and wrapped the elastic band around them. Then I stood up and put it all back just how I had found it.

I would wait.

I would leave it there, go home, and wait. For how long, I was not sure—a few days, maybe. And then I would come back again, and see if the money was still there. I had always mocked Mrs Gwen Hughes, who worked in the front office at school; she wore amethyst crystals and spoke earnestly of their power. But, much like Mrs Gwen Hughes, on that day I was sure I could sense *something*. Animal, wind, or human—there was something in the bush across that wide

14

water, and I was not going to be chased from that clearing by anything or anyone, not even for five hundred dollars.

I climbed down from the tree and called Backflip and we ran flat out back along the bank, up the sandy hill, and through the metal gate to the oval. I was out of breath by the time I got to the bright grass. There, out in the open, with the goalposts all set for a weekend game of football, we fell back to walking. Beyond the gate that we left behind, on the silty bank of the river, no one materialised. Over my shoulder, no one followed.

●

Up on Cedar Street, everything was normal. There was no portent of things to come, no eerie feeling. I went past Woody's and there was Rosie, salting a pile of chips laid out on butcher's paper while Emily Ross and Terry White looked on. Terry—covered in pimples—and Emily, taking asthmatic puffs from her inhaler.

If I'd have known that was the last time I'd see Rosie I would've stopped and looked properly. At Rosie White salting the chips. At beautiful Rosie White in her navy apron, her face inscrutable.

Instead, I went straight on by and didn't even think to notice her at all. No one in Goodwood thought to on that day—no more than usual. Terry White looked on blankly and Emily Ross gently wheezed and everything carried on under the deep green mountain as Backflip and I went across to the Grocer.

Established by Nance Hagan long before I was born, the Goodwood Grocer was the only store of its kind in the vicinity and was thus visited, with great frequency, by every person in town. Men, women, children—everyone went in and out like the tide. As such, Nance's counter was the site of many a conversation. Nance liked to *know*, which was something I could relate to, although I didn't much like the way Nance dispersed her knowledge. Many people came out of the Grocer grasping more than they had bargained for, given all they'd wanted was milk and eggs. Nance dispensed playground gossip, health reports on the sick and elderly, sports scores, implications of impropriety, uncharitable opinions regarding driving skills, her own personal crime book reviews. Nance Hagan had an opinion about everything; and Mum said there was a reason it said *Mixed Business* on the awning—Nance liked to mix everyone's business with her own, and with everyone else's in town.

But the curious thing at the Grocer that day was nothing to do with Nance. It was a girl standing out front who I'd never seen before. She was pale-skinned and willowy and had no expression. I walked past her to tie Backflip to the telegraph pole. The girl looked up at me—she did not smile, she did not frown, she just looked—and then she went back to the book she was reading as she leant up against the glass.

Faded signs for confectionery hung in Nance's windows. The community noticeboard was covered with handwritten advertisements for trailers, lawnmowers, bantam versions of Australorp chickens. The girl read her book and ignored everything around her completely.

There weren't often strangers in Goodwood. It wasn't a town in between anywhere good and anywhere else. Cedar Valley was to the south, and Clarke was to the north, but there was a more direct highway between the two and Goodwood was, on the map, like a vein off the main artery that pulsed gently without the larger organs even knowing it was there.

I went inside and Nance was serving a man my mum's age. She was ascertaining all she could from him with a hail of questions.

They had just moved to town, apparently. Just settling in. Oh yes, that funny-coloured house on Sooning Street. A very long drive—lots of boxes—but a big truck's coming tomorrow with the rest of it.

'We don't get many new people moving here,' said Nance. 'But most people are dead set on staying. It's a lovely little town.'

Nods from the man. He fumbled with his money.

'Have you had a look at the lake? We sell live bait—prawns, pilchards, worms; they generally come in on a Monday. You'll find the soft plastics are best for flathead though.' Nance

17

indicated a revolving rack near the counter hung with tiny coloured lures.

'Ah yes, very good,' said the man, who looked like he wouldn't know the first thing about what to do with them.

The girl out the front kept reading her book like she could've been anywhere. I could see her through the glass. She had a duffel coat on that was a bit too big, and gloves without the fingers. Black nail polish covered her nails and was chipped off in parts. She looked like a little hobo, except her hair was so golden at the ends it glowed white in the sun. She was the prettiest girl I had ever seen in real life.

The man went out and the girl bent her page down and followed him off down the street.

'G'day, Jean. How's your Nan?' said Nance, as I stood before the stacked shelves, trying to remember what Mum had asked me to get. My heart had calmed down after my running. I looked at the rows of cans, thinking about what was waiting back in the tree-hole. Thinking of all the books and tapes that I could buy with five hundred dollars.

3

When I got home, Mum was watering the ferns in the bathroom and humming along to the radio. The two of us lived in a weatherboard house with a nice lawn that Big Jim from next door mowed for us every fortnight. Everything was on one level because the houses in Goodwood weren't big on stairs. It smelt damp in our sunroom after rain, and dog hair stuck to the bottom of our socks, and Mum kept an extensive array of hanging plants. We cohabited with hundreds of books, which lived in uneven piles on our bedside tables, and spread their spines along the living room shelves. Mum owned a big cedar dining table, passed along from Nan and Pop. She waxed it every three months, like clockwork, and the smell of O'Cedar polish would settle in the curtains.

Goodwood was a wood town, historically. Red cedar used to grow thick and tall along the river, all the way from us to Cedar Valley. Toppled, stripped of its bark and cut into smaller pieces, it was transformed into dressers and desks and chairs. Timber cutting caused the town to prosper in the 1840s, and dairy farming followed. By 1992, though, the sawmill was closed and the cedar was gone, and only the Fairley Dairy remained, with its stock of lowing cattle much diminished.

While industry had slowed, Goodwood liked to think of itself as 'progressive' and, as such, 'Being Progressive' was the mission statement of the Goodwood Progress Association, which met at the Community Hall once a month and discussed how the town could progress further. Mum was secretary and reported back, straight-faced, on the various initiatives. These included a proposed mural (Smithy's idea), a proposed book club (Mum's idea), a proposed native garden (our neighbour Fitzy's idea), and the expansion of social events like Fishing's The Funnest, an annual parade led by a selection of keen fisherchildren from Goodwood Primary, who marched along Cedar Street every spring wearing little cardboard fish hats and carrying class-made, hookless rods. There was always a Fish Fry at the Bowlo after and, under brown and blue fluttering streamers, everyone in town would be overcome by the spirit of the lake and the ocean. Gripped by the watery wonderment of it all——they couldn't help it——they would eat and drink and laugh and set down their empty glasses and then they would dance.

The Bowlo was one of two places Goodwood had to drink at. The Bowlo and the Wickham Hotel, which was known as the Wicko—and then a little string of shops along Cedar Street: the Goodwood Grocer, the newsagent, the Goodwood Village Bakery, Bart's Meats, Mountain Real Estate, Woody's Takeaway, a tiny one-horse police station (where Mack was the horse), and so on. Among them were two 'artsy' establishments, as Pop called them: Bookworm, which stocked used books, and the Vinnies, where Val Sparks filled her window with local craft. This, along with the semi-isolated beauty of the landscape and flora, attracted a few artistically minded residents. There was a published novelist called Arden Cleary who lived on the mountain and wrote naturalist fiction; and a potter called Celeste Munch who'd won a ceramics prize in Sydney for her glazed bowls.

Goodwood was flat in the centre, at Cedar Street where the shops were. It was almost flat where we lived, inclining gently towards the escarpment. But our house, from the front, looked like it was wearing a huge mountain for a pirate hat. The rest of the town behind us all happened up the hill, and I often felt like the head of a snail, always under a shell.

That night, Mum and I watched TV, which entailed her yelling *Sale of the Century* answers at Glenn Ridge.

After the lamps were switched off, I dragged Backflip's bed onto the floor next to mine, and she turned in circles three times before settling in a tight ball. I put my heater on low and wrote about the money in my blue notebook under the heading: *Found at the clearing: FIVE HUNDRED DOLLARS*.

Then I lay awake under my quilt and thought about it for a long time, unable to sleep, while Backflip snored and the night hung cold and still outside my unlocked window.

4

On Saturday Nan drove me to Clarke, the closest town with a shopping plaza. *Clarke Plaza: Experience the Lifestyle.* The trees whirred past like steel wool and we listened to Nan's tape of John Denver and she sang along. Just before the bridge, Nan drove gently over a dead kangaroo, which was nothing more than a bump of fur and guts for every car to flatten a little bit more until it became one with the road.

'There're always kangaroos in this spot,' she said.

'There's always dead kangaroos in this spot,' I said.

'So it goes,' said Nan.

The clump of kangaroo offered a soft bumping sound as we passed over.

Nan bought me new sneakers: black Converse All Stars, just like the ones Rosie wore. I put them on straightaway and carried my old shoes in my bag. At every shop we went to, I noted the price of things I wanted and added them up along the way. With five hundred dollars, I could've bought another pair of boots, a Swiss Army knife and *Great Conspiracy Theories of the Twentieth Century* in hardcover, and still had $323.03 left over.

Nan bought wool, *Wild Swans*, and a chocolate Paddle-Pop, which she ate while we sat on the Clarke Plaza terrace in a spot of sun.

My Nan was Joyce Mackenzie. She had been an English teacher by profession, but by 1992 she was long retired. She knitted to keep her arthritis at bay, completed the cryptic crossword in pen, and knew lots of poems by heart, including the whole of T.S. Eliot's *Old Possum's Book Of Practical Cats* and the first five verses of *The White Cliffs Of Dover*.

Nan and Pop had lived in Goodwood all their married life. Nan's family had been dairy farmers. Nan had vowed to marry a man who wasn't. 'Farming's a chancy business,' she'd say. 'Truman Capote wrote that and never a truer thing was said.'

My Pop was not a farmer. He did equipment maintenance for a textile company in Clarke. My Nan fell in love. They adopted my mum when she was a tiny baby.

Apparently Nan and Pop tried their darnedest to get pregnant. But, like trying to make a phone call in a thunderstorm, they had a bad connection. So after several years afflicted with either Nan or Pop's infertility, for tests in those days were inconclusive, they decided to adopt.

Nan and Pop told Mum that when they went to Clarke Base Hospital, a tall handsome doctor escorted them into a big room of cots, and each one had an adorable little baby in it. They walked through rows and rows, looking at all the delightful little faces, gurgling and smiling and perfect and, gosh, it was so hard to choose! But they had to, of course, they had to choose. There was only one baby for them. And as they came upon the cot my mum was in, there she was, all swaddled in a dear little cream jumpsuit, pink-cheeked and perfect, and they said, 'This is the one. This is the one we want to take home and raise as our own beautiful baby girl.'

And the lovely nurses said *Blessed are the pure of heart!*; and by and by the lovely nurses made it so; and it was very good; The End.

Throughout her childhood, especially in an incidence of insomnia or a difficult day at school, Mum would ask to be told the story of how she was Chosen, for the hundredth time. She was delighted at each and every telling, and was often heard retelling the story to her friends, at which point the room of adorable babies inevitably got bigger, and the difficulty of her parents' choice therefore greater, and her ultimate desirability and perfection that much more apparent.

Unfortunately, Mum got older and at the age of fourteen she read an article in the newspaper about the adoption process. It was sobering.

There was no room full of cots. There was no painstaking selection. There was just a mountain of bureaucracy and it took ages and prospective adopters pretty much got what they were given.

Mum wasn't angry. She didn't slam a door in disillusionment. Nan said she came in with the article, and Nan saw what it was, and Pop looked at the floor. My mum did not say one word. She just stood there, and then she knelt down, for Nan and Pop were sitting side by side on the couch. Mum put her head in Nan's lap. Then Nan put her hand on Mum's back, and Pop put his hand on Nan's hand, and Nan put her other hand on Pop's hand, and so on, until it was like a slow motion game of Snap.

The three of them set themselves there like that for some time, as if meditating.

'Eyes were moist,' as my Pop recalled.

So Mum grew up in Goodwood until she moved away for university and married a man whose surname was Brown. That made her Celia Brown. Mum soon got pregnant and then I was born in Sydney. That made me Jean Brown. Then the man whose surname was Brown left us when I was just a baby, and Mum and I moved back to Goodwood. That was how it happened and there we all were; and I was glad to grow up near a man like my Pop and a woman like my Nan.

•

On the way back from Clarke, Nan pulled up at Goodwood's only servo and mechanical repair shop, run by Bob Elver, who was very bald. Elver's Auto. I got out and patted Bob Elver's bony greyhound, Lady, who always sat by the door on a big dusty bed and never needed to be on the lead. I never questioned the fact that Lady's undercarriage revealed him to be male. I was patting and Nan was filling up the tank of her old Sigma when a shiny Subaru pulled up behind her, with the pretty girl I'd seen at the Grocer sitting in the passenger seat.

Bob Elver said 'G'day Jean', and his head shone in the sun as he had a chat with Nan by the bowser. 'Nice day for it. How's Don going, Joyce?'

Lady rolled onto his back and exposed his belly.

The pretty girl looked at me through the car window. She did not smile, she did not frown, she just looked. I stared back at her for a few seconds, but something about her made me turn away. I felt embarrassed. The girl kept her eyes on me for a long moment, like I was a great curiosity. Then she was reading her book again, and her mum was filling up their tank. Nan honked at bald Bob Elver as we drove out and turned off towards home. We left the shiny Subaru sitting in the servo in the sun.

•

The next day was Sunday. Rosie White and her brother Terry went with their parents to the Joneses next door for a barbeque lunch. Opal and Ken Jones hadn't had the Whites over in a long time, and Opal went to extra effort with the salads. The occasion was Terry's birthday, which had been the Tuesday preceding—sixteen candles on a Victoria sponge cake that came in a packet from the Goodwood Grocer. Nance had sold it to Judy White, and then said to Mum later that sugar isn't good for kids with skin problems. Mum said, 'Oh, Nance. Let him eat cake.'

The Joneses had a son the same age as Terry (Jake Jones, a name like a superhero). But Rosie, the oldest at eighteen, was bored and left early to return to her room where she listened to her new tape of Nirvana's *Nevermind* so loud that Judy ducked home momentarily to ask Rosie to turn it down.

Later in the afternoon, Rosie left with her Walkman on—her giant headphones dwarfing her face—and met Davo Carlstrom at the Wicko, where they reportedly drank three schooners and chain-smoked in the beer garden. Smithy, who owned the Wicko and offered gentle musings in a faintly Irish accent, told Mack later that Rosie laughed every now and again, sure, but not as much as usual and that, in his opinion, she seemed sad.

Mack said, 'Smithy, would you have thought her sad if she hadn't disappeared that evening?'

And Smithy, who was often prone to lyricism, said, 'Well, it's hard to distinguish between my sadness and the rest of the sadness in town.'

At that point, Mack, an empathic man, decided to set himself down for a Reschs and a chat, and they ended up drinking past close, even though Mack was supposed to be on duty.

After Rosie had left the pub that Sunday, possibly looking sad, she went home. The Whites ate chops and mashed potatoes and Rosie's stepdad, Carl, went to his shed after dinner and worked with the light on, attracting moths, till after ten. Terry applied his medicated acne cream, finished his homework, and played *Alex Kidd in Miracle World* on his Sega Master System II. Judy washed up and pottered around, watching television and doing puzzles from the large-print puzzle book that always sat on the arm of their couch.

Rosie went to her room, taking the time to say a nice goodnight to her mum and her brother, which she did sometimes, but not that often. Then she closed the door behind her and vanished into thin air.

5

The next morning, around the time that I was arriving at school, Judy White was in the Goodwood Police Station, fretting to Mack, beside herself with panic, while Terry waited outside in the car.

The news was yet to spread to the rest of town.

I had woken in the dark, walked Backflip around the block as the sun yellowed the clouds, eaten my brown toast, and walked to school. In the misty morning, everything felt altogether normal.

Just before the bell rang, I waited by the lunch tables for George, who was coming through the front gates with two of her brothers. She had four in total: Toby was her twin and he went to our school, along with runty Daniel; Vinnie had graduated with the rest of Rosie's year; and Lego Pat was seven and made endless abstract constructions with the three incomplete sets of Lego that George's parents—Noelene and Fred Sharkey—could not afford to replace.

Four of the five Sharkey children, including George, were redheaded, even though both Noelene and Fred were not. George would offer a lesson in recessive genes to anyone who would listen. Spittle would relieve itself from her mouth when she got excited. Then she'd say something droll or self-deprecating; or she'd laugh inappropriately. When George's grandmother, Belle, had died in 1985, a devastated Noelene had ushered George along in front of the open casket. George looked down at Belle, who she was very fond of, and laughed hysterically at her resting face. Poor George. She was dragged out of the church and reprimanded and could not stop laughing for days.

On top of everything else, George had photic sneeze reflex, which meant that she sneezed uncontrollably when exposed to bright light. It's hereditary, and Noelene and runty Daniel had it also. In fact, George's grandfather died sun sneezing at the wheel of his car. He was pulling out of his garage into a bright morning when his head jerked up at an angle, breath burst into his lungs, his eyes shut, and a sneeze came with such force that his foot involuntarily hit the accelerator, propelling his Datsun out over the driveway and into the path of a semi-trailer.

Old Belle, who was soon to be dead herself, saw the whole thing.

'Living on the main road in Clarke has its disadvantages' was what she told the attending officer, in an unfeeling tone.

That's why Fred Sharkey moved his family the forty-minute drive to Goodwood when George was in utero. Goodwood was a safer place for sneezing. There were no semi-trailers passing through; no heavy machinery; just the mountain on one side and the river on the other.

Since the freight train line passed through Goodwood beyond the school, and George's house was beyond the freight line, George was literally from the wrong side of the tracks. The houses on her street had old sinks and white goods decomposing in their yards. Cats mated violently in carports. DOCS arrived on two separate occasions at the fibro house where Emily Ross wheezed out an existence with her alcoholic father. 'The only way is up', George would say, with the same wry expression she had that day in the playground.

The bell rang. The mist had lifted. Toby punched my arm on his way past. Runty Daniel went off in the other direction towards the library. No one missed Terry White, who was due in class just as we were. No one knew about Rosie White, who had vanished into thin air. The sun edged out from behind a cloud and flooded the playground with morning light. As it hit our faces, George sneezed.

And just at that moment, Mrs Gwen Hughes, heavy with crystals, was walking a new student from the front office across the playground—pointing out the demountable classrooms, and the lunch tables, and the canteen, and the hall. The new girl opened her mouth and said something back to Mrs Gwen Hughes and that was when I first saw it: a thin gap between her front teeth. It was surely there, right in the middle; and she looked tiny in her oversized coat; and she really was the prettiest girl I had ever seen in real life.

•

Woody's Takeaway was owned by a white-haired man called Roy Murray. I always thought he should've just called it Roy's or Murray's instead of Woody's, because everyone always asked Rosie who Woody was. She'd look at them, and point to the sign: it said *Woody's* in red cursive with a picture of a cartoon log. The log had a happy, big-eyed face and little wooden branches for arms and legs.

'What town are we in?' Rosie would ask, and that was her deadpan answer.

Roy Murray would open Woody's of a morning and Rosie clocked on around noon and worked till close. Roy was generally well-liked. About as well-liked as his son, Derek Murray, was disliked. Derek Murray: always an unpleasant expression. 'The lights are on but nobody's home,' as my Pop would say.

After school that day, white-haired Roy Murray was standing in the doorway, talking in a quiet voice with Mack. I walked past and wondered where Rosie was, but didn't give it much thought. Mack was too deep in conversation to see me waving, and Roy Murray looked tired in the eyes, like he hadn't slept so well the night before.

I crossed the street and headed home.

It was three days since I'd found the money. Backflip walked around in circles with her ears back, crying with excitement when I opened the back door. I put her on the lead and we set off towards the river.

I decided three days was a good amount of time to have waited. If there *was* someone in the bush across the river last Friday—watching me find the money, watching me put it back, watching me and Backflip run away like a pair of chickens—then they would've collected it after I left and that would have been that. They would've known by now that I hadn't told Mack. And if they really wanted to make sure, they could've watched the clearing for another couple of days and seen that I hadn't returned.

Three days. I had thought of little else since. In my mind, I'd already spent that money. I was on a shopping spree at the Clarke Plaza—at the bookstore, the record store, the disposal store, the Fosseys. I wasn't sure how I would've explained it all to Mum though. *Where did you get those new things, Jean?* I didn't know how well I could lie. And then there was Mack. I was most frightened of what Mack would say. *Jeannie, that's a lot of money. You should have told me.*

Backflip and I cut across the oval and walked along the silty bank, and I looked ahead to the clearing in search of anything disagreeable. I found no such thing. The willow was drooping over into the river. The cows were in the adjacent paddock, eating rye grass and clover. Some of them had little birds on their backs with their beaks up in the winter air.

Backflip launched herself into the water where the river widened. I climbed the willow, pulled myself onto the big branch, and looked up to the tree-hole.

The plastic bag was still there.

I stood, balancing on the branch, as thoughts crowded my mind. Was it that I felt disappointed? I wasn't sure. For the last three days I had been mostly hoping the money would still be there—so I could go to Clarke Plaza and experience the lifestyle. And yet, faced with the money again, I wasn't sure what do to.

I reached up and pulled the bag out of the hole, so I could have the feeling of money in my hands while I considered my options.

The plastic bag came out easily. It felt different.

Almost immediately I saw why: the paper bag was no longer inside. There was no wad of bills. No five hundred dollars.

The money was gone.

Relief and disappointment and confusion, all in one moment.

I stood there, still clutching the plastic bag and feeling its contents with my fingers. It was all scrunched up and folded around. There was something new inside. I opened up the bag and and pulled it out. Then I sat down on the branch and studied it, holding it in my palm.

It was a small plastic horse. The kind they sold at toyshops. Brown and lifelike, with black-painted hooves and shiny flanks. It had a kind face, and little black eyes that were fixed in a pensive expression.

Backflip was getting restless by the fence of the paddock, which came right down behind the dusty road where the cars parked in summer. She barked and the cows startled, snorting through their big nostrils and backing off up the hill. All the birds flew off their backs.

I looked up at the big cows in the paddock, and then back at the little horse in my hand.

What on earth?

Whoever in their right mind would think a plastic horse was a fair trade for five hundred dollars?

Silly old Backflip, barking at the cows. Then trotting down to the bank on the other side of the willow and rolling in the mud.

I held the horse for a time, no longer frightened of anyone in the trees, no longer regretful nor relieved.

Then, deflated, I put the little horse back in the torn bag, and put the bag back in the tree-hole, and Backflip and I walked slowly along the bank towards town.

●

When we got to Cedar Street, something was the matter. There was unease floating like a mist above the rooftops. The sky was clear and absurd. Rainbow lorikeets had gathered in a clump on the awning above the Grocer and they screeched and chattered, and everyone on the street was talking. The town was bursting with bad news. At the Goodwood Grocer, Nance was on the telephone, deep in covert conversation. Val Sparks from the Vinnies had bailed up Smithy outside the Wicko. Bart, in Bart's Meats, was listening to Coral over the counter, who huddled as much as she could with a meat display in the way, as if telling Bart great secrets across the sausages. Tired-eyed, white-haired Roy Murray was also on the phone, by the bain-marie at Woody's, his head hung low. Outside the newsagent a few doors up, Helen was glaring at the absurd sky. The mountain—silent and deep tree green—was all in shadow.

Mum was hanging up the telephone when I got home.

'Did you hear Rosie White's gone missing?'

'No?'

I felt suddenly sick.

'I was just up at Nance's earlier. Apparently Judy went in to wake Rosie up this morning and she was gone.'

'Gone where?'

'They don't know,' said Mum. 'But Jude's beside herself. As you would be. Trace just said it's too early to file a missing person's report. Mack has to wait till tomorrow.'

All I could say was, 'Oh.'

Mum looked at me, concerned, like she'd said too much already. She paused and unworried her tone. 'You know, she's probably just run away. Maybe it's just boy stuff. Nance says she goes out with Davo Carlstrom. Maybe they had a fight or something, who knows.'

I'd seen Rosie and Davo together a few times. Once they were making out in the car park behind Woody's at twilight, against the bonnet of a car, and I watched for longer than I should have.

Mum forced a smile out and I forced one back. At dinner, we made small talk with the TV on. Mum answered Glenn Ridge's questions quietly instead of yelling.

Later, in my room, I wrote the day's happenings in my blue notebook:

ROSIE WHITE IS MISSING.
The money's gone . . . but now there's a plastic horse?!
The new girl is going to our school.

I lay back and thought about Rosie. And the money. And Davo Carlstrom, pressing Rosie against the bonnet of the dusty car, pushing his hands up her skirt and kissing her with all his mouth. She had grabbed his hand and put it higher, like no one was watching except the sky.

Maybe Rosie took the money? Maybe Rosie *left* the money. Maybe Davo and Rosie had a fight. Or maybe she just ran away to the city where everything is full of opportunity.

I wrote down more—all I could think of—and couldn't shake my feelings. What if something terrible had happened to Rosie?

I put my notebook away. Backflip lay in a brown ball on her bed. I could hear Big Jim and Fitzy's TV, muffled from next door. Then, just as I was about to turn my lamp off, Mum knocked and put her head in.

'Goodnight, baby,' she said. Then she strode across my room, trying to be casual, and locked my window.

In all our life in Goodwood, she had never done that before.

6

The rest of that week made me nervous.

There was no word from Rosie, no sightings of Rosie, and no clues as to where on earth Rosie might've been.

On the Tuesday, Mack filed a missing person's report, and spoke to anyone he could find who'd seen Rosie on the day she vanished, or in the days preceding. At school, there was little else discussed, and George and I posited multiple theories on her disappearance. Even George, wiping tears away after a sneezing fit, clear snot running down her top lip and into her mouth, was unable to make jokes.

Kidnapping was the most frightening theory, or any kind of forced removal. The sexual violence that lurked beyond those thoughts was not raised in actual words by either of us, but I heard George's brother Toby utter the worst combination—'raped and murdered'—as he and Brett Hiller walked past us in the hall. They looked like most boys at school did during that time: concerned, but not wanting to appear that way, lest their sensitivity aroused accusations of being a 'fucken faggot', a taunt which the men and boys of Goodwood subjected each other to routinely.

The only boys George and I had any time for at school were Ethan West and Lucas Karras, both of whom had the admirable quality of being tender, an attribute that virtually every other boy in school lacked. Lucas looked at George tenderly when he said, 'Are you guys feeling scared about what happened? Because me and Ethan can walk you home after school?'

How adorable.

'Do you reckon his dad told him to say that?' George said to me after, and we agreed that he probably had. Mr Costa Karras was known to be a gentleman and he had raised a decent son. Ethan West's dad, on the other hand, was a known drunk, and it always surprised me that Ethan had turned out to be tender at all. Old Mal West would shake his cane at the pokies and was prone to getting mouthy. Rumour had it he got himself into fisticuffs on occasion, and I wasn't sure that Ethan hadn't taken a punch or two. Still, Ethan agreed he'd be very happy to walk us home, and a look of concern came over his face at the suggestion that we might be frightened. Then he looked at me for slightly longer than was necessary, and George elbowed me in case I missed it. All I thought was: Ethan was no Big Jim, but he really was very tall. And that, yes, maybe I was afraid. Not of walking home in broad daylight—we respectfully declined the offer of an escort—but the feeling I had in general at that time, along with the unease and the unknowing, was slowly but surely approaching fear.

I wanted to think Rosie had just fled the immutable boredom of takeaway food and the verdant confines of Goodwood. I wanted to think of her among skyscrapers, applying for exciting new jobs and window-shopping in the evenings as the city glistened. I wanted to think that, but the truth of it was that my thoughts were much darker. I worried. I had read a lot of books. I had watched a lot of TV. In my mind—in my deepest fears—Rosie White had met an awful fate; and I knew that George felt the same. Noelene had, after all, immediately locked all the windows in their house, too. It was as if, in the space of a day, all the dusty locks in Goodwood, stiff with neglect, had been bolted and fastened. Keys were fished out from the backs of drawers. Side gates were secured. Mothers of teenage girls held on for longer hugs after breakfast. Fathers peered out across their front lawns, suspicious. Just like that, in progressive and hopeful Goodwood, no one felt optimistic.

I found out from Mack, who told Mum, who was telling Nan when Coral from two doors up overheard and told most people in town, that Rosie's window had been wide open. On a cold August night. Wide open! Like all windows in town before that night, it was never locked, so no one, Rosie or otherwise, had to unlock it. It was just as open as air when Judy came in on Monday morning to tell an empty bed that it was time to get up.

Later on the Monday, Judy White had returned home from the police station and, on Mack's advice, looked closely over Rosie's things, through eyes blurred with tears, desperate to find evidence to indicate her daughter had simply chosen to depart for a new life elsewhere. She found no such proof. The family suitcases were where they always were: in the top section of the Whites' built-in wardrobe. Rosie's toothbrush stood upright next to the three other White toothbrushes, in a Mother's Day novelty mug on the bathroom sink. And Judy could detect no obvious absence of clothing in Rosie's abandoned bedroom. What was gone, along with Rosie, were her wallet and her army disposal backpack. The backpack had been covered with badges and patches and band names, which Rosie had written all over in texta.

For George and me, the lack of Rosie's wallet and back-pack was welcome news. It gave us cautious hope. It meant Rosie had most probably left of her own accord. If someone had opened her window and taken Rosie against her will in order to do terrible things to her, then she wouldn't have had time to grab her bag. She would've been struggling, a hand over her mouth stifling her screams, perhaps the effects of a chloroform-soaked rag held over her mouth and nose rendering her unconscious, much like we'd seen in Noelene's favourite Bette Midler movie, *Ruthless People*. People in that situation don't reach for personal belongings like they're about to run an errand.

But Mack and Sergeant Simmons saw things differently. Rosie may not have been taken from her bedroom. But if she'd taken her backpack, climbed out her window and gone to meet someone in the night? That didn't mean that mystery person, or someone else she came across, didn't do terrible things to her. Because if everything was safe and well, then where was Rosie White?

●

The signs went up around town on the Wednesday. Rosie's brother Terry was seen photocopying them at the library in the morning, leaning over the machine with the lid not properly shut, so the white light escaped and rolled across his face over and over as the copies came out in an increasing pile. It lit up the tears that sat in his eyes, and illuminated the moment he blinked hard enough for them to spill onto the Xerox logo like lonely rain. Terry stared down and let them fall all over his pimples and didn't wipe them off, not even with the back of his hand. When he arrived at the counter to pay (ten cents a copy), my mum's friend Denise, the librarian, said it was on the house. As she relayed the story of their encounter, Terry stood there looking at her like he didn't understand the notion of her charity, wordlessly holding out a blue, crumpled ten-dollar bill in front of his wet face.

He then went to the newsagent to buy Blu-Tac and tape. Helen and her husband Bill also refused his money. Helen said she'd wanted to offer Terry hopeful phrases that she'd been working on all morning in case she saw any member of the White family. When the time came, though, she panicked. 'She'll be right, love,' she said, nodding. 'She'll be right.'

Poor Terry.

I counted eighteen signs on Cedar Street, after he'd done his teary rounds. Faye Haynes, who ran the Goodwood Village Bakery, had allowed two signs on either side of her front windows, and one on the noticeboard inside. There was Rosie in her Year Twelve photo—but with black eyes and heavily contrasted features, due to the unkind quality of the photocopy—and MISSING written in large letters above her head. *Last seen wearing a red jumper, black skirt and black tights on Sunday night. Please help us find Rosie.* Then the number for the police and the Whites' home phone.

I didn't know what good the signs would do in Goodwood. Everyone knew Rosie, and everyone knew she was missing, and everyone knew that if they saw her, they'd tell the appropriate people. But what was Terry White to do?

On my way home, I saw Terry had stuck one on each side of the electricity box on the corner of our street. I looked to see if anyone was around before I peeled one of the signs off, careful not to tear the edges on the Blu-Tac. I rolled the paper up into a tube, scraped the remaining blobs of Blu-Tac off the box with my fingers so there was no trace, and made them into one ball, which I pushed around in my fingers as I walked. When I got home, I stuck the soft blob to the wall above my bed, and slid Rosie's MISSING sign, folded once, inside my blue notebook.

Outside I could hear Fitzy next door, hosing the hedges like there'd never be rain.

•

Davo Carlstrom lived on the wrong side of the tracks, on the same street as George. His house was fibro and slumped in an overgrown lot with a crap caravan in the drive that his uncle slept in, and several shells of old cars which sat under blue tarpaulins, waiting to be tended to. Davo's screen door was one of the first that Mack knocked on that Wednesday, since Smithy said he'd been drinking beer at the Wicko with Rosie on the day she vanished, and also because Davo and Rosie spent a lot of time together in general and most people assumed Davo was Rosie's boyfriend.

He confirmed this to Mack in slightly uncertain terms.

'She's kinda my girlfriend, yeah.'

Around about the time Terry was putting up his signs, George rode her bike up and down her street in a loose figure eight while Mack and Davo talked on the front steps.

Unfortunately, she found it too difficult to decipher their conversation, save for the odd phrase. But she did report that Davo looked genuinely distressed; that Mack called him 'mate' and patted him on the shoulder as he left; and that Davo's creepy uncle watched the whole thing—Davo, Mack and cycling, eavesdropping George—from the steps of the caravan.

'He's a full-on pervert,' was George's summation of the uncle. 'He's been living there for three months. What does he even do all day?'

'Doesn't he fix cars?'

'Davo's dad fixes the cars, I think the bogan uncle just sits around.'

'I think they're all kind of bogans,' I said.

George nodded.

Due to proximity, George, when in primary school, had the unrivalled privilege of having been inside the Carlstrom home. A privilege, because Davo was three years older than us and had grown into the most handsome, the most rebellious and, thus, the most coveted boy in town.

He was blond, his tangled hair touched his shoulders, and he let it do what it wanted. He wore Big W flannos, open over T-shirts. He had a little beard that was lovely and casual, and he played guitar in a three-piece punk band called The Invalids, with Trent Ross from two doors down and Gary Elver, the wayward son of bald Bob at the servo.

I had embarrassed myself at school once by pronouncing The Invalids like it referred to incapacitated old people. Horrible Liz Gordon said, 'You fucken 'tard, it's The *Invalids*,' and pronounced it like Davo and his mates had intended: referring to people who were not valid; people who were somehow illegitimate or untrue.

'That makes the name a bit cooler, hey,' said George later on.

Embarrassed, I agreed.

I appreciated the fact that Davo was quiet to the point of brooding. Just looking at him, a person could see that his eyes were deeper ponds than those of his comrades. Maybe it was because he felt illegitimate or untrue. Maybe he could see a way out of Goodwood but was, for the time being, stuck like the shell of an old car in the yard.

As for horrible Liz Gordon, who often yelled obscenities across the playground, she was a part of a group of rough girls who smoked during lunch by the fence and drank reckless amounts of Passion Pop around the late-night bin fires in Sweetmans Park. Liz Gordon, Talia Edwards, Bec Fisher, Bec Kelly, Kiralee Davis—these were names I longed to forget. They were proudly and deliberately mean. They scratched the caps off cream bulbs and inhaled the nitrous oxide to get high. They had notorious sex with Trent Ross and Gary Elver, and physical fights with each other. My Nan referred to them, collectively, as 'common'.

Liz Gordon once told George she was 'a dead scrag' because George sneezed on her in class. It had been due to Mrs Carr's use of an overhead projector. Mrs Carr had turned the lights off and the projector on and the bulb came alive brightly and George sneezed.

Mucus sprayed on Liz Gordon's milky neck.

'*Gross*,' said Liz. 'You're a fucken dead scrag.'

But George would always have it over Liz Gordon in one small way. George after all was the one who, at age nine, was invited in to play video games with Davo, by Davo's sloshed mother.

'What was it like in there?' I asked.

'Not that nice,' said George. 'His mum smelt heaps like beer. I felt really germy afterwards.'

'Poor Davo,' I said, because of his drunk mum and his stinking house and the fact that Rosie was missing and she was Davo's kind-of girlfriend.

'Yeah, poor Davo—if he didn't do it,' said George.

We both fell silent. I don't think I truly thought, at that time, that Davo had done anything bad. And I don't think George did either. But it was as if we knew, or were starting to accept, that when it came to Rosie, something—and probably something bad—had been done.

7

To celebrate the occasion of Nan's seventy-fifth birthday, Mum and I went to their house for a small dinner party. Pop cooked an easy-carve lamb leg roast and made gravy in the roasting pan. Nan wore a plastic tiara and sat at the head of the table.

Gosh I loved Nan.

Joyce Mackenzie was probably the most forward-thinking person in Goodwood, and yet she was married to my silly old Pop who, on hearing the announcement that Australia would stop distributing one- and two-cent pieces, had begun hoarding them in jars next to his bed, in case he missed them.

'One day you're going to reach into your pocket, Jean, and there'll be none left,' he said. 'How would you be?'

'I think I'll be okay, Pop.'

'Twenty-six years is not enough time for a coin to be in circulation. They should let them live.'

Nan just smiled and shook her head.

She voted Labor; Pop voted Nationals. She read poetry and literary novels; he read instruction manuals. She liked to try new recipes, experimenting with flavours and ordering exotic spices through Nance at the Grocer; he made one meal, once a year on Nan's birthday: easy-carve lamb leg roast with gravy, baked potatoes, pumpkin and peas, served always on the Burleigh Ware dinner set they were given by his parents on their wedding day.

I would look around town and wonder if two married people ever had less in common than my Nan and Pop. And yet they would look at each other across the cedar table and whatever ocean lay between them was bridged, just like that. He would wink and she would nearly blush. They would tease each other and sustain each other and, if music was playing, they would dance. How they loved to dance. Pop told me they had danced for close to five hours on their wedding day. They danced in their living room of an evening to Billie Holiday or Frank Sinatra. They danced very slowly and took it in turns to lead. They danced while everyone was watching, and no one was watching, and the sight of their graceful private universe of swaying and twirling and gliding and rocking would bring joy to the walls of an empty room.

That night, Mack came to the dinner party with his wife, Tracy, and their small son, Jasper. So did Nan's friend Shirl from the CWA, whose husband Clive had died the year before from heart failure, sitting in his reading chair. Old widowed Shirl arrived in Maseur Sandals, which she'd paired with thick socks.

'Joyce!' said Shirl 'I haven't seen you for donks! Happy birthday, love,' and they settled in for a brief, arthritic hug.

Shirl bore a gift basket of scones. Tracy popped a bottle of sparkling. Mack and Pop drank Reschs Dinner Ale because it was a special occasion. Backflip sat patiently under the table, waiting for someone to drop food. Everyone wanted to talk about Rosie.

'It's weird seeing Roy Murray at Woody's all afternoon,' said Mum. 'And Derek Murray—did you see he's been working there this week? It feels funny for them to be open at all.'

'I didn't know Derek Murray had the intellect to fry a bag of chips,' said Mack.

Derek Murray. Roy's son. As my Pop would say, 'Fell out of the stupid tree and hit every branch on the way down.'

'I am not a fan of Derek's face,' I announced to the table.

I wasn't. Derek's face was a big old mess of a thing, and it mainly looked that way because an unpleasant expression had settled in some time ago and had remained there, even if Derek was trying to smile at the time.

Mack had a little laugh.

Mum said, 'Jeannie, honey, don't be uncharitable.'

'What about that bloke Carl? Isn't he her stepdad, not her real one?' asked Shirl.

'Yeah, but he's been around a long time,' said Mack. 'And, you know, I don't really want to talk about the case.'

'So it's a real "case"?' asked Nan. 'You don't think she ran off?'

'Come on, Nan, you know what I mean.'

Mack called Nan 'Nan' even though she was his aunt. Mack was the son of Nan's brother, Lang, who died after the Vietnam War, sitting on his back verandah, cleaning his gun. I only realised in recent years that 'cleaning his gun' was a euphemism. I don't suppose it was dirty at all. I suppose he was though, from the war, and all the horrible things he'd seen and done.

Mack, who was fifteen at the time, found Lang with his beetroot head barely hanging together and a raven standing by his ear, nipping at the wooden boards. Mack was catatonic for two weeks straight. But in the years that followed, he mended and grew into a police officer. By 1992 he was gentle and kind, he loved his family, and could not stand the sight of ravens.

Shirl piped up again. 'I've come up to Cedar Street last Tuesday and I've seen Carl there at the bakery. I don't know if I like the look of him. Faye Haynes says she's never liked the look of him. What do you reckon, Mack?'

'I think they're probably going through a thing or two,' said Mack and tried to eat his lamb. He then tried to change the subject. He commented on the lack of rain and how the lake levels were sure to drop if the dry spell continued. He said Nance had recommended him a John Grisham book called *The Pelican Brief* and it was wonderfully gripping, if not really about pelicans at all. He even asked us if we all knew that Bob Elver's bony greyhound, Lady, was actually male.

But Shirl was ruthless and the rest of us weren't much kinder. As much as Mack evaded, the questions kept coming and, as the night went on, the dinner party did ascertain a few pertinent pieces of information: Carl was not Rosie's dad, but he was Terry's (I knew that already). Judy and Rosie had taken Carl's surname—White—upon the marriage, because Rosie's real dad was a deadshit who left them in the lurch when Rosie was a baby (that was new); Judy White was a mess (everyone knew that already); Davo told Mack that Rosie hadn't given him any indication she was going anywhere, and he had not arranged to meet her on Sunday night in the blanket of darkness; and Davo's bogan uncle, who lived in the crap caravan, was unemployed (I asked that question, and Mack looked at me intently when I did).

The one place Rosie might've gone, according to Mack, was her cousin Tegan's in Ballina. Tegan and Rosie were close. Judy said they sent each other things. Letters, magazines, mix tapes. Cousin Tegan was twenty-one and worked at the West Ballina Transit Centre restaurant, which sat under the Big Prawn. Mack had checked in with Tegan, as well as her mother, who was Judy's sister Alison. Neither had heard from Rosie and both were awfully distressed.

'Jeannie, do me a favour and tell your friend George—and her bike—to mind their own business,' Mack said to me when we were out on the verandah after.

I said I would, and we sat on the daybed in the crisp air while Backflip sniffed around Nan's rose garden. Mack drank his beer and shook his head at the night. Backflip assumed her position and made a slow deposit on Nan's lawn. The smell of it wafted across the garden towards the house and Mack winced. I blocked my nose and ventured to ask, 'Hey, Mack, have you had any robberies recently?'

'Robberies? What d'you mean?'

'I don't know—like, did someone get some money stolen or something?'

'What do you know, Jean?'

'Nothing!'

Mack sighed and looked at me like a man who'd locked his keys in his car. I could hear Backflip rustling in the bushes. The wind had picked up and the trees above were dancing.

'*Jean.*'

I said, 'Well . . .' and thought hard whether to tell Mack about the money. I knew what he would say. He'd be disappointed that I hadn't told him sooner. He'd say '*Jean*' again, in a worse tone. He'd say, 'That's a lot of money. What were you going to do with it? Where is it now? What have you done with it?' And then what was I supposed to say? That someone had swapped five hundred dollars for a little plastic horse?

Just in the nick of time, we were interrupted by Shirl, who came out, tipsy, with her handbag and a piece of cake wrapped in a napkin.

'Bye-bye, Mack. Bye-bye, love.'

The soft sound of cork-lined sandals on the verandah.

'Bye, Shirl,' said Mack. 'You'll let me know if you want me to come do your lawn, won't you?'

And Shirl said, 'Oh, you dear man,' and I got up while Mack was distracted and went back inside.

•

Before going to bed that night I made sure my window was still locked. Then I wrote down all the new information I had relevant to Rosie's disappearance in my blue notebook. Carl White. Rosie's deadshit dad. Davo Carlstrom and his unemployed bogan uncle, whose name Mack had managed not to say. What was his name? I hadn't thought to ask. I wrote: *Bogan Uncle Carlstrom* and put my pen down. I thought about all those cars under their tarpaulins, and wondered what was inside that old crap caravan. I wondered if Davo was lying in his bed thinking about Rosie, too. The wind was squally now and the trees kept wailing. I could almost hear Judy White among them, howling into the night.

8

I woke up early to Backflip's faithful snores, floating up from her bed, and the sound of Mum out in the kitchen, fussing. Backflip got up when I got up. She stretched her front legs out, and then her back legs out, and then she shook all over like she'd just got out of a pond. I filled her bowl with biscuits and made my brown toast. Mum was on all fours on the kitchen floor this whole time, surrounded by the entire contents of the pantry, which she was sorting into piles of either keeping or getting rid of. There was a small third section for odd sauces, the fate of which was uncertain.

'Some of these jams look a bit iffy,' she said and pushed three jars to one side for disposal. 'Remind me not to buy any more from the park market. I just feel bad if Mary Bell's selling them. Does her face make you feel bad or is it just me?'

'Yeah, I feel pretty bad about her face,' I said. Poor Mary Bell. First she was toppled from her position of Secretary of the CWA by Mrs Bart, and now she had to suffer the indignity of selling their iffy jams at the Sweetmans Park Market.

'I just can't imagine what Judy must be going through,' said Mum to the jars and cans. 'I'm going to take her some flowers. Or, no, some food. I think a casserole.'

'I didn't think canned goods went off,' I said.

Mum examined some white beans for a use-by date. She rolled the can around in her hand and looked up as a new thought struck her.

'There's a new girl at your school?' she said, out of nowhere.

'Oh, yeah. There is,' I said, and for some reason I felt startled.

'Evie?' she said.

'Evie,' I repeated. 'Is that her name?'

What a lovely name, I thought. *Evie.*

'Bart said they just moved here. The man was in there yesterday when I picked up the lamb for Pop. Nice-looking guy. Evie's a lovely name, don't you think?'

'Yeah, I guess.'

Then Mum corralled the pile of cans and jars deemed to be unexpired and began putting them back in the pantry with the labels facing out neatly. I ate my brown toast and watched Backflip through the kitchen window: she peed under the flowering gum and then dug a small pointless hole.

•

At school, the normal feeling of things had stopped and the unease had set in. The news of Rosie White was everywhere. It had travelled down telephone lines and across dinner tables and onto the pages of the *Gather Region Advocate*. It had taken up residence in the minds of students and teachers. It sat in the silence between sentences; in the things that people did not say. Goodwood had never been visited by such collective worry, and we were not familiar with the burden of the unknown.

Classes went on as normal but everyone seemed distracted. I walked past three girls from Year Nine in the hall and heard one of them say, 'She has to be dead,' as they walked past. George and I heard Mrs Gwen Hughes, strewn with crystals, say, 'Terrible. Just terrible,' to Mr Cooper in the playground. They saw us and lowered their voices and George swore she heard Mrs Gwen Hughes say, furtively, '*Carl.*'

George and I spent lunchtime in the library by the heater vent to avoid everyone, and the cold. We sat up against the wall and rested our feet on the bottom shelf of the section marked *Australian History*. We went over every memory we had of Rosie.

Most of them were set at Woody's, and had us mainly as bystanders. Rosie saying a wry thing that we may or may not have understood, and us laughing along regardless; Rosie saying, 'Hey, guys,' in that way she did every now and again, as if we were her friends; Rosie offering us unsolicited school-yard advice. That was our favourite. George and I couldn't agree on the exact wording, but it was the time when Liz Gordon and Kiralee Davis had walked past Woody's while we were waiting for our food and Liz had yelled something unkind to George. Rosie made a noise like '*Pffffff*' and gave Liz the finger. Horrible Liz Gordon looked astonished and fit to fall over. Even Kiralee had a little laugh at her. We couldn't believe our luck—having such a bodyguard as Rosie, just for that moment. Then Rosie said something like, 'Don't even worry about it. Those girls'll never get out of this fucken town,' and George and I walked out, puffed up like balloons, triumphant with hot chips.

I remembered seeing Rosie getting driving lessons with Carl White earlier that year. He looked like an impatient teacher, and as I told it to George I realised it wasn't a nice memory. Rosie was gripping the steering wheel with both hands and he appeared to be chiding her as they crawled down our street. She looked, as I remembered it now, scared. Not of the car or the road, but of Carl. The thought of it pained me, and it pained George, and we both sat for a moment and stared off in confusion.

George had seen Rosie and Davo heading down to the clearing several times over the summer, just the two of them, which was obviously for the purpose of sex, we now concluded. George also recalled that her brother Toby asked Rosie out one time at Woody's and Rosie said, 'Sorry, *what* year are you in?' which we deemed a brilliant rebuttal. Considering how much of a pain in the arse George found Toby, she was extremely pleased to hear of the rejection, and it only further increased our appreciation of Rosie.

We sat silent for a while after that, which was an unusual state for me and George. We sat there and tried to remember more, but that was all we could remember.

9

The house directly next to ours was wooden and gabled and in it lived Big Jim and Fitzy.

Big Jim, as his name suggested, was almost a giant. It wasn't one of those instances where someone's called Tiny and they're as big as a house. Big Jim was un-ironically big. Heavy set, six feet and six inches, his head clipped the sky.

Then there was Fitzy. Big Jim's lady. Five foot nothing, and a whole lot of something. Never did a woman of such small proportions take up so much space as Fitzy.

She enjoyed her hair large and auburn, with bright combs holding the whole thing together at the back, and a fringe that looked set to take over her face like a shrub. She wore enormous red-framed glasses in homage to the talk show host Sally Jessy Raphael, who 'spoke' to Fitzy across hemispheres, and who Fitzy earnestly considered 'like a friend'. The glasses were vast and, due to the strength of Fitzy's prescription, an awful amount of Fitzy's visage was magnified. I found the size disparity between her eyes and the rest of her face to be very disorientating during our conversations.

Big Jim and Fitzy chose to cohabit but not to marry, allowing Fitzy to retain her maiden surname of Fitzgerald, which had been permanently shortened and, at some point, granted uncontested usage. Coral, who lived next door to them on the other side, found the situation quite peculiar, and loved to mention it disapprovingly to Val Sparks, who no doubt found it sinful, especially since both Big Jim and Fitzy had left their respective marriages in order to be together, and Big Jim didn't seem to see his kids. Fitzy, on the other hand, had been relieved of her uterus due to ovarian cancer and was, as such, childless.

'Our garden's our baby,' she said, pruning the murraya hedge.

Amid all the unease, that Saturday was a good day, because Big Jim and Fitzy brought home a new baby: a puppy. Backflip was beside herself when they carried it in, and jumped up trying to lick its face, while the tiny dog bleated like a lamb.

Big Jim was a gardener, in a professional capacity, in that his Hilux had *Big Jim's Gardening Services* sprayed on the side with his phone number and a picture of a red wheelbarrow. His small talk was endlessly concerned with either fish, birds or plants, often punctuated by his favourite expression: 'You can plant a dead stick in the ground here and it'll grow.' Then he would look up at the sky and say, 'Fish are biting today I reckon,' as if the information was bestowed upon him from the clouds.

Big Jim provided constant commentary on our gardenia or our grevillea or our lavender. 'Nice and healthy, that is,' as he caressed a leaf and smelt a flower. He offered unsolicited lessons in botanical names. '*Tropaeolum majus* is what that one's called. That's the Latin.' Or, 'How about the difference in the pH level in the soil from your place to ours, Jean? We're just next-door and look at the difference of colour in the hydrangeas. That's the alkaline.' And my eyes would glaze over as I'd say, 'Wow, would you look at that,' and Mum thought it was hilarious how boring one man could be about plants, a subject she found quite interesting if anyone else was talking.

Big Jim called their new puppy Myrtle. I learnt, from Big Jim telling me all about it, that myrtle is an evergreen shrub. They'd gotten Myrtle from Big Jim's mate Merv's recently pregnant terrier, who was called Periwinkle. 'And do you know what the definition of myrtle is in the dictionary, Jean? The lesser periwinkle! That's the dictionary definition! Get it, Jean? How good is that?'

'It's very good,' I said.

It was Mum's suggestion, as we all sat in their front yard and the dogs tussled, that I should go up to Bart's to get a bag of bones. 'Little meaty bones,' she said, as a welcome to Myrtle.

I was pleased to be excused, and I stood in front of the sausage display while Bart fixed some little meaty bones in a plastic bag.

'How've you been, Jean, good? How's your mum?'

'Yeah, good. Big Jim and Fitzy got a puppy. It's pretty cute.'

Bart stood behind the counter in his butcher's striped apron. The collar of a canary-coloured polo shirt sat under his kind face. On the wall behind him was a cluster of framed photographs. There was Bart and Mrs Bart with Pearl, in a riding hat. There was Bart at the lake, grinning, holding a giant fish, flanked by Roy Murray on one side and Carmel Carmichael on the other. There was Bart and the Mayor and a group of men from the council. And Bart holding an Excellence in Small Business Award certificate, the photo of which hung next to an array of other laminated local business prizes, and thankyous from the school and the CWA and the Goodwood Progress Association and the Bowlo, and a poster for last year's Fishing's The Funnest parade.

'You been worried about all the business this week?' asked Bart.

I looked at my feet and said I was.

Bart said, 'Yeah,' sympathetically.

It was the last conversation I would have with Bart, not that I knew it at the time. Not that I'd paid much attention to any of the conversations I'd had with Bart, really. I was young and he was old. He'd say a friendly thing and I'd nod along. But he always did have time for a chat, no matter who was waiting. That was something I remember thinking during our last conversation: that Bart always seemed to have the time.

'She'll turn up,' he said confidently. 'Don't you worry yourself too much with all the things people are saying.' He tied a knot in the bag of bloody bones. Cartilage poked out at strange angles and red juices gathered in the plastic creases. 'This is a safe town.'

Backflip and I walked past Woody's on the way home and, even though I half-expected to see her, Rosie wasn't there. There was just one of Terry's signs hanging in the window, next to a poster for the Clarke Show. And Derek Murray, frying chips and laughing his unpleasant face off with Trent Ross. *Ha ha ha ha*, went Trent and Derek, and I wasn't sure how Derek Murray could be laughing. The one place where Rosie's absence was most obvious was behind the counter at Woody's. She stared out from the photocopied Year Twelve picture and the memory of her hovered there—like a ghost, or a mist, or a web—reminding everyone that she was gone.

I remember thinking that day that there was nothing much worse than a missing person. Rosie had vanished and all that was left was a hole where she once was. Or in this case, all that was left was Derek Murray. I looked at him, filling the spot where Rosie should have been, emptying chips from the wire basket onto a sheet of butcher's paper on the counter, surrounded by the thick air. I thought he must've felt like he'd walked through a spider's web and got some stuck in his hair.

10

As it turned out, there was something worse than a missing person: two missing people.

Bart often fished on a Sunday. A lot of men in Goodwood fished on a Sunday. There was a cluster of boats on the lake that bobbed up and down all week waiting to be taken out. Bart's was a Savage fibreglass half-cabin cruiser in white and royal blue. Bart loved his boat. He spent many a Sunday in peaceful solitude on Grants Lake with the motor off and the anchor down, fishing and drinking beer and eating beef sandwiches.

The Sunday in question, Mrs Bart prepared Bart's sandwiches, and Bart packed his gear and popped a sixpack into his little esky from the bar fridge in the carport. The McDonalds' carport was like an aeroplane hangar and heavy with cars. Bart mostly drove a white Commodore and Mrs Bart drove a Mazda 323. Then they had a Hilux for when they did farmy stuff and an old Corolla that once belonged to burly Joe and usually sat on the far left, next to the bar fridge and deep freezer, and was kept mainly for the use of Mrs Bart's sister Jan, who 'never married' as Coral would say, and visited Goodwood via bus several times a year.

Bart took the Hilux out to the lake that day, with his rods in the tray. Faye Haynes, who ran the Goodwood Village Bakery, attested to the fact that Bart had stopped in briefly for a coffee scroll. Then he pulled off again, eating it out of the paper bag, and was seen waving to several people on his way down Cedar Street, including Nance, whose counter in the front window of the Goodwood Grocer was positioned so she could witness everything that happened on the main road during daylight hours. Bart wore his yellow windcheater and Nance saw it, and she saw him wave, and she saw him drive off towards the lake, and that was the last of him she ever did see.

Bart would have driven the long road out of town alongside the river, then the stretch that sidles around the base of the mountain in shadow. He would've gone past the rest stop just before the bridge, and flattened that old dead kangaroo a fraction more into the bitumen. Then over the bridge, nice and high above the lake, and eventually—after two kilometres of fast flat road—onto the wide patch of browned grass where cars park near the boat wharves.

Grants was a big, meandering lake. So big that if you stood at its widest point and looked to the other side, a person standing there would appear as small as a fleck of sand. The lake turned corners around the foothills of the mountain and had several secluded horseshoes that bent into the shore like giant private pools. Pop took me out lots when I was younger, or when he was younger, but his age meant that his boat was more patient than most, and I doubt it'd been taken out in nearly five years. Not like Bart's much-used cruiser, which was found later that afternoon by Big Jim and Merv, who were doing some fishing of their own when they noticed the unusual sight of Bart's boat nodding sideways in the wind.

As they approached, they wondered if Bart was tricking.

'Bart?' they yelled.

No reply.

They came up on his cruiser, cut their engine and bumped his boat with theirs as they peered over.

There was Bart's gear, and Bart's beer, but no sign nor sight nor smell of Bart.

Merv boarded Bart's boat while Big Jim kept theirs steady. As Big Jim later recalled, Merv looked at him dead serious, shaking his head, saying, 'Mate. *Fuck*. He's gone.'

They surveyed the water for a further few minutes or so. Brown and choppy, it offered no glimpse of anything human. Merv wanted to tow the boat back with them, but Big Jim insisted on dropping Bart's anchor so whoever was going to come looking would know where to look.

'Good thinking, BJ,' said Merv as they headed back full throttle to the wharf and their car, their faces flushed with worry.

There were no phone booths between the lake and Goodwood, so they sped back to town in Merv's ute and called Mack from Merv's house to tell him what they'd found.

Mack said that as soon as he got the call he knew how bad it was. Bart was an experienced boatman—one of Goodwood's finest. He knew Grants Lake like the back of his hand. He'd been out there every week for the past eight years. He was known to be a stickler for safety rules and regulations. A man like that didn't usually end up, on a relatively calm day, relieved of his boat.

By the time Mack got the call it was almost six and winter dark. It put him in the awful position of having to knock on Mrs Bart's door with bad news and no ability to make it any better until the sun rose the next morning. Mrs Bart, on answering the door, crumpled. Mack told Mum and me the next day that it was the hardest door knock he'd ever done, and that no matter how much he rubbed them, he could still feel the difficulty of it there, on his knuckles.

On the Sunday evening, though, Mum and I were blissfully unaware. We heard Big Jim arrive home next door, but he didn't come over to tell us the news. Fitzy said later that he came inside—wordless, most unusual—and got down on all fours on the living room floor. The big man just crouched there like a table while Fitzy asked the table over and over again what was wrong.

•

The following day, Bart's Meats was closed and Mrs Bart was pacing. Everyone on Cedar Street knew the bad news by mid-morning. It filtered through the school gates and into our classrooms, while Mr Cooper and Ms Carr and Mr Davies and Mrs King huddled in the doorways and corridors to discuss possibilities and ramifications and how-could-it-bes.

George said, 'Two people. What are the odds?'

I did not know the odds.

All I knew was that I'd just seen Bart two days ago, tying up a bag of bloody bones, and now he was gone.

Bart and Flora McDonald had only been in Goodwood for eight years. They weren't lifers like most of the other shop-keepers on Cedar Street. They had their son, Joe, who was grown up and lived in Sydney and a daughter, Pearl, whose mind sat somewhere on the rainbow spectrum of autism and who found solace only in horses. When she was younger, Pearl had festooned her bedroom with horseshoes and bridles and her full set of My Little Ponies. The latter gave the entire room the effect of a pastel equine kaleidoscope. By the age of nine, Pearl could name the gross and microscopic anatomies of horses, as well as donkeys and zebras: external, digestive, reproductive, skeletal and so on. She was a walking encyclopaedia of equestrian terms and trivia. And Pearl watched a horse movie every night before bed: *The Black Stallion*, *The Man From Snowy River*, *National Velvet*, *Phar Lap*, *Black Beauty*. Nan told me there was a very specific movie roster at the McDonald house that no man or mountain could disturb.

As she grew, Bart and Mrs Bart bought Pearl a horse—an Appaloosa with a snowflake coat—which Pearl called Oyster.

When they'd lived in Sydney, the McDonalds drove Pearl out to the stable lot they rented, a fifty-minute drive, three times a week.

It wasn't enough. Pearl became difficult to manage on the remaining four days, and more and more despondent when she wasn't with Oyster.

So, after many long evening discussions over chardonnay and crackers, the McDonalds decided to leave the city and move to Goodwood. Bart opened Bart's Meats, a rural version of his store in the northern suburbs of Sydney, and Mrs Bart experimented with new glazes for her pottered crockery, made jam, and ascended with lightening quickness to the position of Secretary of the Goodwood branch of the Country Women's Association. Meanwhile, Pearl, at twenty-two, spent all her days with Oyster, along with Apples and Pears, the two pintos they had since acquired.

Bart was good at gifts. He was an intuitive and imaginative giver. Not only had he sated Pearl with horses, he expressed himself lovingly through his generosity to Mrs Bart, too, and had done so throughout their long marriage. For one Christmas: a star. Mrs Bart was very fond of stars. She enjoyed gazing into the sky over Goodwood, where they shone so brightly. 'There's nothing brighter than country stars,' she would say. So Bart bought her one, from the Sydney Observatory, and he named it Flora—verified by a certificate that arrived in the mail. Flora the star was in the Phoenix constellation, and flickered away endlessly. Flora the woman—or Mrs Bart, as we all knew her—was so thrilled she cried.

For Mrs Bart's forty-fifth: a piano. Mrs Bart had always wanted to learn, and longed for the kind her mother had owned: a Richard Lipp. There wasn't one to buy in Goodwood, or Clarke, or Cedar Valley, or even Sydney for that matter. So Bart had one driven by truck from Melbourne and it arrived on the morning of Mrs Bart's birthday and she was so thrilled, she cried.

Three years later, for Mrs Bart's forty-eighth, Bart gave his wife a rose garden. Full of flora, as it were. *I never promised you a rose garden, but I got you one anyway*, said the card, which also contained a map and directions that led into the foothills of the mountain. Mrs Bart followed the map on horseback. She arrived at a clearing, which was filled with a rose garden that Big Jim had planted especially at the direction of Bart. She dismounted and knelt and—the thrill of it!—all those fragrant coloured flowers. The very special thrill of the map and the ride and the clearing and the roses. Mrs Bart cried and cried and cried.

But on the day after Bart went missing, Mrs Bart did not cry. She paced. And in the days that Mrs Bart spent pacing, her sister, Jan, stayed with Pearl. Jan loved her niece, and happened to be in Goodwood at the time Bart went on his fishing trip of no return. Jan and Pearl rode all day, the horses' hooves mimicking Mrs Bart's own feet, as they paced around the paddock, along the river trail, and into the foothills of the mountain.

Pearl struggled to express her sorrow about the absence of her father—and that of her mother, who was gone for five days in the shop, unable to show her grief to Pearl, and hoping always that Bart would be the next one to cause the bell above the shop door to ring.

Jan knew that Pearl, in her own words, 'didn't do feelings'. So Jan kept Pearl busy doing what she always did: riding, grooming, pitching straw, bucketing manure, feeding, watering and hanging up her saddle at the end of the day. Of an evening, Jan would hear Pearl out in the stables talking to Oyster, whispering at times—saying in her strange mono-tone, 'It's alright. It's alright, gentle Oyster'—and Oyster responding every so often with snorts and whinnies.

•

After the divers dived, and nothing was recovered, a simple drowning was still the most popular theory. Mum was convinced of it. He'd tripped and fallen, maybe hit his head on the way over. Or he'd had another heart attack. That was not unlikely. Bart's heart was known to be weaker than most—he'd already had an episode a couple of years earlier, on the riding trail with Pearl. So maybe he'd had another, this time on his boat, and gone over and under. There was a wind; maybe they didn't dive in the right spot. Maybe, said Big Jim, the boat had drifted for a long time before he and Merv had found it. Bart could've been anywhere down there, for who knew what varied paths him and his boat might've floated along.

That was the thing for Mack, though: Bart's lack of floating. He was known to wear a life vest. He was a councillor, an elected man, a pillar of the community. He had completed a First Aid and Cardiopulmonary Resuscitation course through St John's Ambulance. He drove safely, and offered well wishes, and gave great gifts, and every now and again he'd take a mate fishing with him. Roy Murray sometimes, or Irene Oakman, who also 'never married', wore much purple, and was known to prefer the company of women. Irene Oakman said that on the three occasions she fished with Bart, he wore his life vest and had provided one for her also.

So, Mack wondered, why didn't Bart float?

Pop said sensibly, well, Bart might've *been* floating. There were many marshy banks where no roads neared for many kilometres. The police boats travelled the perimeter as best they could, but in some areas the marshes prohibited access for a good ten metres out from shore. They were matted like brambles and hooked plastic bags and other passing jetsam. The police hadn't sighted Bart in any of the bends, in any of the marshes, above or under the water. But it was a big lake.

When the Clarke police had finished their search and directed their investigations towards other avenues, many people in town continued looking. Mack did, as did Big Jim and Merv, bald Bob Elver, Irene Oakman, Smithy, and Carmel Carmichael who owned the Bowlo and bore the unfortunate burden of a name that few people could easily say. It was nice—the community spirit. All of them out there all week, taking time off work, utilising boats they didn't often utilise, and meeting at the Wicko for steaks after—sombre and, increasingly, drunk.

'He'd've been out there for us,' said Smithy. 'He'd've looked till he found any of us. Otherwise—what? We'll all sit around and say, "Oh, we should've looked." None of that. You either shit or get off the pot. So we look.' And they all agreed.

The Clarke police didn't have an opinion on that, but they did seem to have an opinion on Bart, in that Mack said that Sergeant Simmons said that there's no such thing as a coincidence.

First Rosie vanished. And then Bart. 'And now, Mack,' said Sergeant Simmons, 'you can believe in people's good nature all you want, but this is a small town. What are the odds of two people going missing, exactly one week apart, in a town this small?'

Mack did not know the odds.

'There's gotta be a connection,' said the sergeant.

And, bless his heart, that was the first time the possibility of a connection had occurred to Mack.

'What, like a serial killer?' asked Mack.

'Nah, not a fucken serial killer,' said Sergeant Simmons, half laughing. 'But, mate, a connection.'

11

'Do you think they're connected?' I asked George.

'What is?'

'Rosie and Bart,' I said. 'Them disappearing.'

'Oh,' said George, eating her sandwich, 'I don't know. Do you?'

'I don't know,' I said, eating my sandwich.

I wanted to tell George about the money—and the absence of the money, and the plastic horse—but something made me continue to keep it all to myself. It had occurred to me that morning on the way to school that I'd forgotten all about it. So much had happened, and there was so much else to think about. What with Rosie, and then Bart.

On its own, money in a tree didn't necessarily mean anything. But the more I thought about what Mum said Mack said Sergeant Simmons said—that there is no such thing as a coincidence—the more I worried.

'Do you mean like a serial killer?' asked George.

'No, God. I don't know. I don't think so.'

'Because they're totally different. Rosie is so young and cool and all in her room. And Bart was old and on his boat.'

'Yeah,' I said.

'And, I don't know . . . Bart drowned, didn't he? Or he had a heart attack and fell in or whatever.'

George put the rest of her sandwich down, like she was no longer hungry. She frowned. I didn't know what to think. Except that I should go to the clearing later and check if the horse was still in the bag.

'He did seem to drown,' I said.

•

Ethan West was my age, a good foot taller than me, and blond and tanned. His nose went a bit red in the sun and he often smeared zinc across it when he swam at the river, his body lean and well-proportioned and admired. When he swung off the big branch that hung over the water, his arms were as long as spears. I admired them, and so did George. Ethan would lope on down with Lucas Karras and we would all drink pilfered beer and swim at the twilight of summer, when it was too cold for the cooler kids to hog the clearing.

In March that year, Ethan had begun his practice of looking at me for longer than was necessary—and then George would elbow me or cough. George never missed a long look, and

George never missed an opportunity to make it clear that she never missed a long look. 'He *looks* at you,' she would say. And I would say, 'Not as much as Lucas looks at you.'

Ethan's parents had moved themselves and their two sons from a town in Queensland even smaller than Goodwood. Ethan's little brother Petey was mostly barefoot, even in winter. Ethan's mum was an avid member of the CWA and presumably didn't have time to shop for kids' shoes. And then there was Ethan's dad, who used to be a dairy farmer before he shattered all the bones in his left leg in a horrific accident involving his herd and a metal fence. Unfortunately, Ethan's dad had been in the middle, and there's nothing like the weight of cows to break a set of bones.

Ethan told us that Mal West could no longer do physical work, with a cane and a bung leg, so they'd moved to Goodwood to be near family, and Mal had become terribly depressed. He drank enough beer to fill the river and he got mean when he was drunk. He was angry at cows. He was angry at fences. In fact, the Wests were the only family I'd ever known to knock down their own fence when they moved in. Ethan's mum planted English Box where the fence had been, and shaped it into squared solid blocks with a shiny pair of topiary shears.

Ethan missed the cows, and during the times we'd all spent at the clearing, he would walk up to the fence and put both his spear-arms out until a docile cow approached. The herd was unsure at first. With other people they would snort, or hoof the ground, or toss their big heads. But Ethan was like a magnet for them. He was a beacon. He stood at the fence, offering nothing but himself, and the cows gathered near in a huddle and stared forth, as if his very presence calmed them into a bovine trance.

'Hi, Jean,' said Ethan West, appearing beside me as I walked out of the school gate that day, his nose red in the winter sun.

'Oh, hi,' I said, and we walked together as the rest of the school wandered in various clusters up the hill towards Cedar Street.

'You wanna go see the cows with me?'

Ethan's boots made a clopping sound. He scuffed them along the ground like it was too much of an effort to lift his long legs up enough in order to get his big feet off the ground.

'When, now?'

'Yeah,' he said, with his hands in his pockets. He was being very casual about the whole thing, even though this was the first time he'd invited me to go anywhere just the two of us.

'Is Lucas coming?'

'Oh, nah,' he said.

All I could think of was that I wanted to check the tree-hole, and that the tree-hole was at the clearing where the cows often were.

'I have to go home and get Backflip,' I said, wondering if I could check for the plastic horse while Ethan entranced the cows. He looked down at me and stared for a moment too long before his eyes found the ground again. He was no Big Jim, but he certainly was tall.

'Can I come?' he asked. 'To get Backflip?'

I wasn't sure what to say.

Liz Gordon and Kiralee Davis jostled by us with George's brother Toby, who punched my arm on his way past. I wasn't really in the mood for company, but I didn't know what to tell Ethan. He looked expectant. There was something about him that seemed almost fragile, or hidden away.

'Okay,' I said.

And that was how Ethan West and I ended up spending the afternoon together.

When we got to my house, he waited outside with his hands in his pockets while I went to get Backflip. I told him he could come in, but he declined.

Mum gave me a bemused look and said, 'Is that Ethan West waiting outside?'

I said, 'Yes, that is very clearly Ethan West waiting outside.'

Mum was plainly entertained. I sensed that she had to restrain herself from winking.

We walked past Bart's Meats on the way to the river and I was quite interested to discuss the disappearances with Ethan and get his particular opinion on the whole thing.

'Full on about that business, hey,' he said. 'My mum's all upset about it.' And then he changed the subject to cows.

We stopped briefly at Woody's, so Ethan could get a chocolate Moove. Derek Murray took Ethan's money and said, 'How's it going?' in a way that indicated he didn't give two shits about the answer.

'Yeah, sweet,' said Ethan, oblivious, and Derek Murray had already turned back to the deep fryer.

We arrived at the paddock fence next to the clearing and Ethan offered me a sip of his Moove. I said: 'It's so weird that Rosie just isn't there, don't you think?' and Ethan said of the cows, 'I knew *they'd* be here, though. They get moved from the other paddock to this one on Saturday at dusk. And then they'll go on back to the other paddock this Saturday.'

'At dusk?'

'Yeah, at dusk,' he said, putting his arms out. 'Kevin moves them back and forth every Saturday at dusk.'

I knew Kevin Fairley owned the Fairley Dairy. He was a friend of Pop's, kind of, in that they used to boat together on occasion. Also, I knew Nan had concerns for Kevin because farming's a chancy business, and Kevin was in it all alone. But, alone or not, Kevin Fairley was not much seen in town since his wife had passed, and I wondered how Ethan knew the specifics of his routine.

'I help him out a bit, every now and again,' said Ethan, which cleared that right up.

'Why dusk?' I asked.

'Oh, because it's better for them when it's dimmer light. They get less stressed out when you move them. Kev moves them at dusk and he talks all slow and quiet. Then they settle into the new paddock better.'

The cows moved slowly towards us—or towards Ethan, really—and Backflip started barking and carrying on. I shooed her off towards the water, where she thankfully found the ducks more interesting than the cows. I watched her wade in, panting, and the ducks disperse. I watched her stand still in the water and shake herself, and the ducks flap off in fright.

Then Ethan and I stood by the fence and looked at the gathered cows, as planned, while the slow, loping animals mooed and ruminated. Ethan told me that cows have four digestive compartments; they drink about a bathtub of water a day; and they sit down when it's going to rain. He also told me that some people milk reindeer.

We talked a good while by the fence while Backflip ate the best part of a fallen branch. I could feel Ethan move a bit closer to me every so often. His leg finally touched my leg about half an hour after we got there and then we sat down under the willow tree on the bank and then we lay on our backs next to each other and looked up at the canopy and let there be silence except for the birds.

Ethan had big lungs. The air went in and out much louder than mine and for a while it was all I heard. Just air and birds. I kept staring upwards and so did he. His spear-arm lay by his side, and then he shuffled himself around so his arm ended up touching my arm, as we lay there on the ground. Soon he had put his hand over my hand and held it. I wondered if perhaps he would turn his head towards me. I wondered if he was going to kiss me, and if he'd taste like chocolate milk and paddocks.

Backflip had sat down right next to me, having dragged her half-eaten branch up from the bank like a trophy. She stank and panted away with her eyes closed in joy.

A cow mooed.

Then Ethan sat up abruptly, looking at his watch.

'Shit,' he said, getting up and dusting his jeans off with his big hands. 'Jeannie, I gotta go.'

Not many people called me Jeannie. It was nice.

'Okay,' I said, propping myself up on my elbows.

'I gotta go get Petey from Lego Pat's house,' he said. 'Mum's been all worried about him walking home by himself since Rosie got—you know.' He paused and looked over his shoulder. 'Since she's been missing.'

It was as if that last word was very difficult for him to say. *Missing*.

He said it over his shoulder to the cows.

I looked up at him and he seemed to be in a whole different world all of a sudden. The world of the missing, maybe. Somewhere very far away—like even the thought of Rosie took him there and he couldn't easily come back. I wondered how well Ethan had known her. I wondered if he'd found her inscrutable or desirable or free.

'Hey, can you not tell anyone I work for Kevin?' He was looking back at me now, full of concern.

'Oh, okay,' I said. It seemed like a strange thing to be kept private. 'Why, is it a secret?'

He laughed—a bit too loud. 'Oh, nah, it's just between me and Kevin, you know?'

'Oh. Sure,' I said. But I didn't know.

Then he picked up his bag and put it over one shoulder.

I watched him walk back along the bank towards town.

When he'd gone, I climbed the willow and stood on the branch as tall as I could muster, which was much less than Ethan West could've—he would've had no trouble popping whatever he wanted in a high tree-hole. I could see the white plastic bag poking out just a fraction, just as I had left it.

I looked around the clearing and saw no one. Just Backflip, panting on the ground near the willow. I pulled the bag out and felt the shape of the horse inside, running my fingers along the bumps of its hard mane and along its snout. I thought about Ethan. His breath went in and out as loud as Backflip's. I had thought no one came to the clearing in winter, but maybe Ethan did? Maybe he came down here to visit the cows all year round and sat in this very tree. Or maybe he just helped out Kevin up in the paddocks on Saturdays at dusk.

I reached up and put the horse and bag back in the hole and climbed to the bottom of the willow where names and initials were carved into the trunk. I had carved mine with George's Swiss Army knife when I was thirteen. JEAN. George had carved her initials near mine: G.S. The newer carvings were paler, since they hadn't seen so much weather. The newest carving, in fact, looked brand new. It was right around the emptier side of the trunk, down low. RW 4 DC, it said, clean as a whistle, and as soon as I saw it my stomach fell.

Rosie White and Davo Carlstrom. Sitting in a tree.

•

That night Mum and I went to Nan and Pop's for dinner. Nan made a lentil soup that was so warming I took my jumper off at the table. Pop went back to the shed after dinner to potter around, and Nan and Mum and I sat in front of the fire. I was permitted to watch television while they drank wine.

Nan was terribly upset about Bart. So was Pop, but he hid his feelings about it in the shed. He was quieter since Rosie vanished; and quieter still about Bart. But Nan could not be quiet about any of it. She had talked non-stop at dinner and then non-stop after. How could this happen? Why can't they find him? She took a big sip of wine and slouched back in the armchair, shaking her head at how big the lake was.

Mum tried to coax Nan out of her low mood by teasing me about Ethan West.

'Jean had a hot date this afternoon,' she said.

'We looked at cows,' I said, without turning around from the television.

'They looked at cows. This is what the kids do these days,' said Mum.

'Don't marry a dairy farmer,' said Nan. 'It's a chancy business.'

Nan got up and put another log on the fire. She pushed it around with the poker and stood up for a while with her arms folded. Then she sat back down, deep in thought. Pretty soon she was talking about Bart again.

'Do you remember Don's 70th? Bart brought over *all* those scotch fillets. And he wouldn't take any money. He was just like that. He has time for everyone. Remember when he gave Mrs Bart a rose garden? And that piano? He was so generous. Oh dear, Celia. I think it must've been his heart again. Do you think? He's had another heart attack and gone over into the water.'

Nan went on for quite a while like that, switching confusingly between the past and present tense when she spoke of him.

'There was no one he didn't have time for,' she said.

'Except . . .' said Mum, and there was a pause. Then the silent sound of a penny dropping and Nan saying, 'Oh. Yes,' and crackles from the fire.

'Except who?' I asked, turning around from the TV.

'Jeannie, honey, don't be a creep,' said Mum. 'This is our conversation.'

'Except who?' I asked again. 'Nan?'

They both looked at me and said nothing, and then Nan looked at Mum as if to apologise for what she was about to say.

'Except Carl White,' she said.

12

After almost three weeks without a daughter, Judy White began making brief appearances in town, having finally left the house where she had hovered, in and out of view—sometimes in front of the living room windows, sometimes just inside the screen door, sometimes in the wooden frame of Rosie's window, and always in her dressing-gown.

I saw her go into the Grocer on the Saturday, properly dressed, and saw Nance anxiously fumble with the arrangement of her counter display, as if it was suddenly quite urgent. Then, when Judy had chosen her grocery items and arrived at the counter to pay, Nance clasped her hands together as if in prayer and offered her worried condolences. Judy tried her best to smile but her face could not make one. She looked grim.

I passed her as I went in and tried to make eye contact, so I could offer a look of support, but her head was hung low, as if her shoes were the only horizon she could find to quell her seasick heart.

Then she crossed the street and started off on what I assumed to be the long way home, so she didn't have to go past Woody's.

•

Davo Carlstrom had also been keeping a low profile, and had only been seen at the Wicko once since Rosie vanished. Smithy had to ask him and his bogan uncle to kindly leave, because Davo got so drunk he was threatening to lose consciousness in the front bar.

Perhaps due to his rebellious disposition, people looked sideways at Davo now. People spoke about him in tones of disapproval, heavy with question marks and the occasional accusation.

'It's just like "Hazard" by Richard Marx,' said George.

George didn't really look sideways at Davo, though. George looked sideways at Davo's bogan uncle, every time she walked up her street. Especially since he dressed most days in an Adidas tracksuit and had lined up a row of empty beer cans on the front fence, as if waiting for the energy to fetch his gun.

After some effort, we discovered his name was Lafe and that he'd been a mechanic in Albion Park, where he'd fallen on some kind of hard times, hit various kinds of bottles, and ended up in Goodwood, mostly drunk and living in his brother's crap caravan. This only added more cause to the fact that the Carlstroms were not particularly appreciated in town. Davo's mum, Linda, worked at the Ingham Further Processing Plant, which was a good hour away—or four hours if you stopped at the Royal Tavern in Cedar Valley every night on the way home. George and I were horrified by whatever 'further processing' meant when it came to chickens; and mothers in town were, historically, horrified by the fact that Linda was never home.

'No wonder,' said George's mum, Spray n' Wiping their counter. 'He's been left there while Linda goes out drinking his whole life.'

'No wonder *what*?' asked George.

Noelene paused and said, pointedly, '*You know.*' Gravid with disfavour.

The uncle, Lafe, had only been in the caravan for three months, and had apparently been given a further three to sort himself out and move on. Davo's dad was loyal to his brother, but his loyalty was strained by the renewed attention on his family. While previous decades had shuffled past in the sleepy town of Goodwood with little interest from law enforcement, suddenly it wasn't such a good thing to look like a criminal, especially when your nephew was 'connected', as they said, to an ongoing investigation.

In an attempt to create a more positive impression, or maybe just because he needed the assistance, Davo's dad—Dennis Carlstrom—soon wrangled Lafe into helping him fix the comatose cars that he bought at the Clarke Wreckers or through the *Trading Post*, planted in their yard, and covered with tarpaulins. I thought it was an improvement when Lafe changed from his Adidas tracksuit to his khaki coveralls and actually started doing something with his days, but George said that he often left his buttons undone in particular places, so you could see a bit more of Lafe than you were supposed to. Towards the end of that second week after Rosie vanished, George walked past the Carlstrom house to see Lafe leaning against his caravan with his buttons gaping, looking her right in the eye, leering, and then down at his nether regions. George was horrified and ran home.

•

On the better side of town, Carl White's routine seemed largely unchanged. He went to work, driving up Cedar Street with his radio on loud enough to hear through closed windows. He did whatever it was he did in his shed till the wee hours, as faithfully reported by Opal Jones next door, for she could see the fluorescent light from her bedroom window, and the tiny cloud of moths and night bugs that hovered there, well into the night. Mainly, though, Carl White sat in front of the pokie machine nearest to the ladies toilets at the Bowlo and slotted in coin after coin after coin.

Carmel Carmichael, who had a good view of Carl's favourite pokie from her spot behind the bar, said that to look at him going about his business, you couldn't tell if the man was upset in the slightest. You couldn't tell if he was anything at all—except gambling, he was certainly doing that. But the more people thought about it, the more people felt that Carl White's lack of emotion—given the recent gaping hole in his family—indicated something unsavoury.

When Mum and I were returning books at the library, Mum's friend Denise the librarian said, 'He's a bit cold, don't you think? Given the circumstances?'

Mum said diplomatically, 'Well, we don't know what they must be going through,' which didn't seem to satisfy Denise at all.

Only a few months earlier, Mum and I had been watching the news when the government awarded Lindy Chamberlain over a million dollars in compensation for wrongful imprisonment. Mum had said to me, speaking over the television, 'Do you know why they convicted her, Jean? Because they thought she was unemotional. That and her religion, which people didn't like. Everyone thought she was in a cult and should've been crying more. You know what I think? I think everyone grieves in their own way.'

So I wasn't sure what to make of Carl White. Except I did have some feelings when I walked past the White house, which I was prone to do at that time, and saw Judy, hovering in the bay window in her dressing-gown. She looked seasick, like she was standing on the deck of a ship, swaying in the still air. I felt that it would've been nice if, at least one time, Carl had been there beside her.

●

Mack, Tracy and little Jasper came to our house for a barbeque on the Sunday, two weeks after Bart had vanished, with a potato salad and a bag of sausages. Mum invited Mrs Bart and Pearl too—through Mack, who was visiting the McDonald house most days—but Mack advised that Mrs Bart had thankfully declined, and the only outings she had any room for, emotionally, were either CWA- or horse-related.

Backflip and I went walking through the foothills that morning and passed Pearl and Oyster on the trail. Oyster and Backflip weren't natural friends, so we kept a wide berth, but I waved at Pearl and she waved back and I could smell Oyster's horsey aroma.

I wanted so badly to offer my condolences. I wanted to say something comforting, but—much like Helen with Terry White that day at the newsagent—I panicked and got flustered and said, 'Have a good one!'

Have a good one. Her dad had just been swallowed by the lake—and she was going to have a good one?

Pearl rode out of earshot. The smell of Oyster receded. I felt foolish, verging on heartless, all the way home.

After everyone had eaten, I stacked the dishwasher and Mack brought in the empty meat tray, dripping with bloody juices. I rinsed it and he got another beer from the fridge, and I was on the verge of telling him about the money when Mum and Tracy came in laughing together with more plates, and Mack hugged Tracy from behind tenderly, and everyone settled on the couch while Mum made tea.

The conversation over lunch had touched on various topics. Mum, who worked as a proofreader at the *Gather Region Advocate*, had gone up to four days working at the paper; Myrtle had learnt her own name; Ethan West had taken me to look at cows and wasn't that hilarious and isn't he tall; and Mack had been doing the work of several officers for the past two weeks, while the Clarke station was slowly reducing its support. Meanwhile, Jasper fed pieces of apple to Backflip under the table and Mum and I pretended not to notice.

Everyone was trying to talk about nice things, but everyone was dying to talk about Rosie and Bart.

Luckily, one curious item of information had come to Mack's attention since the last time we had all spoken. And against his better judgement—with the encouragement of several afternoon beers and Mum's persistent questions—he eventually told us. Apparently, about a week before Bart disappeared, which was around the time that Rosie disappeared, the McDonalds' old Corolla—the one that sat unused most of the time in the carport—had been stolen.

Mrs Bart hadn't gone to town on the Monday. She'd stayed home, glazed two ceramic salad bowls, and gone riding with Pearl. On the Tuesday morning she had secretarial business at the CWA so she packed her purse and went to her car—the Mazda—only to realise the Corolla wasn't in its spot. The bulk of the Hilux had been concealing its absence.

Bart had driven off in the Commodore earlier and was already at the shop, so Mrs Bart went back inside to call him.

'Bushka, the Corolla's gone,' she had said.

'Is it now?' Bart had replied.

'Yeah, you didn't notice?'

'I don't reckon I did,' said Bart. 'The Hilux is in the way.'

'Why wouldn't they've taken the Hilux? Or the Commodore?' said Mrs Bart, very confused about the whole thing.

'Maybe they were after fuel efficiency,' Bart said, in an amused tone.

'Bush, the car's been stolen, what are you? Cracking jokes?'

'Sorry, honey, I've got people here—we'll talk about it later.'

'I'll call Mack,' she said.

'No, no, no—I'll pop over there in a minute and fill him in,' said Bart, and they hung up.

Mrs Bart assumed Bart had popped over to the station. In fact, Bart told her that evening that he had; that Mack had filed the relevant paperwork; that they'd have to wait and see, and if it didn't turn up then he'd call the NRMA and file a claim.

The problem was, Bart never went to the station.

Mrs Bart had been satisfied that the matter was being taken care of, and remembers mentioning it maybe one other time towards the end of the week. 'Any news from Mack about the Corolla?' she'd asked Bart over one of their steak dinners. To which Bart had said something along the lines of, 'Not yet, but I'm sure it'll turn up,' and didn't seem concerned about it at all.

Then she'd been distracted with Pearl, and Jan had arrived, and Bart had gone fishing and never come home, and she hadn't thought of the old car since. Until Mack was visiting and it dawned on her, as she was seeing him off in front of the carport, that she'd never spoken to him about it directly.

'I don't suppose it matters,' she said absentmindedly, staring at the horse sheds, 'but did you find anything on the Corolla?'

And that was the first Mack had heard of it.

Since that confusing conversation, Mack had gone over the events around the stolen car with Mrs Bart thoroughly, a line of inquiry which alarmed her a great deal, for she'd never known of any other instance, in their long and good marriage, when her husband had lied to her.

'Why would he? What's going on?' she pleaded, as Mack sat at her table making notes.

After ascertaining what Bart had said about the car, and what Bart had, or in this case, had *not* done, Mack didn't know how to pose the next question, for fear of alarming Mrs Bart further. But all he could think of was Constable Simmons's mocking face.

'Flora, do you know—I mean, from what you gather, did Bart know Rosie White . . . well?'

And just like that Mrs Bart burst into tears.

13

According to Mrs Bart, Bart knew Rosie White as well as he knew most people who worked on Cedar Street. Woody's was two doors up from Bart's Meats. The back of both businesses exited onto the same lane, which adjoined the same car park. They shared two dumpster bins, along with their immediate neighbours: the newsagent, Bookworm, and the Goodwood Village Bakery, where Bart bought his coffee scrolls. There was a big car park where Derek Murray sometimes did burnouts to impress his very few friends; and an awning that sheltered the back doors where Rosie, and now Derek Murray, would smoke on a fold-out chair. Bart also smoked, even though he continually promised Pearl he was giving up, and he occasionally allowed himself a cheeky one under the awning too, after he'd turned off the fluorescent lights, locked the front door, and put the garbage in the dumpster bins as the light faded over the mountain.

Mrs Bart said Bart was fond of Rosie, as he was fond of everyone really, but he just hadn't spoken of her since she'd vanished, even though Mrs Bart had raised it at dinner every night that week. This—said Mrs Bart—was odd. It was something she kept coming back to in her mind. The thought of it came and hovered there—teasing her, testing her, confronting her. It was just so *unlike* him. For Bart to be uninterested in a person he knew? A person who was in some kind of trouble? A person who was *missing*?

'He just didn't say anything about it all, which was . . . *odd*. Because everyone was talking about it. *I* wanted to talk about it,' she told Mack, sniffling, and he nodded. 'But you know, he hated Carl, so I'm not sure. I mean, it's probably nothing. It's nothing!'

Mack did know there was bad blood between Bart and Carl. It seemed that a lot of people in town knew. For instance, when Bart was thrown a party at the Bowlo one time, just for being an all-round terrific guy, everyone knew not to invite Carl. Much like they knew that Carl never took his boat out on Sundays anymore, as of two years ago, because that was Bart's day and they tended to avoid being on the same body of water at the same time.

I'm not sure Mum or Nan knew why, they just knew that it was; and similarly, as much as Mack had an inkling of it, this was the first time he'd ever ventured to ask, ever so gently, 'Why did Bart hate Carl?'

Mrs Bart shook her lowered head.

'Oh,' she said, 'it's not good.'

Mrs Bart shuffled in her chair. She pressed her fingers against her temples and Mack waited patiently until she gathered the wherewithal to explain, slowly, the dark history of her husband's ill feeling.

Bart and Carl had been cordial enough to begin with. The Whites and the McDonalds didn't socialise together as couples, but both men drank beer at the Wicko and the Bowlo, and Carl bought a good deal of topside. Judy White had attended Mrs Bart's floral art workshop at the CWA a few years back and had considered membership for a time, but never seemed to get around to it. Carl didn't seem to approve—which was odd, come to think of it. What's not to like about togetherness and craft? But in any case, Judy was busy seeing Rosie and Terry through high school and working as a nurse at Clarke Base Hospital. She was on duty the night Bart went to Emergency in the summer of 1990, after he'd suffered a mild heart attack while horseriding with Pearl. Bart had spent four days in the hospital and Judy was a nurse in his ward on two of those days. On the second occasion, she administered his medication and Bart asked her if she could please raise the blinds. She went to the window and lifted both her arms to untangle the cord, which Bart had made a mess of earlier, and Bart saw her dress hike up as she reached, and then he saw her thighs, which were black and blue and purple and red, like someone had taken to them with a belt and not let up.

Bart thanked her kindly and did not say a word. But he did go home and tell Mrs Bart that someone was laying a hand on Judy and he had a good idea who that person was.

'What do I do?' he had said. 'What can I do?'

Mrs Bart had not known what could be done.

A few months later, after Bart had fully recovered, Mrs Bart met with Nance and Helen and Faye at the Bowlo for a chardonnay. Carmel Carmichael had brought out a delightful surf and turf platter and they'd had a lovely time. They sat at the table inside looking out the big window onto the green. Carl White was also drinking there that day, heavily, with Roy Murray and Mal West.

As she was getting ready to leave, Mrs Bart excused herself to use the ladies room, which was at the end of the carpeted hall past the pokies. Roy and Mal had left, and Carl was having a flutter on his favourite machine closest to the toilets. Mrs Bart said, 'G'day Carl,' as she walked past, and he hopped up and followed her to the bathroom door, which she only realised when she felt a hand on the back of her thigh, at which point she shrieked and turned to find Carl, hungry, smiling at her with glazed eyes, saying, 'Come on, baby,' and groping for the small of her back.

It should be mentioned that Mrs Bart was an attractive and charismatic woman. She wasn't Secretary of the CWA for nothing. When the McDonalds moved to Goodwood, she turned heads. And so did Bart, in his rugged, handsome way. Mrs Bart had the face of a morning television presenter, or a pageant winner grown up. She injected a youthful energy into her secretarial duties, encouraging a younger membership than the association had ever enjoyed before. Nan always said she was a 'good girl'.

She was also quite strong, as it turned out, as she struck Carl White across the face so hard he fell all the way over. She stepped around him, saying nothing about it to her friends, and went home to tell Bart.

Bart was beyond recognition in his rage. 'Mortally angry' was how Mrs Bart described it. She spent the first part of the evening angry herself, and the second part trying to calm Bart down. But wild horses couldn't stop Bart. He backed the Hilux out of the drive (choosing the biggest car at his disposal), and drove to the White residence. That was where he found Judy doing one of her puzzles in front of the television, and Rosie and Terry somewhere off in their rooms, and Carl out back in his shed.

Mrs Bart didn't know what happened. All she knew was that Bart came home without a scratch on him, and that Carl White—as reported by Opal Jones next door—looked like someone had run him over with a trailer. Unwilling to explain his injuries to anyone, Carl simply avoided town for the most part, and made Judy buy him cases of beer and nurse him at home.

When he got home that night, after smashing Carl, Bart had spooned Mrs Bart closer than ever, and while he didn't shudder or move at all, she felt his tears fall onto the back of her neck and roll down the inside of her nightie.

14

In the third week after Bart vanished, Mum's need to be active in the face of anxiety took her beyond organising the pantry, and she began sorting through the back sunroom where she stored most of her 'secondary' books.

Much like Nan, Mum had always been a big reader. She told me she spent all her time at Goodwood High reading and dreaming of her life in the big city. She'd considered Melbourne but chose Sydney. It was much closer and, when it came time, she could fit all her things in one carload.

Nan and Pop knew she'd be leaving. Nan wanted Mum to have a tertiary education—an arts degree to be specific—and Mum was happy to oblige. She was so very fond of all the books and she walked through the sandstone buildings at Sydney University and felt like she was in Paris. She found a sandstone house near the harbour and drank at the Forth and Clyde Hotel. She smoked roll-your-own cigarettes and was enamoured with Gough Whitlam.

Mum was eight months pregnant with me when she left her job as a proofreader. After that she caught the ferry to Circular Quay and back, just to be on the water. I grew into a toddler and caused her much delight. Then my dad left. He walked out the door one day, leaving five hundred dollars on the table, and never came back. Five hundred dollars didn't last long, even in those days. I was two years old and she had to make a decision. She moved back to Goodwood to be near Nan and Pop. She missed them and they wanted to help raise their granddaughter. But Mum felt like a failure. She'd returned to the town that she spent her whole youth desperate to escape from.

At first, Mum's involvement in town events was ironic. She was depressed, but she had a great sense of humour. She wrote long letters to her friends in Sydney, mocking the craft, mocking the meetings, mocking the mentality. But over the years she settled. Her mood lifted. She enjoyed having the time to read. She stopped fighting it. She made friends. Her interest became genuine. She loved walking Backflip in the foothills of the mountain. She loved living close to Nan and Pop and Mack. At some point it occurred to her that she truly enjoyed taking minutes for the Goodwood Progress Association and attending CWA dinners at the Community Hall.

Mum said, 'Growing up's working out what makes you happy, Jean. Not what you think might, or what you think should, but what actually does.'

In 1992 Mum worked as a proofreader at the *Gather Region Advocate*, three and then four days a week. She always had a pile of books on her bedside table, lining the shelves in the living room, and then overflowing into the sunroom. She'd been saying for ages that we could set up a desk there and, one day, get a computer.

For days she fussed over piles of paperbacks and had sneezing fits with the dust.

Next door, Big Jim and Fitzy seemed equally eager to get on with things, especially Fitzy, who didn't like to dwell on sadness. I felt bad for Big Jim, because he *was* sad. Bart was his mate and during the previous week when he'd been going off to the lake with Merv every day, looking for him—any glimmer or glimpse of Bart—he'd trudged out to his car as if he was going off to war.

Fitzy waved him off, with a big forced smile, and welcomed him home with the same one every evening. Big Jim was a patient man, in my estimation.

It's not that Fitzy wasn't nice. Fitzy was catastrophically nice—even if she did have far too much hair for one person and a confusingly strong prescription. But to put it plainly, Fitzy had such bad luck with her coordination that she could have caused an accident by standing still and waiting for one to find her.

The previous Christmas, when Fitzy was hanging coloured lights along the front of their house while balancing on the top step of Big Jim's ladder—the step everyone knows not to balance on—the ladder got sick of Fitzy and made a dash for the ground. She dangled from the awning making the sound of a cat fight while Big Jim, who had rushed out in terror, yelled 'Let go hon, I've got you!' from below. When Fitzy's arms finally relented, which happened fairly quickly, the weight of her fall, on top of Big Jim, ruined a generous section of their murraya hedging. Big Jim sprained his lower back and was forced to pass himself back and forth on a foam roller in their sunroom for ten minutes a day until it healed.

The year before, Fitzy slipped out of the Wicko, as if on a sheet of ice, and collected Val Sparks from the Vinnies next door as she was on her way inside for a glass of port. The two women lay mangled on the pavement in front of the doorway, with Val moaning 'For Christsake, my knee' and Fitzy yelling, 'Val, can you hear me? Val!'

Unfortunately, Val could hear Fitzy loud and clear. She was practically wearing her like a throw. Poor Val. She was the most pious person in Goodwood. A little porcelain nativity scene adorned the wooden shelf behind her counter all year round. And yet, entwined with Fitzy, as her knee swelled quickly towards a chronic case of bursitis, she was forced to take the Lord's name in vain.

Most recently, in June, Fitzy went to meet her work friends at Panda Garden, the Chinese restaurant in Clarke. She drove down the long road that heads out of town by the river, while bugs ended themselves on her windshield, dazzled in the glory of her high beam lights. Fitzy was singing along to her favourite tape, *Wilson Phillips* by Wilson Phillips, and looking forward to a plate of pineapple pork, when a kangaroo pronked out of the tree line, a blur of fur in Fitzy's headlights. She swerved, clipping the kangaroo and continued off the road, over the dirt and leaves towards the metal guardrail that stops cars from hurtling off the high bank, just before the bridge. Thankfully Fitzy hadn't been travelling at too great a speed, and thankfully the silver wattle she ploughed through slowed her down further. She came to a stop on the guardrail, which bent forward and over, under the weight of her Honda Accord.

'Any faster and I would've been up to my neck in the lake,' she said to everyone in her retellings.

Fitzy had cried a river on the side of the road that night, imagining herself prone in the lake, and waited for a passing motorist. It turned out to be Kevin Fairley on his way home from a big shop at Woolworths and a meat pie in the Clarke Plaza food court. Kevin drove Fitzy home, comforting her and smelling like pie. Then bald Bob Elver towed Fitzy's car back to Goodwood the next day. It needed a new radiator, a new bumper, and a new bonnet. The guardrail and the silver wattle, however, could not be saved. They were removed pending replacement. Fitzy championed a stronger, doubly reinforced rail at the next council meeting and this met with agreement from Bart. But much like the proposed new picnic tables in Sweetmans Park, the proposed restoration of the Community Hall, and the proposed resealing of Woodland and Pioneer Streets, Goodwood was still waiting.

On top of her tendency to ruin things, Fitzy was a taxing conversationalist. She was as boring about jam, and hedging, and the weather, as Big Jim was about plants. Man, could Fitzy kill the weather. It'd be the nicest day of the year—sun shining, perfect clear skies—and I would wake up feeling inspired for a day of swimming at the river, but having Fitzy talk to me about it for ten minutes, after she'd caught me off-guard as I was leaving, I'd wish for rain.

Then it'd rain, and Fitzy would pop up behind a hedge in a raincoat and rain hat, just doing a spot of weeding in the downpour, and there I'd be for the next eternity, listening to her bang on.

That's what happened that day, while Mum was sorting through the secondary books. Up popped Fitzy, just after the rain had started and I was standing on the front verandah.

'Oh Jean, there you are', she said, and then without drawing breath, 'You're going to love this. I'm trying to put together a rainfall map for Goodwood. Which is difficult because the Bureau of Meteorology—they are quite private about their procedures—did you know that of all the three thousand rainfall measuring sites in Australia, Goodwood doesn't have one?'

She looked incredulous, water dripping off her hat. Her eyes enormous behind her thick glasses.

'I have written and written. Because it would be so good for Jim to have proper analysis for work. And for you kids to know for school. But "our" (air quotes with four fingers) rainfall is really just Clarke's rainfall, because that's the closest site.' She did a little disbelieving headshake and flipped raindrops left and right. 'But you know as well as I do that sometimes you drive to Clarke, and it's raining there when it's not raining here! Or vice versa. Even last week when I went up there to go to the RTA, the ground was wet! And we hadn't had a drop since the 12th. So it's not accurate for Goodwood. And I told them that. It's just not accurate. So I don't know what to do to make it official, because the Bureau won't budge. But to make it unofficial we're going to get our own! A rain gauge! Jim's such a honey, he's been at the library looking up pictures. I think it's a good way for him to get his mind off things. We're gonna mount it out back and go from there.'

'That's a very good idea,' I said, just as Myrtle rushed out of their front door and rolled in a puddle, and Fitzy started high-pitch yelling while Myrtle flipped around, and I made my escape.

Out of our front gate, saying my hasty goodbye to Fitzy and swampy Myrtle, I went left towards town. And that's how I ended up on Cedar St in the rain on the same day Derek Murray had a big fight with his father, Roy.

15

Roy and Derek Murray lived a short drive from Cedar Street, on the mountain side, with Roy's wife Doe. Doe Murray was never seen in town, as she suffered from what Nan called 'a terrible affliction of nerves'. Nan said she was as nervous about the cracks in the pavement as she was about the cracks in the sky. I'm not sure if she was scared of lightning, or falling meteors, or acid rain, or noxious weeds—but whatever it was that might befall Doe, from above or below, left her little room to get out of the house.

Doe Murray's birth name was Josephine Mae. She met Roy at a mixer in the mid-seventies, a couple of years after Roy's first wife had died from killing herself with an overdose of sleeping pills. Poor baby Derek Murray was only three months old when his mother shuffled off, suffering as she was from acute postnatal depression, coupled with a life-long bout of chronic low-grade sadness.

When Roy brought his new lady friend home to meet his infant, half-orphaned son, Derek couldn't say 'Josephine'. So he called her 'Doe-pheen', which was soon shortened to 'Doe', and that's how she was known forever more, to everyone in Goodwood.

Nan knew a little bit of Doe from yesteryear, before my memories began. Apparently, Doe hadn't always been so nervous. When she first started appearing on the arm of Roy, drinking white wine at the Wicko of a weekend, she was talkative and sweet. Her Korean heritage was interesting in a white-bread town like Goodwood, and she offered Nan a delicious recipe for kimchi. She was well liked for her dry sense of humour, even if she could be a little too timid at times. But over the years, as Derek grew into a young man, Doe sunk into their weatherboard home, and ventured out less and less. I had only seen her once—at Woody's, sitting in the far back booth, where no one else ever sat. Mum had said, 'Wow, there's Doe Murray,' as we walked past. 'It's like seeing a ghost.'

Nan and Mum had read several books on psychology and had a theory on almost everyone, including Doe, who they declared to be the most panicked person in Goodwood, apart from Helen at the newsagent. One time, when I was little, Mum had encountered Doe in a full-blown attack near the corner of Cedar and Pioneer streets. Doe had come up to Woody's to look in on Roy, and wound up in the gutter around the corner, shaking like a tail, with her head between her legs. Mum bent down and asked, 'Are you feeling faint, Doe?' and Doe accused the sky of sinking, and the sun of malevolence, and the air of being too thin for her lungs to find it. Mum sat down on the kerb and put her arm around Doe's shoulders, emptied four potatoes from a paper bag in her shopping, and said, 'Well, there's not much I can do about that, but why don't you try breathing into this?'

They sat there for some time until Bart, of all people, walked past and saw their predicament. He went to fetch Roy Murray. When Roy relieved Mum, he hoisted Doe up like she was a sack of potatoes, gave her a Valium (which she expertly swallowed without water), and hobbled her into his waiting car. Mum collected her own potatoes off the ground and went home.

Nan said of the incident that agoraphobia often knocks on the door when a person's in their thirties. Doe had been in her thirties at the time. Mum said that, usually, something unpleasant triggers it off, but neither of them had any opinion as to what that might've been. Derek Murray was, by all accounts, a bit of a shit. But Roy Murray loved Derek blindly, so one might assume that he loved Doe in the same way. Then again, no one had much of a handle on their relationship, given her constant absence from town. The only thing you could really tell about Roy Murray was that he ran Woody's well enough for it to be the busiest culinary establishment in

Goodwood; he held the town fishing record for Biggest Catch (for an eighty-seven-centimetre dusky flathead he caught in '89); and that I saw him get into an awful fight with Derek on that rainy day in August.

If we'd had a rain gauge, it would have certainly declared that a lot of water fell on Goodwood that day. The cracks in the sky had opened, and the gutters were rushing like brown rivers when I got to Cedar Street under an inky sky. My shoes were sopping, so I went into the newsagent for some shelter, and flipped through *Rolling Stone* while Helen stood in the doorway and worried about the deluge.

'It's a wonder we don't all wash away,' she said pointedly to no one.

Under the awning in the front of Bart's Meats, waiting for the worst of it to pass, I tried not to look at Joe as he gazed out from behind the steamed glass. I tried not to notice how much he looked like his dad, Bart. I tried to ignore how wet Terry White's signs were getting—the ones he'd wrapped around the telegraph poles on the street. Rosie's black-and-white face was frozen in time, and missing, and now getting drenched. A gust of wind had peeled one almost off its pole and it flapped like a sail. Everything felt cold and bleak as Helen frowned from beside the Lotto signs and Faye Haynes, in the bakery window, stared into an arrangement of coffee scrolls.

As I went past Woody's, I almost didn't look in. I didn't want to see the terrible absence of Rosie. But something caught my eye at the back of the shop near the rear door. That was when I saw them: old white-haired Roy Murray and his son, Derek, looking fit to kill each other good and proper.

Derek had his head down and was shaking it angrily, left and right, like a horse trying to buck off its rider. Roy Murray's face was right up close to Derek's, hot and aggressive, and he held up a quivering finger, right under Derek's nose. Derek stared back with an expression even more vulgar than usual. He spat out some words and his bottom lip curled under. Then Roy's mouth moved, too, and spittle escaped onto Derek's disagreeable face. The rain was so loud on the tin awning that I couldn't hear anything they were saying. It was like a silent movie overdubbed with gunfire. But I did see Derek shove his father with both hands to Roy's chest, and I saw Roy fly backwards into the wall. He looked stunned at the might of his son. Then Derek pushed the back door open hard and disappeared out of it, slamming it behind him. And Roy Murray appeared to be winded as he whacked the straw dispenser off the counter in frustration, so all the straws dispensed themselves on the lino like a game of pick-up sticks.

My eyes must've been very wide when Roy saw me there on the street looking in. I decided it best to pretend nothing had happened, so I smiled at him. He did not offer a smile in return. He just looked down ruefully at the big blue mess of straws. Then he bent over, with great difficulty, and slowly began the tiresome task of picking them all up.

16

George and I spent most of the next week, at recess and lunch, lying on the carpet in the library next to the heater vent.

I told her about Roy and Derek. She didn't seem surprised. She said Derek had got into a fight with her youngest brother, runty Daniel, on the oval the year before. Daniel came home with a bleeding nose and without his favourite football. The worst bit was Derek was six years older than Daniel and a full foot taller. George and I agreed that it just wasn't cricket.

'What did your parents say?' I asked.

'Dad said Derek Murray is dumb as a box of hair,' said George.

Due to our newfound interest, we uncovered the following facts: Derek Murray repeated Year Nine and dropped out in Year Ten; he spent a lot of time smoking bongs and playing video games; he did burnouts in the car park behind Woody's;

he did donuts at the cul-de-sac of trees near the clearing; he had, up until Rosie vanished, always rejected Roy Murray's requests that he work at Woody's, even though he hung around there like an unpleasant smell; and he never seemed to have a girlfriend. The last part was gleaned from Toby, who George went to for information relating to boys. Toby had said, 'Fucken Derek Murray? What a toolbox. When we're there with girls? He clears the clearing.'

'Toby made a little pun?' I asked.

'I was also surprised,' said George.

Toby had apparently made another whole sentence, too, as if Derek Murray's detestability inspired him to communicate.

'As if girls give a shit about Derek's Kingswood,' he had said. And, as girls, George and I had to agree.

The heater vent in the library rattled. I rolled my cold hands around in front of it as if it were a fire. Miss Lopez, our librarian, wheeled around a trolley full of books, carefully choosing the right spots on the shelves to put them. George was flipping through *The Pictorial History of Australian Prime Ministers* and stopped at Harold Holt.

'You are just like Bart,' she said to Harold's picture.

George held the book up so I could see it. 'See? Look at his kind face.'

Harold Holt was posing in his spearfishing outfit on a beach in black and white. He looked very happy to be near the ocean. On the opposite page he was more prime ministerial, in a suit and tie; no snorkel. He did look a bit like Bart, just ever so slightly. I stared at Harold while George held the book up and nodded, and then just beyond the book I saw Evie come in the doors of the library and wander up to the counter with an armful of paperbacks. She put her pile on the counter and waited there for Miss Lopez to wheel the trolley back to her station.

'There's that new girl,' said George, turning her head.

'Yeah,' I said. 'Evie.'

'Have you spoken to her?'

'No,' I said.

Evie looked down at her book pile, examining the back of her hands.

'She's really pretty, hey?' said George, and rolled over onto her back, putting aside *The Pictorial History of Australian Prime Ministers* and using her bag as a pillow.

The fluorescent light above flickered. George looked up as the globe twitched and came on suddenly and compelled her to sneeze three times in quick succession. George and I started cracking up—just as Evie handed over her books to Miss Lopez and turned to leave. She must've heard us, because Evie looked right at me as she walked out and she smiled, with a brave and proper smile. The gap between her teeth was magnificent. Her smile filled her whole face and flooded it over with joy. It gave me the strangest feeling—like pins and needles. Evie walked out and George was lying on her back, laughing and blowing her nose into one of Noelene Sharkey's handmade hankies.

'Ah, fuck,' she said, and sighed.

I kept on looking at the spot where Evie had been.

I felt like there were many lit sparklers, tingling across my face.

•

After school that day, George wanted me to go with her to meet Ethan West and Lucas Karras on the oval, where they were planning to kick a football while we were to sit there and watch.

It was unestablished at that point as to whether Lucas was George's official boyfriend, because she was very odd about the subject and seemed able to constantly dodge my inquiries without giving a straight answer. All I knew for certain was that they'd had unsatisfactory sex, at least once, on the oval that autumn; and who knew what else had happened thereafter. Georgina Sharkey was always talking, and yet no one was better at evading an unwanted inquisition.

On the particular night in question, I was present with a group from school and I'd spent much of the evening wishing I was home with Backflip. George had got drunk. And Lucas had not even had to be that charming. He was merely pleasant enough, and as George told me after, there had to be a first time for everything. So she'd left me with the others by the goalposts, and given herself over under the moonlight near the river, while I drank warm beer.

When they returned, after what seemed like less than ten minutes, Lucas looked all puffed up, like he was leading a parade, and George looked like she'd just seen a disappointing fireworks display. She kicked me, indicating it was time to go, and we had walked home along Cedar Street under the tall and naked trees.

George's seventeenth birthday had been two days earlier. 'I am a whole year past my age of consent,' she had said. 'So, I don't know. I consented.'

That seemed like an insubstantial reason to have sex with Lucas Karras to me, especially given the fact that he ended most sentences with an upward inflection—like every single thing was a question? But I did appreciate that Costa Karras had raised a pleasant-enough son and that Lucas couldn't help the way he talked.

'How was it?' I asked.

'I don't know, maybe it's been hyped up too much. Like when we finally got to go to Pet Porpoise Pool in Coffs Harbour,' said George, in a more amused tone than I'd expected. 'You know how when you blow up a balloon and let it go? And it just goes *pffffffft* in circles really fast?'

I was laughing by then and George was laughing, too. She seemed genuinely entertained by parting with her virginity.

'Poor Lucas,' I said. 'A bit of an anticlimax?'

'Not for poor Lucas,' said George.

We walked to the corner of my street, where George goes the other way to the wrong side of the tracks, and I go up the hill towards the mountain. There was not much moon. That was when we could still walk our separate ways, alone in the dark, and not even think a bad thing could happen. That was when Goodwood was still peaceful and quiet—'a safe town' as Bart McDonald would say—and Rosie was months away from being missing.

'Maybe it was his first time, too?' I suggested, in Lucas's defence, standing on my corner.

'Nah. He fucked Liz Gordon's little sister twice—he told me.'

'Amy Gordon? Isn't she thirteen?'

'Apparently she's very mature,' said George, smiling. 'Either way he kind of sucks at it. But, shit, Jean, what do I know? I bet all the boys here suck at it. I bet Toby sucks the worst, followed by the rest of Year Twelve.'

George had ambled off towards the train tracks that night, looking much the same as she had before this momentous event had transpired; and I had wandered up the slight hill towards the mountain feeling strangely disappointed about that and, as a result, about everything.

I was not sure what I thought about Lucas and George— back then in autumn, or that afternoon on the oval. I was not sure what I thought about Ethan West, either. And yet

I agreed to half watch them kick the football back and forth to each other while we lay on the grass and ate hot chips fried by Derek Murray.

We listened to them jeer each other jovially when a kick was bad. We watched them show off when a kick was good. George mock-clapped. Lucas yelled at us in good humour. Ethan looked up a few times to see if I was watching, and George elbowed me and coughed.

'Where do you think she is?' she said, after a lull in conversation.

'Who?' I asked, as the faces of Rosie and Evie both popped into my mind at the same time.

'*Rosie*,' said George. 'Who the fuck else is missing, Jean?'

'Bart?'

George looked annoyed. The mood turned. Ethan had fallen over and Lucas was being uncharitable about it.

'I don't know,' I said. 'But, you know, I don't think she's dead.'

I'm not sure if I really thought that or not, or if I just said it to be it optimistic. Maybe I was trying to reassure George; or reassure myself.

George ate the hot chips very slowly off the butcher's paper. She put them in her mouth one by one and chewed them carefully and swallowed and took another.

'I do,' said George. 'I think someone did something to her.'

Then she pushed the chips away. I folded the paper over them and we sat wordless for a long time. Ethan had picked himself up. His knees were muddy. Lucas looked out of breath. George lay back on the grass and closed her eyes. I watched the football go up and down and up again. I flinched at the dull *ooof* that echoed across the oval with each kick.

17

Mack had spent three days asking everyone he saw in town if they'd seen any sign of the McDonalds' stolen Corolla. Nance, who kept a close eye on Cedar Street from her counter, had not. Neither had Helen or Bill; or Faye Haynes; or Smithy; or Val Sparks; or Carmel Carmichael; or Robin Clunes, who ran Bookworm; or Roy or Derek Murray. Mack asked everyone in every house he happened to have business in, as well as their neighbours, his neighbours, our neighbours, and the ladies at the CWA. It was a no from Carl White, and a no from Mal West, and a no from Davo Carlstrom and his bogan uncle Lafe.

Mack went around especially to see Judy White when Carl wasn't home. When asked how she appeared, he said she quivered. Not in an obvious way, but when she'd made him a cup of tea, the milk went in shakily and she spilt a few drops on the counter.

Mack took his mug and they sat on the couch for a spell. Judy shook her head and said, 'There's just nothing,' and Mack had to agree—that after three weeks there was no sign whatsoever of Rosie.

It wasn't as if Mack hadn't followed any leads; it was that there were no leads to follow. If someone had meddled with Rosie, they hadn't left a trace. If Rosie had run away, she hadn't left a trace either. If she'd headed off to her Cousin Tegan's, she had never arrived.

Mack had spoken to Tegan and Alison on the phone three times since Rosie disappeared and they were near inconsolable. And just to make sure they weren't trained actors, Mack called the Ballina police and asked them to sniff around. Tegan went to work every day at the Big Prawn; Alison went to work every day at North Coast Cleaning Services. They lived together, mother and daughter, in a fibro two-bedder. The Ballina police reported that Cousin Rosie from Goodwood was nowhere to be seen.

'You know how many long-term missing we've got in New South Wales as of July?' asked a serious-sounding Constable Marcon in Ballina.

'A few hundred?' guessed Mack, on the other end of the phone.

'Mate, we've got eight hundred and sixty-one long-term missing. That's long term. And we got another four hundred more recent cases. You see the kind of number we're dealing with? My brother heads up Missing Persons in Sydney. They're slammed. Around here we're dealing with runaways all the time. A lot of people don't want to be found. You reckon you got a runaway?'

Mack didn't know. Some days he reckoned that, sure. Rosie brooded. She kept to herself. She had an air about her—what was it?—like she was closed off from the world. Or damaged. Like she didn't want to be talked to. Maybe she did just run. But why would she? And even so—if she did or didn't—most days Mack had darker thoughts. All he knew for certain was that unless he was dealing with a bunch of terrific liars, no one in all of Goodwood had seen Rosie after she shut her bedroom door that Sunday night. And no one had seen her since.

Again he asked Judy, as they sat in the Whites' musky, carpeted living room, if there was any reason that Rosie would leave. Again Judy said not that she could think of. Again Mack asked, were there any problems at home? Again Judy said, nothing out of the ordinary. Again Mack persisted, but this time, with his new-found knowledge of Carl, he persisted more strongly, and in a more direct fashion.

'What about Carl, Jude? Do you think he could've had anything to do with this?'

Judy didn't answer. She just looked horrified, like Mack had brought shit in on his shoe and wiped it all over her good rug.

'I'm sorry, but I have to ask,' Mack said.

Judy quivered. Her tea was like a rough sea in her cup as she held it.

Finally, she managed to say, 'He's got his faults but he's not a monster,' and looked at Mack grimly. And Mack was left with nowhere much else to go.

'I'm not saying he is, Jude. All I'm doing is my job. You know how sorry I am—I'm so sorry—I'm just trying to piece this thing together.'

Judy became colder as Mack continued, and eventually he thanked her for the tea and stood up to leave. As he did, he asked one last question, and that was answered with a no: Judy White had not seen the McDonalds' stolen Corolla.

After their awkward encounter, Mack drove out to the browned grass where the cars park by the boat wharves. It was his seventh trip there since Bart had vanished; he'd been keeping notes. He drove out of town along the long road that hugs the river and rounds the mountain; he passed the rest stop just before the bridge, where a fresh kangaroo was mangled on the road, just a few metres from the old one. Ravens were nipping at its flesh and Mack drove right through them, as they flapped off, and tried to suppress the nausea he always felt when he saw them. He drove past the spot where Fitzy hit the railing; and, just after, he went over the high bridge, above the brown water, and along the fast flat road where he liked to ponder. Eventually he pulled up to the spot where the boats bob, and the river became the lake.

He stood there and stared out with his binoculars, hoping the two glass circles would reveal a glimpse of Bart. When they didn't, and Mack had done his customary search of the bankside marshes, he got back in his car and drove back over the bridge towards town.

Past the rest stop on his way home, Mack could see Kevin Fairley's little dairy, and his cows eating grass in the paddock. Kevin rarely came into town. He mostly did big shops at the Woolworths in Clarke so they'd last him enough time to stay on his farm and be with his cows. He had been blessed with a wife for forty years, Susan, but she died of cancer at Clarke Base Hospital in 1988, the year we had a bicentenary parade at school. Kevin sought comfort in his herd. While he was forced to sell off almost half of them when Susan got sick and could no longer lend a hand at milking, he still had forty-five cows—a mix of Jerseys, Friesians and Brown Swiss—and moved them weekly from paddock to paddock, wherever the grass grew greener. Kevin Fairley was known to moo to his cows, on a daily basis. He lowed and made deep sounds. His cattle dog, Remington, barked, and Kevin mooed and the cows mooed and the man and the dog and the cows made a three-part harmony under the silent sky.

Mack drove back into town that day, turned off along the road near the clearing, and went all the way alongside the river to the Fairley Dairy.

'G'day, Kevin,' he said, when he found Kevin in the sheds.

'Constable,' said Kevin. 'To what do I owe the honour?'

'Ah, just off on a drive, thought I'd pop in,' said Mack, even though he'd not once popped in to the Fairley Dairy before.

They shot the breeze a little. Kevin was sorry to hear about the troubles—he'd seen Nance at the Fosseys in Clarke and she'd been very pleased to fill him in. Mack agreed it'd been a tough few weeks.

'Not a good thing,' said Kevin, shaking his head.

'I don't see you much in town,' said Mack.

'I don't come much into town,' said Kevin. 'You know me.'

But that wasn't true. Mack didn't know Kevin at all, because he didn't come much into town.

'Big job doing it all by yourself.'

'Oh, I manage okay,' said Kevin. 'Don't know how to do anything else is the truth of it. I get some problems with off-flavours from time to time, but I manage okay.'

'How's that?'

'Lately a bit weedy. Usually a bit barny,' said Kevin.

Mack nodded and had no idea what Kevin was talking about. Then he brought up the stolen Corolla and asked Kevin if he'd seen it.

'I seen how your paddocks run along the road out of town just now when I was driving in, so I thought I best come and ask you,' said Mack.

'Well it's a good thing you did,' said Kevin, and told Mack the short story of what he'd seen.

Three Saturdays ago, he'd been moving his herd from the paddock that almost spills into the lake into the paddock that starts at the dairy and ends up closest to town, next to the clearing. The road out of Goodwood was long, since it had to meander around the river. But if you walked from the clearing where the willow was—where the money was—and down along the edge of the river, along the brim of Kevin's paddocks, you got to the bank of the lake in less than half an hour.

That's where Kevin was walking, but in the opposite direction—towards town—when he saw an old white Corolla parked on the road that forked off from the clearing and headed into the bush, where it stopped a short time later in a cul-de-sac of trees. He could see the road from his paddock, and that's just what he did. He saw it; and on that day, there was a car there.

'It looked like it needed a moment to itself,' said Kevin.

'The car did?' asked Mack.

'That's right,' said Kevin, and Mack wrote it down.

Kevin didn't know the car belonged to Bart. He thought Bart drove a Commodore. Or a Hilux. And that Mrs Bart drove a little blue Mazda. Mack said that was all true, but some people never have enough cars.

Kevin was sure he'd seen the car on the Saturday at dusk, because he always moved his cows to that paddock on Saturdays at dusk. Mack asked him if it was there the following Saturday, at dusk, but Kevin didn't know. He'd moved his cows, but he'd walked high on the paddock and hadn't had a view of the clearing. He was sure, however, that on the Tuesday after that, at dusk, it'd been gone. He'd seen a report on *Four Corners* that made him worry about his heart, so he'd started taking an evening constitutional, and he started them that Tuesday, two days after Bart disappeared. He'd walked all the way along the perimeter of his paddocks with Remington, and they went right past the clearing. The car was gone.

'So it could've been there for over a week?' said Mack.

'Well,' said Kevin, 'I suppose it could've,' and the two men were quiet for a moment. 'Or it could've been less.'

Then Kevin said he was feeling much better in general after some exercise—the best he'd felt since Susan passed—and that the lovegrass in his south paddock was flowering very early this year. Mack put his notebook in his pocket and had complicated thoughts.

'What do you make of it?' asked Kevin.

'At this point,' Mack said, 'I couldn't tell you.'

He walked back to his car and Kevin escorted him along by the big milking sheds. Remington stood sentry in the doorframe. The moo of a cow punctured the air.

Kevin smiled. 'It's hard not to moo back, isn't it?'

Mack felt bad for Kevin. A man in his sixties doing it all by himself. It was a chancy business, too, farming. Nan had always said that. Drought, disease, the lack of rain, the price of milk. And every day without Susan.

'Sure is,' said Mack. 'Really had to stop myself there.'

Kevin nodded and silently studied his paddocks.

On his way home Mack drove back past the clearing, easing off down the road that ends in the cul-de-sac of trees. It had rained on Goodwood since the Corolla had been parked there. It had poured down—on the day that Roy and Derek Murray had their fight at Woody's—and the ground offered no indication of tyre tracks or any other clues. Mack stood, as the trees sang with birds, and felt as small as a wing among the ancient trunks and branches.

18

Big Jim and Fitzy mounted their rain gauge on a wooden post in their garden on a fine day in early spring, as jasmine flowers scented our yards and Backflip ate dirt under the eucalypt. Big Jim was in a terrific mood, after spotting a pied oystercatcher on Grants Lake that morning—so far inland!—and bored us to tears with descriptions of its handsome plumage. I had to remind myself, in a moment of great intolerance as Big Jim hung over our fence with his newly updated second edition of *A Field Guide to the Birds of Australia*, that at least Big Jim was in some ways preferable to our neighbours on the other side. At least Big Jim mowed our lawn and brought us herbs and vegetables. And at least Fitzy, when she wasn't crashing into something, was nice.

Our next-door neighbours on the other side, Con and Althea, were ancient and peculiar. They hung plastic bags to dry on their clothesline, used their hose as a broom, and were far too old to talk to. Like most women in her family, Althea was known for her uncanny ability to determine the sex of unborn children. It was something about the way a woman carried, and she'd examine from the front, the side and the rear before making her forecast. With an unchallenged success rate, she was like the Nostradamus of Goodwood, and often wore too-tight skirts with the slip showing. Mum and I, having not had a pregnancy for Althea to witness, had not spoken to her much. We were, however, intimately accustomed to the sound of Con and Althea's automatic roller shutters, which went down, noisily, around seven every night, and rolled up again every morning at six. What they did in their house-cave of an evening, with no shred of external light—from sun, moon, streetlight or stars—we had no idea.

Coral, on the other side of Big Jim and Fitzy, was also ancient, and breathed the air of other people's business. On most days, Mum couldn't stand to look at her, but on some days Coral had some pretty great information, and we lowered ourselves to listening to it on the footpath, where a little circle of neighbours would gather as Coral held court. She wore noticeable hearing aids—brown shells that gripped her hairline and fed little tubes into plastic cocoons in her ears—and yet she seemed to hear everything, and more immediately than anyone else. She heard first when Bart had the heart attack on the horse trail and was sped to Clarke Base Hospital by Mrs Bart's sister Jan, who 'never married'.

She heard first when Nance found a lump in her breast, which thankfully turned out to be a fibro-adenoma. She heard first when Fitzy flattened the railing and almost ended up in the lake, only to be returned safely by Kevin Fairley, who smelt like pie. And she heard first that Mike, the kindly man who cleaned the storefront windows on Cedar Street every second Monday, had actually spent four years in a maximum-security prison. In her retellings of these particular events, Coral also seemed to imply that there was something untoward about Jan and Kevin, whose chauffeuring of people in need took on the scarlet hue of extramarital scandal.

Not only did Coral hear things first, she was also the first person to tell everyone else about it. She didn't really stand next to people when she did either, but rather huddled with them, even when her information wasn't that exciting. I think the huddling had become a habit. After spreading salacious gossip for so many years, she had to look around three times and lean in to tell you it was Tuesday.

But while all the very exciting things that had gone on in Goodwood up until then had buoyed her on each trip to Cedar Street and back, the events of 1992 changed Coral.

Rosie's disappearance was one thing. Coral didn't think much of Carl White, because he was always playing the pokies at the Bowlo when she went in for a shandy and she didn't trust a man who was so loose with his pennies. She felt sorry for Judy White, because she put up with Carl, and didn't even get to put up with him over a nice steak dinner. Not once had Coral seen Carl and Judy having dinner together, at either the Bowlo or the Wicko, and every man should take his wife out for a nice steak dinner every now and again. The Wicko even did a Sunday roast from June till August. Besides, Rosie had probably run off with a boy. That Rosie, she had an unfamiliar attitude, and Coral didn't understand her dark sense of fashion any more than she understood Davo Carlstrom and his outspoken poverty.

But Bart. Goodwood's own Bart McDonald. Bart was seldom out of Coral's thoughts.

When the McDonalds had moved to Goodwood, Bart was undoubtedly 'the most handsome man we've had', as Coral declared to Nan at the CWA craft circle. '*Coral*,' said Nan, amused, 'I'm clutching my pearls.'

Coral thought Mrs Bart was nice enough. Maybe not nice enough to have been elected Secretary quite so soon, and perhaps Coral had in fact voted for Mary Bell, whose unfortunate face had held the position for almost two decades prior. Coral was one of the only people in Goodwood who referred to Mrs Bart by her given name of Flora. According to Coral, Flora was just Flora. But Bart was an absolute gift of a man. *So* terrific, *so* kind, *so* interested in Coral's myriad opinions. Before Bart opened up shop, Coral ate red meat twice a week, on Thursdays and Sundays. Having lived through both world wars, she was thrifty and had a tendency to ration. But when the fluorescent lights of Bart's Meats flickered alive on Cedar Street like the heady glow of a fresh carcass, Coral became ravenously carnivorous. Every day, from Monday to Saturday, she rolled her tartan shopping trolley past our house, past the seven bottlebrushes that lined our street on the way to town, around the corner by the Wicko, and up to the main shops with the sole purpose of seeing Bart, having her wonderful daily chat with Bart, and buying a tiny portion of lamb.

'Coral, you look absolutely delightful,' Bart would say in good humour. Or, 'Looking younger every year, Mrs McLeod.'

Poor Coral. Mr McLeod had been dead so long that Mum couldn't find the memory of his first name, even though she'd heard it spoken numerous times, and had to ask Nan. Nan said it was Charles. He was a fighter pilot for the RAF Bomber Command until he fell out of the sky in 1944, leaving Coral both husbandless and childless (since they hadn't got around to having any yet).

After Big Jim mounted the rain gauge, and he and Fitzy scanned the sky in the hope of a dark cloud, the sound of Coral's trolley rolled past on the pavement. I was sitting in the living room as Backflip twitched in her sleep on the rug. Coral was off to look in on Joe, who was really such a poor consolation for Bart. Since Bart had vanished, her trolley went slower than usual, as if her whole life's purpose was diminished, and time was no longer of any essence.

•

Mum had organised her secondary books into three piles: a pile to keep; a pile to donate to Bookworm; and a small box of crime novels for Mack, who was making a concerted effort to read.

At five-thirty, he arrived to pick up his selection, and then drive us up to the Bowlo. He carried them out and put them in the back of his police car while Mum gave Backflip a bowl of biscuits on the back pavers. Then we got to ride in the police car, siren off, towards a nice steak dinner. Tracy and Jasper met us there, as well as Denise and Brian, and Opal and Ken Jones, who were having a rare night out. Opal Jones wrote for the *Gather Region Advocate*, so Mum knew her professionally, as well as from around town. But the reason they were there was Ken Jones, on Mack's invitation.

Ken and Mack had gone to Goodwood High together and still knocked around as friends, as one of a smallish group from the class of 1978 that had never moved away. Mack felt sorry for Ken because Opal wore the pants in the Jones house and rendered Ken emasculated at every given opportunity. Mack, an empathic man, told Mum he was going to get that poor guy out from under Opal's thumb, one fishing trip at a time.

I didn't care much about the predicament of Ken Jones. Most interesting to me was the fact that the Joneses lived right next door to Carl and Judy White. And judging by the look on Denise's face—which was wide-eyed and conspiratorial whenever Opal said pretty much anything—I figured that fact was quite interesting to her, too.

Everyone except me ordered steak with chips, vegetables and their choice of sauce, and I ordered the vegetarian cannelloni. Mum proceeded to get a bit tipsy since she wasn't driving. The Bowlo was brightly lit and brought out everyone's pocks and creases. It was a funny place of an evening, since its main activity happened in the daytime, when old people in white trousers and pale yellow shirts ran heavy balls along the green, as slow as snails, and drank from jugs of shandy. On Wednesday nights, Carmel Carmichael poured beers and made small talk with the regulars at the bar, old Mal West included, his cane resting against the adjacent stool. The bistro was carpeted, large and underpopulated, and had the feel of a wedding reception centre for a couple with no imagination.

When our dinner arrived, everything smelt like meat and sauce, even the cannelloni. Mack did a good job of fielding questions from Opal Jones, who acted like a hard-hitting journalist, even though she only wrote articles about sad things, like lost cats, or happy things, like people being reunited with lost cats. Mack said, under questioning, that no, he had not become aware of anything untoward about Davo Carlstrom. Davo's as upset as everyone. More so, in fact, since he and Rosie were, you know, close.

'Close as in her boyfriend?' asked Opal, like we should all know what *that* meant.

142

'Yeah, they were going out,' said Mack.

'You know it's always the boyfriend,' said Opal, raising a glass of chardonnay to her lips and winking as Ken Jones hushed her meekly.

'Ah, Christ, Opal,' said Mack, irritated.

'So nothing new at all? There's just nothing?' demanded Opal Jones.

'Not nothing,' said Mack defensively, 'just nothing right now. And we're having a nice steak dinner, so come on.'

Denise, who had been quietly eating her steamed vegetables, made her move. 'But, Opal,' she said, '*you* must've heard something? Living right next door?'

Brian and Mack and Ken Jones stared at their plates in a stoic, detached fashion. They pushed their steak knives through their scotch fillets. Jasper smeared tomato sauce all over his plate with his fingers. All other eyes turned to the fountain of information that was Opal Jones. She breathed in and nodded at each of us, cherishing her moment as keynote speaker. Then she launched, like a ship into the ocean. Spray and waves rolled off in her wake. No one knew an intimate detail like Opal Jones.

Rosie had, after all, vanished just after having lunch at their house—and Opal was very insistent that we all knew that they were some of the last people in Goodwood to have seen Rosie; and the second-last people in Goodwood to have served her a meal, which was a barbeque lunch of sausages and bread and two very interesting salads that Opal had found in the *Women's Weekly Dinner Party Cookbook* at the library. That was nice because Denise had recommended the book, she'd just updated the cooking section, and the two women clasped hands for a moment over the salads—they were a triumph!—and then Opal went on.

Poor Terry was very depressed. That much was obvious with just the way he walked now. He didn't even walk, he slumped. He just slumped and shuffled around town, putting up his signs and whatnot. It's just not right; he's so young. What a thing to happen. And with no warning whatsoever, just poof! Honestly, there was no hint of what was to come at the barbeque lunch that they'd had with the triumphant interesting salads, even though Rosie didn't stay very long. But you know how teenagers are. And who makes Terry's lunches now? Opal was quite worried that Judy didn't.

And as for Jude, well you never see her. She hovers sometimes in the window, or behind the screen door. It looks like she hasn't gotten out of that dressing gown for weeks. Opal knocks and she knocks, and she knows Jude's in there but Jude doesn't answer. Then later, when Jude hovers, she won't return a wave. It's just so sad.

'Isn't it nice that so many people sent flowers?' said Denise, as a kind of question-statement.

It *was* nice. But so many flowers that they ran out of vases pretty much straight away! I mean, of course they did. Who has that many vases, just waiting for a tragedy? And, actually, that was the last time Opal had spoken to Jude properly, when she dropped over some empty vases at Terry's request. He's such a nice young poor boy.

Sympathetic nods came from Denise.

And then—with a distinct change of tone, like winter blowing across the table—there was Carl White. He always used to be so good for a barbeque lunch. He'd bring such lovely topside. The man can really cook beef. Very tender. Just the right amount of pink. Gosh, him and Jude, they were so in love! But then, time carries on, over the years. The kids get older and you just don't socialise as much. It's hard to put a finger on. He didn't seem to like her going out as much, maybe that was it. And now, honestly? It's peculiar only because you just can't tell what he's feeling. Not peculiar as in off; or maybe it *is* a bit off? It's just, that even living right next door and seeing him come and go, you can't tell anything's even *happened*.

Ken Jones looked at Mack apologetically.

'Exactly!' said Denise. 'That's what I said to Celia,' and Mum nodded to indicate that Denise had indeed said that. Denise breathed deeply and calmed herself. 'I think he's a bit cold. Don't you think, Mack? Given the circumstances.'

Mack dipped a chip in his mushroom sauce and didn't venture an opinion.

'It's just *very* sad,' said Opal Jones, 'and such a mystery.'

The table fell quiet and hung on the last word. *Mystery.* Knives and forks became audible. I pushed my cannelloni around my plate. And Mack deftly moved the conversation on to Jasper who, unfortunately for him and Tracy, had just learnt to whistle.

'It's like living with birds,' said Tracy, looking exhausted, and Jasper demonstrated, making an avian sound with his tiny lips.

'Aaaaaw,' went Denise.

After drinking two Cokes I needed to pee. I excused myself and headed to the toilets, past a nice portrait of the Queen and then the poker machines, which announced themselves with little rings and jingles. I walked the same route that Mrs Bart had when Carl White had groped her. And sure enough, like it was his second home, there was Carl White, sitting at the poker machine closest to the ladies toilets.

The mess of him in the Bowlo that night was a sight I would not soon forget. He looked like a blank man. Like his brain had stopped working some time ago and the rest of him was just sitting around unawares. He pressed an illuminated button, and another, and another. The machine went *bling bling*. Coloured lights flashed on and off. Scrolls of kings and queens and cherries and moneybags went flipping around like a windmill, stopping in different formations, promising the world. The blank man just stared and pushed and slotted; and every now and again he raised his schooner glass and drank.

I walked past him quickly and was glad he didn't look up. I was gladder still that the jangly cartoon noises of the machines drowned out any stray voices from the bistro.

•

On the way home, Mum was tipsy and Mack was quiet. The Bowlo was on the road out of town, along past the oval. Mack drove the short distance slowly and looked to be having faraway thoughts.

'You all right, Mack?' asked Mum.

'Yeah, yeah,' he said, watching the road.

It didn't seem like Mack was all right. The back of Mum's head looked concerned. She endeavoured to cheer him up.

'I could take or leave Opal Jones,' she said, deadpan.

Mack laughed.

'I could leave her just fine,' he said. 'Poor Ken. The poor bugger.'

'What a thumb to be under. In that nail polish?' said Mum.

Mack chortled. The mood lifted a millimetre. Mack turned the gentle corner into our street and, as he did, as if Fitzy had willed it, it started to rain. Little droplets, falling widely on the windows.

'It'll come together, Mack. They're out there somewhere. Both of them are out there somewhere,' said Mum.

Mack was quiet.

Mum went on, full of wine, 'And you're gonna find them. I know you will, Constable Mackenzie. Hey, did you ever find anything out about Bart's Corolla?'

We pulled up outside our house, the engine idling.

Mack looked through the windscreen at the dark road, lit dimly by the moon, and the raindrops like pencil lines in his headlights.

It seemed like he wasn't going to say anything. It seemed like he'd sigh or evade or say you-know-how-it-is. But he didn't. He stared at the road. He shook his head. 'Ah, Ceils, bloody hell,' he said. And quite unexpectedly he unburdened himself slowly, while we sat in the warm police car and the rain fell.

The news about Kevin Fairley had Mum and I quiet. Mack told us of his drive out to the lake; of how helpless he felt when he went there. He told us how he'd driven back to Goodwood past the Fairley Dairy and, being reminded of its proximity to the road out of town, had felt compelled to stop in. He told us about the Corolla that Kevin Fairley had reported seeing on the road next to his south paddock, just near the clearing, parked alone in the cul-de-sac of trees.

Mum stared out into the night.

'That is weird,' she said and thought for a time. 'That's definitely weird.'

'Isn't it,' said Mack.

I sat in the back and said nothing, hoping they might forget I was there—which seemed to have already happened, given how unusually forthcoming Mack was being.

Mum was quiet a while longer, then she asked, 'So it was sitting there for over a week?'

'Nah, I said it *could've* been sitting there for over a week,' said Mack. 'It might've just been a couple of days. We don't know. But it might well've been over ten.'

'Ah,' said Mum, and did silent calculations.

'It's just—it's really funny that Bart didn't report it,' said Mack.

The rain got harder. Our house, with the front light on, looked sodden and heavy with grey mist.

'I guess the obvious reason not to report a stolen car is when it wasn't actually stolen,' he said.

Mum turned her head to look at him. I could see from the side that her brow was furrowed. She was almost squinting.

'You think Bart stole his *own car*?' she asked, incredulous.

Mack shook his head like he didn't want to know the answer. He kept on staring straight ahead. He was silent for a time before he spoke.

'Honestly? I don't know. I just think it's pretty strange for a car thief to steal a car from someone's house, and then leave it in that dirt road next to the clearing for however long it sat there, and *then* drive off in it,' he said.

The rain pelted. The gutters ran with water. Mack turned on the windshield wipers, even though we were parked.

'Oooh-eee,' said Mum, and blew out a puff of air.

I thought about the Corolla, sitting on the road that goes right past the clearing. I hadn't seen it. But you can't see the cul-de-sac from the clearing because all the trees are in the way; and I never walked the road way. I always walked by the river so Backflip could go splashing. I thought about the money, sitting in the tree, right in the clearing. I thought about the plastic horse. I thought about Ethan West, moving cows with Kevin Fairley at dusk.

'Ethan West works for Kevin,' I said from the darkness of the back seat.

'He's Jeannie's new boyfriend,' said Mum.

'He is not,' I said.

Mack didn't say anything. He looked at me in the rear-view mirror, and then he turned right around in his seat to meet my eyes.

'He helps move the cows,' I said. 'At dusk.'

'Does he now?' asked Mack. Then he turned back to the road. 'Kevin failed to mention that.'

We all sat there and wondered what it could mean, if anything at all.

Then Mack broke the silence. 'Fuck. I don't know,' he said curtly, and turned his blinker on to pull out again, in a way that summarily ended the conversation.

'Well,' said Mum, 'I don't know about that either. He is very tall, though, isn't he? Ethan. I might have to have another glass of wine.' She fumbled with her keys, and fumbled with her bag, opening the door to let the rain in.

'Night, Macko,' she said.

Mum went in the gate and up on to the verandah, little raindrops catching in her hair, and stood there opening the front door under the light, not looking back.

'Jean?' said Mack to my reflection in the rear-view mirror, because I wasn't getting out.

I sat there a moment longer, contemplated it, went through potential outcomes in my mind, dwelled a little on Mack's unfavourable mood, and decided that, no, this was not the time to tell him about the money.

I unbuckled my seatbelt and got out.

Mack pulled off into the rain with his right blinker flashing.

When I went inside, Mum had put the kettle on and was under the ferns in the living room, shushing Backflip, who went around in circles, crying with excitement at the very sight of us.

'Backflip you're so *brown*,' said Mum, ruffling Backflip's ears. 'Backflip Brown, Jean Brown and Celia Brown,' she said, in a very jovial mood. Backflip was delighted. The rain was heavy still and the muffled voices of Big Jim and Fitzy floated in from their little patio. I stood in our back doorway and listened.

'How many millimetres do you reckon, hon?' said Fitzy's voice from over the fence.

Mum looked at me, cracking up. Big Jim and Fitzy, watching their rain gauge, making their estimations.

I sat down on the couch and felt heavy and complex. The kettle started whistling. Mum turned on the radio in

the kitchen and cellos sang. She hummed along, swaying.
I wondered about Ethan. Was it some kind of secret that he
worked for Kevin Fairley? What else could he see from high
up on the paddocks? Why did Kevin never come into town?
And then there was Bart. That was the main concern. The
Bart that was emerging compared to the Bart that I knew.
The Bart that Goodwood knew. Councillor, butcher, pillar
of the community. Loving father to Pearl; faithful companion
to Mrs Bart.

I didn't think of him as a lying husband or a thief of his
own car.

Mum sat down in our pink velvet armchair with her tea
and Backflip joined us on the rug.

'What do you think about what Mack said?' I asked.

Mum puffed out air again. Shook her head. Sipped her
tea. Stared at the wall.

'I don't know, baby,' she said. 'On the one hand, I think:
it's a big lake.'

It was a big lake. Bart could've been in there anywhere,
dusting its silty floor, and no one would've been the wiser.

'But, on the other hand, I don't know,' she said. She put
her mug down on the side table and leant back in the big soft
chair with her hands behind her head. 'Maybe Mack feels like
Bart might've been different to what we all thought.'

19

I sat on the bench outside the police station for close to twenty minutes after school the next day. I was determined to tell Mack about the money, and paralysed by the fear of what he might say.

Across the road, spring was sprouting flowers along the edge of Sweetmans Park, under the ancient fig tree. Burly Joe was in the window of Bart's Meats, organising sausages into separate flavoured piles: pork, thin; pork with garlic and herbs; pork, thick; beef, thin; and so on. Bill was outside the newsagent smoking his cigarette.

Goodwood was heavier than ever. It had a different feel of an afternoon. Even with the season changing and green shoots appearing in the dewy branches, everything felt dark and heavy with grief. There was grief in the awnings, and grief in the wheels of our cars, and grief at the bottom of our glasses. Smithy, who served many a glass from behind his beer-soaked bar, told Nan it was just like *Watership Down*.

'That book scared the daylights out of me when I read it to my son,' he said, 'but that's how it feels around here now. Like we're the rabbits and the field is filling with blood.'

As a former English teacher, Nan appreciated the reference, if not the sentiment. I heard her telling Mum that Smithy was prone to malaise, and that people ought to pay attention to it, even if he shrouded it in charm and poetry.

But how were people to notice Smithy's sadness when it was so hard to differentiate between his and the rest of the sadness in town? Val Sparks knew it all too well. Her piety strained under such taxing circumstances. 'It must be God's way,' she kept saying to my Nan, the atheist. But even Val seemed concerned about the kind of God we had, if taking people from their boats and their bedrooms was the right way to anything. When I went past the Vinnies, Val was standing in the doorway, holding her porcelain baby Jesus and staring fearfully at the Wicko next door, as if Smithy's grief might be infectious.

'God bless, love,' she said to me.

'Hi, Val,' I said back, and walked across the road to the bench outside the police station, where I sat and deliberated. I went over my story. I decided how I was going to say it all out loud. I considered the various excuses I could proffer for not having told Mack earlier. By the time I worked up the courage to stand up it was almost four o'clock.

When I walked in I could see the top of Mack's head above the pinewood counter. He looked up at me, starting to stand. He looked like Roy Murray did these days, which was tired in the eyes. I felt a pound of regret in my chest and wished I'd chosen a day when Mack was refreshed and bright-eyed with adequate sleep.

'Jean?' said Mack.

'Hi, Mack,' I said.

'What are you doing here?' he asked. 'Something wrong?'

'No. I don't think so. I mean, maybe.'

So far it was going about as well as I had imagined.

Mack leant on the counter and said, 'Why don't you come around here and sit down.'

I walked around, through the little pinewood gate that went up to my waist and presumably kept criminals from getting Mack. We stood awkwardly for a moment before Mack gestured to a cheap, black vinyl chair. The cushion went *whoosh* as I sat down. Then Mack settled behind his desk again, looking like he was preparing for bad news.

'What's up, Jean? Is Ceils okay?'

'Oh yeah, she's fine.'

'You want to have a chat?'

'Yeah, okay. No, I do. Let's chat.'

Mack leant back and clasped his hands behind his head.

I moved around in my chair and the vinyl squeaked. I chewed my bottom lip. Then I launched—much like Opal

Jones had at the Bowlo the night before. Much like Mack had in his police car in the rain. Much like Fitzy did, apropos of absolutely nothing, all the time. Without any prompting from Mack, I unburdened myself of everything: the money and the tree-hole; the clearing and the plastic horse; my fear that I'd kept my secret too long; the amount of time I spent worrying about what might have happened to Rosie, and to Bart. I spoke quickly and nervously. I raised questions; I digressed. And then suddenly I had finished and, mercifully for both of us, I stopped talking.

The quiet was relieving.

Mack squinted at me. He had a pen in his hand, which he'd picked up sometime after I started speaking. He held it above his notepad but wrote nothing.

'So,' he said.

'So yeah, that's everything. I haven't been back to the clearing in a while, but last time I was there it was just the same, the bag with the little horse. And no one really goes there in winter. Except maybe Ethan does. I thought I should probably tell you about the whole thing.' I tried to stop myself talking again by breathing. Mack looked at me and made a straight line with his mouth.

'Well, what do you think?'

'It's a hidey-hole,' said Mack.

'In the tree? Yeah. It's up above the big branch of the willow where—'

156

Mack cut me off. 'I know, Jean. It's a hidey-hole. We used to use it when we were your age. I used to hide weed in there when I was in high school.'

'You smoked weed?'

Mack seemed so cool all of a sudden. I couldn't wait to tell George.

Mack went on, 'So you found five hundred dollars in the hidey-hole on the Friday before Rosie disappeared?'

'Yeah.'

'Five hundred?'

'Yeah. I counted it.'

'In a plastic bag?'

'In a brown paper bag, which was in a plastic bag.'

'And then you went back . . . when?'

'The Monday. And it was gone. But the little plastic horse was in there.'

Mack wrote the days down and tapped his pen on his desk.

'And you didn't think it worth telling me until now?' he asked, in a tone that I had imagined correctly in all my pre-enactments of this conversation.

I hung my head and remained silent.

He let out a big sigh, breathing all the air out through his nostrils.

I sat while he scratched some words on his notepad and tapped his pen and had faraway thoughts.

'Well, I guess we better go have a look then,' he said.

•

Mack and I walked across the oval in the sun, out the gate, and along the silty bank. He was a man of few words on the way; he mainly asked me to tell him everything again, so he could get it clear in his mind.

I found the money two days before Rosie vanished. Then the day after Rosie vanished the money was gone. I hadn't taken the money. I didn't know who took the money. I didn't know who left the money.

'And you didn't see the car?' asked Mack as we neared the clearing.

'No, I always walk this way along the river so Backflip can swim. I don't ever see the road.'

Mack nodded. He looked up towards the cul-de-sac and sure enough there were far too many trees in the way to get a look at it. You'd have to walk up the hill by the cow paddock and along the road to the very end.

'Do you think they're connected?' I asked. 'The money and the Corolla?'

'I think your head's connected to your arse, Jean,' said Mack.

I tripped over a stick, just managing not to fall all the way over, and corrected my footing, feeling ridiculous about myself.

We got to the clearing and the cows looked on, chewing with their mouths open, their big bodies attracting flies and birds.

'Hello, ladies,' Mack said to them kindly.

I always knew Mack to be a kind and gentle man.

He stood on the bank and raised a hand to his brow, squinting up to the tree-hole.

'You better go up, Jean, I can't see it from here. The branch bends.'

I climbed up the willow, onto the big branch, heard Mack telling me to be careful. I wavered and balanced, and looked up at the hole.

I saw no fraction of white plastic.

There was nothing there.

I put my hand up and felt inside the hole as best I could.

Crumbling bark, gritty dirt, rough hollowed edges.

I looked down at Mack, staring up at me, his face full of sun. I felt all the wind go from my sails.

'It's gone,' I said.

•

On that same afternoon, about the time I was arriving home, deflated and confused, Goodwood erupted in violence.

George went to the oval after school to meet Lucas Karras, where he planned to kick a football and she was expected to watch. She watched for a little while, expecting him to stop kicking at some point and come sit by her on the hill. That point never seemed to arrive.

'How long are you going to kick that for?' yelled George.

'What's wrong with it?' yelled Lucas.

'Fuck this,' yelled George, and walked towards the railway tracks that cut the town from her delinquent street. Lucas fetched his ball and followed, only to be deterred by the swiftness of George's pace. He yelled her name twice, gave up, and headed off home.

Mack and I would've just missed them on our way across the oval in the other direction, towards the clearing.

When George got to the corner of her street she could see the kerfuffle outside the Carlstroms' house. Davo's immediate neighbours were standing behind their screen door looking on. They were an elderly couple, Edna and Gus Field, who were often quoted in the *Gather Region Advocate* as describing any change to Goodwood (mainly those initiated by the Goodwood Progress Association) as 'an outrage'. George said later, 'If Edna Field really wanted an outrage, she finally got one.'

As George got closer, she crossed to the other side of the street to give the shouting a wide berth. She admitted to me later that she was genuinely scared. The sound of tools hitting the shell of a car clanged in her ears. Male voices became louder and more aggressive. It was Davo, yelling at his bogan uncle, Lafe.

'It was about Rosie,' said George. 'Davo was really losing it.'

'Like what kind of stuff?' I asked.

George struggled to be specific. All George heard, which she claimed she could testify in court with a fair degree of certainty, if the need arose, which she hoped it did, was Davo was yelling something like, 'You have no fucken idea,' followed at some point by, 'You're a fucken dog.'

Evidently, given what transpired, Lafe did not take kindly to being equated to a canine.

As George got to the pavement opposite the Carlstrom house, Lafe took Davo around the shoulders, grabbing his shirt and shaking him about. George caught something like, 'If you fucken . . . *something*,' from Lafe. Again, she could not be more specific as to the content. 'It was very rough and tumble,' she said later in her own defence.

Davo swung his arms and clipped Lafe around the ears. Lafe held him tighter and shook harder. There were grunting noises. Davo went red in the face. Then he got his knee up and boofed Lafe in the stomach, and Lafe went over onto the weed-infested, overgrown grass.

The crap caravan stood over them and made the whole scene look even more depressing.

Rearing back and catching his breath, Davo kicked Lafe in the torso, but Lafe grabbed Davo's shoe and twisted, which brought Davo to the grass too, flailing in the dandelions. Then the Carlstroms' screen door was flung open and Davo's dad Dennis stormed the lawn.

He picked up Davo by the arm and dragged him, blood now running from his nostrils, into the house.

Lafe was left in the weeds by himself.

He just lay there and said, '*Fuuuuuuuuuuuuuck*'—a word George heard quite clearly given its deliberate elongation. One of Lafe's empty beer cans took the opportunity to fall off the fence.

George watched Lafe for a minute, wondering if there was anything she should do.

Edna Field went inside, presumably to call the *Gather Region Advocate*.

Eventually George went home and took a long shower, and Lafe may well have lain in the grass all night.

•

On the right side of the tracks, Opal Jones was reading aloud to Ken from the *Women's Weekly Oriental Dinner Party Cookbook*. They were thinking of having Denise and Brian over some time, because although Brian was boring, Opal liked the way Denise listened. Ken Jones told Mack he would've rather heard the phone book read aloud than one of Opal's cookbooks, but Opal got annoyed when he resisted, so he'd learnt not to resist. Mack had shaken his head and said, 'Maaate.'

Opal Jones heard the noises before Ken. She says Ken was so interested in her recipe recitation that he might not have noticed if she hadn't cocked her ears to the disturbance and stopped reading. She turned down the volume on the TV news.

The sound of glass breaking. The sound of a thrown plate smashing against a wall. A woman screaming. A man, in thunderous tones, booming something Opal Jones couldn't decipher. The sound of the front door slamming and Terry White running out of the White house and off towards town. Opal Jones was practically hanging out the window by then and she saw him go. Then more smashing—glass, crockery, it was hard to tell—and muffled whopping sounds. *Whop, whop, whop.* It went on and on, followed by some thuds. Dull, brutal thuds. Someone falling. Then silence, except the sound of Opal asking Ken if they should call Mack.

After a few more minutes, Terry White ran back along their street and back into the White house, and the door slammed behind him.

Opal called Mack.

When Mack arrived, it'd been about fifteen minutes since the last smashed glass. He knocked on the Whites' door and Terry answered, in tears. Carl White, Opal attested, had reversed his car out from under the jacaranda and departed just minutes prior, with the look of a man possessed. That's how Opal described him: *possessed*. Carl White was haunted; he was bedevilled; and no one could argue that any of this was an improvement on blank and unfeeling.

The last thing Opal saw was Mack leading Judy White down to his police car, with Terry following a few metres behind. Judy had refused an ambulance, but she had trouble walking the short distance, and appeared to wince as Mack put his arm around her middle in an attempt to help her along. Her face did not resemble the woman Opal knew: it was entirely different colours.

Mack drove Terry and Judy the familiar forty-minute drive to Judy's own workplace. Her eyes had been beaten back into their sockets, so she didn't see much of the journey, but she knew the way with her eyes closed. Terry helped her out of the car. Another nurse, one of Judy's friends who was on duty, admitted Judy White. After twenty-five years of working there—apart from her brief stints in the labour ward with Rosie and Terry—it was Judy's first time as a patient at Clarke Base Hospital.

20

The Goodwood Progress Association met the following evening in the Community Hall and was grossly down in numbers. Bart McDonald, the co-president, was missing. Judy White, who had been absent the last meeting also, was in the hospital. Helen, who only ever came to the meetings to panic, was too distressed by recent events and had taken ill with a cold compress and a Valium. And Fitzy, upon hearing about Judy, had driven her car into the parking sign pole outside the Vinnies, much to Val Sparks's horror, and was at home wearing a neck brace and waiting for rain.

Smithy, the remaining co-president, who was both present and accounted for, ran the proceedings.

Spirits were low.

Without Fitzy, the movements towards lobbying council for an official Goodwood Monthly Rainfall Map, a native garden, and a reinforced guardrail for the bridge, were hereby postponed. Without Bart, any preparations towards the Fishing's The Funnest parade seemed gauche. And without Helen, whose newsagency's wall would bear Smithy's proposed mural, since it was the end building and faced the picnic tables at Sweetmans Park, there could be no progression with designs or a painting schedule.

The only thing left to discuss, thankfully without Judy, was unofficial business: Carl and Judy White, and whatever it was that had transpired between Lafe and Davo in the Carlstroms' front yard the day before.

Mum reported back when she got home.

Apparently, Davo Carlstrom sustained a bleeding nose, no actual break, and red rosy bruising to his cheeks and clavicle. Lafe—who was a prick of a thing, according to Smithy— drank five schooners at the Wicko some time later. He was speckled with grass and had a split lip and some roughing to the forehead. He was bigger, older and stronger, and had clearly got the better of Davo in the scuffle.

Smithy had inquired politely as to the cause of the dispute.

Lafe said, 'Ah, you know how it is. Davo's not over his fucken girlfriend.'

'You mean Rosie?' said Smithy, gently correcting what he considered to be Lafe's lack of respect for the missing.

'Whatever,' said Lafe, and left.

Smithy, who was often prone to say something profound,

told the meeting, 'Many a time a man's mouth broke his nose', and everyone agreed.

Meanwhile, Judy White had three broken ribs, two beaten-closed eyes, and severe lacerations to the backs of her thighs. A belt had been utilised. The buckle had caused the most damage.

While Judy was being treated for her injuries, Terry White was staying with the Joneses, waiting to be picked up by his Aunt Alison who would take him to stay with her in Ballina while Judy recovered. Alison told Mack that the further Terry could get from Carl the better. Cousin Tegan had taken a week off from the restaurant under the Big Prawn to hang out with Terry. She was to take him to the Richmond River, because everyone in the White family knew of Terry's fondness for rivers.

Mack had arrested Carl White first thing that morning, as Carl was sitting in his shed drinking a beer. He hadn't slept. Mack told Tracy, who attended the meeting, that Carl had said, 'You don't understand her. She did most of that to herself. She's lost it.' Mack was disgusted. He was, that afternoon, preparing an Apprehended Domestic Violence Order on Judy's behalf.

The Goodwood Progress Association was in deep shock. How could this be, in Goodwood? How could this be, in such a *safe* town? And what did it all mean about Rosie White?

'You know what I always thought was a bit funny?' said Carmel Carmichael. 'Jude used to come in for a wine with the girls—but only if Carl dropped her off and picked her up again. Like she's a big old baby!'

Faye Haynes snorted in disapproval.

Smithy chimed up with his opinion: Bart never liked Carl. He knew there was something off about him. But Bart was a gentleman. He didn't say a bad word about other people. He just made it clear that something was off and we were to make up our own minds about that. Now Bart's gone, so we can't ask him, God rest him in that beautiful lake. But Rosie White and Judy White. Now, what's this terrible business? What kind of man puts a belt to his wife? Puts her in the emergency department? That is not a man: that is a monster. He has the demons inside. 'I have a mind to think Carl White has done something awful last winter,' Smithy concluded. 'And now he's done this to Judy to keep her quiet. May the cat eat him and may the devil eat the cat.'

Mum resisted the urge to take minutes.

Tracy nodded as Smithy spoke, then took her turn to offer an opinion, which was hotly anticipated given her spousal proximity to Mack.

The meeting leaned in.

'That Lafe Carlstrom is a piece of work,' she said. 'I seen the way he looked at me at the Wicko one time. I did *not* like that look in his eye.'

That was all from Tracy. She never was a woman of many words.

The meeting leaned back. Smithy put a hand on Tracy's shoulder in commiseration. Carmel Carmichael, crestfallen, had another Scotch Finger. The Community Hall creaked with memories. Mum found herself anxious and had the urge to rearrange something. The meeting wound up early and everyone shuffled out into the warming air, with grief lining their light spring jackets.

•

The next day, Mrs Bart got up early. She rode Apples and Pearl rode Oyster, and they caught the first of the white morning light as it capped the top of the mountain like snow. Pearl had been distressed for weeks now and Mrs Bart wasn't faring much better. The two of them had made a pact to ride every morning together, in a concerted effort to make facing the day less of a concerted effort. So far, ever so slowly, it had been working. Pearl spoke more about Bart, now that she had a riding partner. Mrs Bart listened. Then Mrs Bart spoke about Bart, and Pearl listened, the sound of hooves interrupting them pleasantly. More often than not, though, they spoke of the horses, which was a much easier subject to broach before breakfast.

After they'd eaten, Pearl performed her morning dressage ceremonies with her My Little Ponies, then joined Jan to muck out the stables and check the pasture for fireweed. Mrs Bart backed the Mazda out of the carport and headed out of town towards Clarke. She drove the long road along the river, bumping over the dead kangaroos before the bridge, then she soared high above the brown water, trying not to look at it or to dwell on what might lie beneath. She sped along the two kilometres of fast flat road in a blur. And then she made sure to accelerate even faster as she approached the browned grass near the boat wharves. This was the first time since Bart vanished that she had been able to set wheel anywhere near the lake.

As she sped past the fishing spot, she couldn't help but turn her head. There among the bobbing boats was Bart's half-cabin cruiser, ghostly and floating. She swallowed hard and two tears let themselves out, stinging as they left her eyes and rolled down her cheeks. Later, Mrs Bart told my Nan that, involuntarily, she'd said, 'Oh no, no, no,' aloud to herself in an effort to push on.

When Mrs Bart arrived at Clarke Base Hospital, she was shown to the shared ward that contained Judy White. The nurse who escorted her shook her head and said, 'It's unspeakable,' as they pushed through big white double doors. Mrs Bart agreed, and therefore did not speak.

Judy White was sitting up in bed staring out the window. She was as surprised to see Mrs Bart as Mrs Bart was to be there.

When Nan asked Mrs Bart, 'Why did you go?', Mrs Bart just said, 'I felt compelled,' and Nan left it at that.

Judy White was a wrecked ship. There were no flowers. There were no vases. There were no sympathy cards. Just Judy, who quivered at the sight of Mrs Bart, a look of shame and humiliation filling her swollen face.

In an instant, Mrs Bart regretted her visit. She stood there not knowing what to say. Judy White had attended her floral art workshop; they knew each other to say hello, like everyone in Goodwood knew everyone. But that was really it. They had no bond whatsoever. They were not friends. Mrs Bart was not expected. Only then, in their shared losses, did Mrs Bart feel some kind of connection; only that day, upon waking, had she felt herself compelled.

Judy White said, 'Mrs Bart, you didn't have to come.'

Mrs Bart said, 'Call me Flora.'

Judy quivered, and stuttered, and began to make excuses. 'I'm such an idiot,' she said.

Mrs Bart replied, plain and firm: 'No. You're not.'

Then, pulling up a cheap plastic chair, Mrs Bart sat, and Judy lay, and Mrs Bart took Judy's hand, and the two women sat in an uncomfortable silence, until time passed and they no longer felt uncomfortable. They willed themselves into a state of ease. Just the two of them. Without having to plan it. There was nothing to say. All of it was unspeakable.

They merely set themselves there together—these two very different women—in unexpected solidarity.

Eventually, when the quiet current between their palms had exhausted itself, and their restorative silence was complete, Mrs Bart took her hand from Judy's, giving it a gentle squeeze as she did, and left.

Who knows what Judy White thought of the whole episode.

But Mrs Bart—Flora—felt compelled, and then regretful, and then empowered, and then somehow absolved.

21

During the afternoon while Mrs Bart and Judy White held hands in silence, Nan did her shopping at the Goodwood Grocer, stopped for a middy of shandy at the Wicko, looked in on Val Sparks at the Vinnies, and baked a silverbeet lasagne. Our phone was ringing with a dinner invitation as I got home from school.

Nan's cooking was generally thought to be the finest in Goodwood. When the CWA ran bake sales, Nan's cakes sold out by lunch. When she was still interested in competition, in the form of the Clarke Show, Nan held first prize in Biscuits and Muffins from 1984–1990. When Denise needed advice on updating the cookbook section at the Goodwood Library, she consulted with Nan, and hoped Nan would bake for the occasion.

When Rosie White went missing, Nan left a shepherd's pie on the Whites' doorstep and rang the bell before rushing off to her idling car.

'People need to grieve without bother,' she told me. 'But hot food always helps.'

When Bart went missing, Nan baked a banana bread (Pearl's favourite) and left it with Jan while Pearl was in the stables. Then she drove to Bart's Meats, where Mrs Bart was pacing, and left a spinach and cheese pie (Mrs Bart's favourite) on the front step. She gave a wave to Mrs Bart through the glass. Nan had wrapped the pie in a tea towel and left a note on top. It said, in cursive, *Flora, I cannot imagine. I wish you every strength. From Joyce Mackenzie.* That evening, when Nance closed the Grocer and walked home along Cedar Street, she was pleased to see that Mrs Bart had stopped her pacing, for a moment at least, and was eating a piece of pie.

When Mum and I arrived for dinner, Pop and Mack were drinking Reschs on the front verandah. It was always Reschs for my Pop. He drank the Pilsener at home, because you couldn't get the Draught in a bottle. But it was Reschs Draught or the highway when Pop went to the Wicko—he refused to drink any other beer.

Nan set the lasagne in the centre of the table, alongside a lovely spring salad. Pop clinked Mack's glass as he sat down. His beer sat inside a holder that said *Goodwood's Good For Wood*, with a picture of the sawmill and a cartoon man winking at a blushing lady. Mum sliced bread. Cutlery sounded. I could feel Backflip's fur against my ankles. Everything was the same; but nothing felt normal.

Dinner conversation at Nan and Pop's used to be light-hearted and free. It was homey and sophisticated and sometimes gamy; peppered with little puns from Pop, and humorous forays into politics and town business. Mum and Nan would have a glass of red wine and practise their amateur psychology. Nan knew best about everything, without having to make a song and dance about it, and everyone agreed—even Pop, who voted differently and had far less tolerance for oddity. We all looked to Nan like she was an oracle.

That night was different. Not about Nan, because she was still the authority on everything and sat at the head of the table to show it. But the tone had taken a turn. The talk was frenetic and sprawling. Voices were raised higher than usual. Everyone had an opinion. Everyone wanted to know about Judy and Carl; and Lafe and Davo; and Rosie and Bart.

Carl White was a deadshit, beyond all measure. An absolute disgrace of a man. No one thought 'monster' was too strong a word; the guy was on par with the devil. Lafe was not much better, although no one knew exactly why they felt that so strongly—it just seemed to be a common understanding. Davo was questionable, but the general consensus was: innocent till proven guilty. Judy was a martyr, a quivering mess of loss. And Rosie was a mystery. Rosie was just *gone*.

'Plus, I think Smithy's terribly depressed,' said Nan, cutting into the half-eaten lasagne when it was time for seconds.

Talk of Smithy led to a discussion about Goodwood in general, and the atmosphere that had overtaken Cedar Street and beyond. Everyone at the table was concerned, but no one more than Nan. Her trip to the shops that day was troubling. Everyone seemed to suffer. She could cut the air with a knife. The newsagent, the Bakery, the Grocer, Woody's, Bart's Meats. There was not a shop Nan had visited that didn't smell of grief. The corner block of our street, with the Wicko and Vinnies, was especially affected. Nan worried most about Val Sparks and Smithy.

On account of her piety, Val Sparks was particularly sensitive to the spiritual and emotional climate. Since the Vinnies was next door to the Wicko, she had come to believe that Smithy's melancholy was seeping through their joining wall. It was weighing on her more than the disappearances: this thing, this feeling—Smithy's heavy heart song—that hung in the air. It dusted her shelves with sorrow, and Val predicted that soon it would reside on every shelf and in every cracked brick in town.

Nan suggested that Val change her window display to make it look more sunny. She did. She rearranged her collection of Celeste Munch's pottery and made her pyramid of CWA jams into a square. She draped Coral's newest knit—a bright red scarf—across the foreground. Then she replaced the craft circle baby bibs with some general thrift items: two porcelain cats, one porcelain Dalmatian and a handsome wooden clock.

Quickly, she changed her mind about the clock. She worried that it would only point to time. And time—when people are missing and sad—is not a friend.

Nan said the new window looked very fresh. Then Mrs Gwen Hughes stopped in with her crystals and suggested Val burn a smudge stick of sage, in an act of cleansing. Val said, 'What a good idea,' to Gwen, and Gwen left satisfied.

Then Val said, 'I would never,' to Nan, and accused sage of being pagan.

Nan had looked out through the window, over Val's new display. The parking sign pole that Fitzy had crashed into with her car had been left slanting. It severed Nan's view of the street. She agreed with Val that it needed urgent straightening.

'God bless that woman, but she's a walking accident,' said Val. 'I look at that pole and think the whole town's askew.'

Mack piped up that he'd done what he could to talk to Smithy, but Smithy was acting strange. Mack had been into the Wicko the previous evening to ask about Lafe Carlstrom. Lafe had left sprinkles of grass under the bar stools from his scuffle in the yard.

Smithy told Mack all he had to tell and went back to humming 'Whiskey in a Jar'. In regards to anything personal, he was unforthcoming. All Mack could muster was a cryptic statement, which may have been quoted poetry—'the fields are filling with blood'—and Smithy had said it to the beer taps rather than to Mack directly.

'Smithy'll be all right—I'm more worried about Terry and Jude,' he said. 'And I'm mostly worried about what I'll do to fucking Carl White if I see him showing his face in town.'

The unusual instance of Mack cursing at Nan's table went by without comment. There was an aura of despair in the dining room. Mum leant back in her chair as if resigned to tragedy. Pop didn't have any puns. Mack looked exhausted. Backflip sat under the table waiting for someone to drop food.

'Well,' said Nan to the lasagne, 'most of you are too young to remember, but this whole time we're in right now? It reminds me of the war.'

•

When we got home that evening, Mum pulled up two chairs on the pavers and we sat and watched the garden. Big Jim and Fitzy had their back door closed and were quiet. Con and Althea were safe behind their roller shutters on the other side. Backflip sniffed around under the big flowering gum by the back fence, but she was too brown for us to see in the dark and all we could hear was her snuffling.

Mum made us peppermint tea and I held on to my warm mug.

I thought about everything everyone had said at dinner. I thought about walking to the clearing with Mack. I had no idea who took that plastic horse from the tree hole. I had no idea who *left* the plastic horse in the tree hole. I had no idea what anything had to do with anything else.

Mack and I had walked back to Cedar Street with few words. I said, 'Don't tell Mum,' and he nodded that he wouldn't.

Then, before dinner that night, Mack had pulled Mum and I aside about Bart's stolen Corolla, 'Don't tell Nan,' he said, and we nodded that we wouldn't.

I looked at the dark garden and imagined Bart: emerging from the lake, dripping with brown water, running past the paddocks, finding his Corolla, and driving off somewhere else to be gone.

22

George, who had always been fond of a conspiracy theory, found the whole thing highly suspicious.

'So, Bart didn't report his car stolen. And he lied to Mrs Bart about it?'

'Yeah,' I said, as we sat cross-legged on the grassy hill at lunch.

George looked perplexed. She stared off towards the fence.

'And so, okay, if he did steal his own car: first, would that be called stealing, and second, why would he do that?' she said.

I thought about it. 'I don't think you'd call that stealing,' I said.

I remembered that when the divers searched for Bart—and we huddled on the shore of the lake with the other concerned townsfolk—we'd heard the police from Clarke speculating that Bart had done a runner. Toby had driven us there that day—George had made him. He'd smoked cigarettes and kicked tufts of brown grass while we watched the divers. We'd wanted to stay longer but Toby complained of boredom, and the lack of a dead body, and we reluctantly agreed to go home.

The huddle from town included Big Jim and Merv, who'd brought Coral along with them at her insistence; as well as Irene Oakman, Carmel Carmichael, Smithy, and several fisherdads who spent their weekends on the lake. They all spoke over each other, and then not at all, and then over each other again when it looked like the divers might have something.

They never did.

But Sergeant Simmons from Clarke stood at the back of the group with Mack and two other officers, casting doubt over the likelihood of Bart's drowning.

'Fellas, he might not be there to find,' said Sergeant Simmons, looking cocky.

Why would he think that?

Was it that Bart had debts? Was it that Bart had a secret lady friend stashed in a nearby motel? Was it that Bart had an entire double life with a different family in a different town and decided now was the time to make a break for it and be gone?

The latter was George's most recent theory and she was very fond of it. She'd read an article in the newspaper a while ago about a podiatrist in England who had a whole other family secreted in a town only twenty minutes away from his wife of twenty years.

'He had two sons in the first house and two daughters in the second house, and the women had no idea! They just thought he fixed feet and was normal.' George spoke fast, nodding. 'Seriously, it happens all the time.'

'I don't think all the time,' I said. 'And when would Bart have had time for a whole other family?'

George didn't have an answer to that. She frowned. Bart opened Bart's Meats six days a week and fished on Sundays. He rode in the foothills with Pearl of an evening, under an orange sky. He took Mrs Bart out for nice steak dinners; he met his mates at the Bowlo or the Wicko most Fridays. He knew our names, our families, our months of birth. He chose thoughtful gifts and was always generous. He asked questions and he listened when we answered.

'I don't think Bart did a runner,' I said, after we'd gone around in several of these circles.

'But I'm just saying that if he did run somewhere, he would've needed a getaway car,' said George.

I lay back on the hill and looked up at the bright sky, squinting.

'I still think he seemed to drown,' I said.

George lay back too and looked up at the bright sky and sneezed.

'Bless you,' I said.

She sniffled and wiped her nose with her sleeve. She sighed. 'He did seem to drown,' she said.

•

Davo Carlstrom had slept late and spent until lunchtime lying on his bed, smoking. His mum, Linda, had left for work at the Ingham Further Processing Plant. Her day consisted of breading chicken limbs, which rolled away on a large conveyer belt to be packed in plastic, and then in boxes, and then into trucks and, eventually, into supermarket freezers. Linda and her colleagues wore sanitary gowns and gloves and masks and, under them, frowns. Due to her work, and the way it gradually sickened her, the Carlstroms did not consume any chicken. Linda rolled home most nights after the men had eaten, and was met with silence and disapproval. Her face was puffed and beery from too many schooners at the Royal Tavern.

When Davo woke, Dennis Carlstrom was toiling with an automobile in the yard. He'd dragged home a wounded 1980 Torana from the wrecker just outside of Clarke. Pop told me *torana* was an Aboriginal word meaning 'to fly'. Dennis and Lafe Carlstom, who had bent themselves under the bonnet, were determined to make it fly once more.

Relations between Davo and Lafe had been frosty in the few days since their lawn fight. Lafe drank by himself in his caravan. Davo stayed out late and avoided his house. He'd been seen on the oval, drinking; he'd been seen in Sweetmans Park, drinking; he'd been seen at the Wicko, drinking, and 'steaming' as Smithy said, which was Irish for drunk. George saw Davo walking up their street at night, off towards the dark, looking abandoned and savage.

Davo had been nothing like himself since Rosie vanished. His shoulders were less broad. His back was more stooped. His rebellious good looks became anguished and dishevelled. He'd lost weight in his face and chest, like a tyre with a slow leak.

But that day, after he slept late, he got himself out of his smoky bed. He wore his favourite Big W blue-checked flanno over a black T-shirt and jeans with no knees. He walked in heavy boots that were neglectfully untied. He ambled up his delinquent street, across the train tracks, up to the shops under the mountain. He went past Woody's, averting his eyes so he didn't have to see the place where Rosie should have been. Then he crossed the road directly and went straight into the Goodwood police station.

Mack's head was just visible above the pinewood counter. Posters for domestic violence services and Neighbourhood Watch hung crooked and faded. There was a smell of Pine O Cleen and Nescafé. Mack looked up and said, 'Davo. What can I do for you?'

Davo leant on the bench with his arms folded. He looked shrunken. He was pained. Mack could see it. It sat in his eyes like the grief that floated all over town. Mack stood up and said, 'Davo? Mate?'

Davo pulled a little plastic horse from his pocket and put it on the pinewood counter.

•

At the same time, down the hill from Cedar Street, the bell rang to announce the end of lunchtime and we had school assembly. The entire student body of Goodwood High was corralled into the gym, where blue plastic chairs were set in rows. A little demountable stage was wheeled out with a microphone on it. Kids from all years filed in noisily.

I sat next to George in the back row, closest to the big double doors. The light from outside poured in the high windows and made white squares on the dusty wooden floor. George talked at me while the chairs filled up around us. Our principal, Mr Cooper, stood waiting by the microphone. Teachers lined the walls. Mrs Gwen Hughes stood alone and rubbed her amethyst necklace like a mystic.

Evie came in behind us.

There were three spare chairs to my left, and then the aisle. I saw her out of the corner of my eye. She stopped before the double doors in the white light and looked at the section assigned to Year Twelve. She could've sat in any row.

She could've sat in any chair. But she came to our row and shuffled along three seats and sat down right next to me.

It was the closest I had ever been to her. I'd seen her in the library; in the playground; in the canteen; at the lunch tables. She was always by herself and often reading. She always seemed as if she was in a faraway and much more interesting world.

George, on my other side, was talking away, even though I had stopped listening properly. Bec Fisher and Bec Kelly, reeking of Impulse, sat down in the two seats next to Evie, and our row was full.

Mr Cooper began to speak. It was a tough day to be Mr Cooper. He was never good at addressing difficulty, and this was a particularly difficult time. For us as a school and for Goodwood as a town. All of us knew Bart McDonald. He was a terrific bloke. Very generous to the school. He put together the meat tray for the raffle; it was always a great tray. He was very generous, a really terrific bloke. We all think of his family, and—of course—Rosie. As for Rosie, *cough cough*, she just graduated last year—as we all knew. Worked up there at Woody's Take Away—up there. Really terrific young girl, with a lot of potential. It's a very difficult, very tragic time—but if we all just stick together. Terry White—we all knew Terry. Terrific kid. Year Eleven student here at Goodwood High. It's a very difficult time for Terry and his family. Terry is absent for the time being as we can all understand. Let's all keep hoping they come home safe and sound: Bart and——*cough cough*——Rosie.

Beads of sweat had sprouted all over Mr Cooper.

'Have mercy on that poor man,' said George.

He soldiered on. Matters of upcoming exams and sports couldn't have come soon enough. He began to recover his voice. The Gather Region Athletics Carnival was imminent. Goodwood could be very competitive, he said, particularly in cross-country.

'Maybe because everyone wants to leave town so bad and no one has a car?' whispered George.

He moved swiftly along from sports to aspiration in general. He found his stride. Mr Cooper claimed that we, the students of Goodwood High, would be successful Twentieth-Century Global Citizens. In eight short years we'd inhabit the Twenty-First Century and beyond. He reminded us of our school motto. 'Strive for the Summit,' he said, which always made me think of the deep green mountain.

'And once you get to the summit, go down the other side and don't look back,' whispered George.

The Goodwood High School band performed a shaky version of 'Top of the World' by The Carpenters. The clarinets let the whole thing down. Poor Emily Ross. I had no idea why someone with so much asthma would choose a wind instrument. George and I clapped loudly to compensate for the lacklustre applause. We loved assembly. Especially George.

A school counsellor from Clarke High made a speech over half-moon glasses. She was going to be at our school on Fridays for one month in case anyone needed to talk about their feelings. She had an inkling that some of us might be sad or anxious, or even scared, but not to worry because she had a degree in psychology and was not afraid to use it. Apparently, beyond all things, it was important for us to seek help early.

'Before it's *too late*,' whispered George.

Mr Berg made a short speech about a new Safe Town program. 'A safe and caring environment' where students could meet and discuss things they were nervous about: recent unsettling events, walking home alone, stranger danger.

'As Mr Cooper said, Rosie White was a student here. She graduated just last year so many of you will have known her reasonably well. As a school we pray for her safety. Even those of you who don't believe in God can pray in your own way.'

Some boys a few rows in front of us laughed. One wolf-whistled in a tone that suggested a distinct lack of belief. Mrs Carr glared at them and performed one of her reprimanding coughs.

I was thankful that Terry White was in Ballina.

I could sense Evie next to me the whole time but I didn't turn my head. I stared at the stage and tried to look at her out of the corner of my eye. She crossed her arms. She leant back in her chair. She tilted her head sideways towards me and then straightened it again.

Toby laughed with the laughing boys.

'How is he related to me?' asked George, looking genuinely confused.

Mr Cooper was up on the wheel-out stage again. The boys had been shushed from all angles and Toby was swinging his legs in his chair. Mr Cooper was winding up with a rundown of training session times. 'Do you know what the best sportspeople do?' he asked rhetorically. 'They strive for the summit. That's what they do.'

'Up, up and away,' whispered George. I was smiling.

Evie shifted in her chair, she got closer. Her arm touched my arm.

I felt a little jolt from it, like electricity coming down a wire. Like a spark plug in a car under a tarpaulin. George went to uncross her legs and accidentally kicked the chair in front. Jackson Harrington, who we felt sorry for on account of his size, turned around and gave her an aching look. 'Sorry,' whispered George, looking contrite. She stared at the floor.

Evie kept her arm touching mine. I didn't move. The wings of birds beat in my chest. Evie stared straight ahead. I did the same. I breathed in and out slowly, trying to be calm. I felt her braveness. I could feel it through my jumper, through her jumper, and all the way to where her skin would be.

She moved one leg over her ankle. Her arm pressed against me harder still. Then her fingers reached out, only a fraction, and she touched me just below my shoulder.

I didn't make any sound. I didn't move at all. I closed my eyes for a moment and I could feel Evie breathing. Slow and gentle. She moved her fingers up and down against my arm and everything tingled—and then Mr Cooper said, 'That's all, thanks everyone,' and the room erupted in standing and talking. George bent over and pulled her bag out from under the seat in front, muttering something about science.

Evie pulled her hand away and uncrossed her arms. She leant down for her bag. Bec Kelly stuck her gum to the leg of her chair and shuffled out with Bec Fisher. Evie got up. She didn't look at me; she just put her bag on one shoulder and went straight out the double doors into the white sun.

George raised a fist. 'To the summit,' she said as she turned towards the light. 'I'm fizzing at the bunghole.'

She blinked and sneezed and fumbled around in her pocket for a hanky.

I could feel Evie against my arm still. My skin was covered in goosebumps. The light was so white outside. How blinding and brilliant it was. I smiled, dazzled. It looked like a faraway and much more interesting world.

•

After Davo put the plastic horse on the counter, Mack stood looking at it. They both did, the two of them—grown men—stared at the little plastic horse like children. Mack remembered the barnyard collection he had as a boy—his menagerie lived in a plastic stable, and one year Mack swallowed a yellow tractor. His dad, Lang, bought him sheep and cows, but Mack always wanted more horses.

Mack forced himself to look up.

Sergeant Simmons from Clarke came in from the other office. He had an arm full of manila folders. He put them on the desk near the counter and riffled through them. Davo hardly noticed.

'What's this then?' Mack asked, while Davo stared at the toy horse.

'I think Rosie did a runner,' said Davo.

'Did the little horse tell you that?' asked Sergeant Simmons, looking up from his folders.

Davo looked pained. He was not amused. He started shaking his head as if to say *fucking pigs*; like he might turn tail and run right out of there.

Mack turned and glared at Sergeant Simmons, who looked very amused. Sergeant Simmons winked and walked back to the other office.

'Mate. Davo,' said Mack. 'Why don't you tell me what's going on.'

Davo looked like he might cry. He fondled the horse with two rough fingers, stroking it along its brown plastic back. Mack looked on. He had the urge to pat the horse, too. Lang's beetroot head flashed in his mind. Spilt blood and the beak of a raven. He winced and felt nauseous.

'Why don't you come around here and have a seat,' said Mack kindly.

Davo picked up the horse and passed through the waist-high gate next to the counter. Mack sat down at his desk and gestured to the cheap black vinyl chair opposite. The cushion *whooshed* when Davo sat down.

Mack noticed that Davo was thinner. He noticed his slumped shoulders. He could see the grief coming off him like mist.

'Why do you think she's done a runner?' asked Mack.

Davo held the horse in one hand on his knee.

'Because she left this for me,' he said.

'And what's that?' asked Mack.

Davo looked at him like he was dim. 'It's a toy horse,' he said.

'I can see that,' said Mack. 'But why'd she leave it for you? Where'd she leave it? And how do you know it was her? How do you know it's for you?'

Davo ran the little horse along his leg, trotting. 'Because I gave it to her,' he said.

23

Davo and Rosie had been seeing each other for almost nine months. It had started slowly. Rosie was so beautiful. She was always aloof. Davo found her impossible to figure out. He was older by eighteen months, but he'd seen her around at school for years. There was electricity when he saw her. She'd hardly have to look at him and all he could do was feel it, charging down the wires.

The other girls at Goodwood High were rough and eager. He'd had sex with them on the oval, or in the back of his car, or in the bushes at Sweetmans Park. He always went home empty. He drank a lot of beer to forget his mother; his mother had long forgotten him. He didn't want to just fix cars in the yard with his dad, and now his fucking uncle. Rosie was different. He had really wooed her. He stood out the front of Woody's until she'd smile. Then she finally smiled: and he died. He took her to the clearing to go swimming in summer. She'd be hot and then she'd be cold. One minute, his hands were up her skirt, finding her skin wanting, finding her covered in goosebumps and pressing his hand higher. The next, she'd walk right past him, by the beer garden at the Wicko, ignoring his waving and looking the other way.

By the start of March, she seemed to be won over. They didn't see each other all that much. Davo always wanted more, but Rosie would recoil if he pushed her. She'd stay in her room with the stereo up loud. She'd sit in Sweetmans Park under the grand old fig tree, reading magazines, listening to her Walkman. He pressed her to open up to him, slowly, like a flower. He felt around for the pieces of her difficult life. But she would show him only tiny fragments. They lay in his bedroom, smoking. They lay at the clearing, in the dappled shade.

The clearing has a big willow tree and there's a hidey-hole in its trunk, up above the high branch that goes out over the water. Over summer, Davo would leave Rosie presents. He left her two cigarettes wrapped in paper. He left her nasturtium flowers. He left her a mix tape. It was always when they were going to meet there. He would leave her a present, usually on the way home from the Wicko the night before, and he loved to watch her climb up and find it. Then they'd have sex—fast and slow—under the willow tree, on his laid-down jacket, while the cows looked on and the birds sang in chorus.

Rosie wanted to leave Goodwood. She always had. Davo tried to make plans for them both, but she wouldn't hear it.

She was so independent. So brave and alone. He could never tame her or make her his own. She spoke always of her Cousin Tegan in Ballina. She was older and cooler and free. She had a good job at a restaurant and maybe she could get Rosie a job too, right there under the Big Prawn. Rosie wanted to move to Byron—Tegan had told her all about it. Rosie would say to Davo, while they lay in the clearing, 'We're getting out of this one-horse town, one horse at a time.'

Davo wished they could ride out together, but it was always *one horse at a time*. Maybe he could catch her up, he thought. He decided on her next present.

The last time they met at the clearing to swim, before the weather got too cold, he had left his present and arrived late. When he got there, Rosie, in cut-off jean shorts and one of Davo's Big W flannos, was holding the little plastic horse. Davo had bought it at the toyshop at the Clarke Plaza and kept it in his glove box.

'One horse at a time,' she said, properly smiling. She smiled like that and he died. She undid his jeans in a fever and he pushed himself inside her—on the dry leaves, while the sun dipped low and the dusty sky dimmed the mountain.

After, Rosie carved their initials in the trunk with her Swiss Army knife: RW 4 DC.

That was March. The weather cooled. They met a few times a week, but Rosie always put the brakes on and Davo always tried to speed things up.

Then, in April, Lafe arrived. Rosie didn't like him at all. She would not say why, no matter how much Davo asked her. She just stopped wanting to go to Davo's house altogether. She gave a wide berth to the whole delinquent street. Lafe stayed in his caravan, drinking and leering. Davo never understood what he'd done that was so wrong. But Davo couldn't go to Rosie's house either and she'd never explained why. She just said, 'It's not a good vibe,' and wouldn't go any further. She never said one word about her stepdad, Carl White, but Davo knew there was some kind of problem. He knew that something wasn't right. One time she had little brown bruises—just one time—wrapped around both her wrists. Davo had put his fingers on them tenderly and Rosie had jerked her hand away.

It was cold on the oval. It was cold at the clearing. They met in the day and found a small patch of sun. They drank at the Wicko and sat by the fire.

Then it was August. That week before Rosie vanished. She had worked as usual at Woody's and Davo hadn't seen her at all. He'd tried, but she'd gone silent. Then, out of the blue, she called his house on the Sunday morning. Linda, already half drunk answered and slurred Davo's name. Lafe said something revolting from the doorway.

Rosie asked Davo to meet her at the Wicko, and so he had. She seemed kind of normal, but not normal at all. There was just something different about her. Maybe she was sad. He couldn't quite tell. She laughed at his stupid jokes. She endured when he was lost for words. But there was *something*. She seemed so far away, but was smiling to reassure him, or to reassure herself. It was there in her eyes——this dark intensity——and she looked down at the table more than usual, and avoided his glances.

She'd said, 'David. One horse at a time.'

No one ever took him seriously enough to call him David. He liked it.

They said goodbye in the beer garden. She was going home for dinner; he was staying on. She kissed him with her tongue, with all of her mouth, with her hands on his face. He got hard in his jeans——just the impossible smell of her.

And then she was gone.

•

Mack leaned back in his chair. He had a pen in his hand, but he hadn't written anything.

Davo held the horse. Mack chewed at the inside of his lip. The two men sat in silence. Sergeant Simmons's voice said, 'Ah, fuck's sake,' muffled from the other office, with the sound of rustling paper. Davo looked at Mack starkly.

'I went down the clearing last weekend,' said Davo. 'First time since summer. I dunno why.'

Mack nodded.

'I just went to sit in our spot I guess. Just be there a bit, even without her. And this was there. In our hidey-hole.' He held the horse up in case Mack hadn't seen it enough already. 'I can't believe it. She left it for me,' he said. He was quiet for a time. He looked like he might crumple. 'She *left*.'

Mack said, 'Okay. Okay.' Nodding, thinking.

He wrote some words on his pad. *Last weekend—horse. The clearing*.

Then he looked Davo straight in the eye and asked him plainly, 'Mate, what about the money?'

Davo looked back, his brow furrowed. 'What money?'

•

After school I stopped at Vinnies and asked Val Sparks if she had any army coats or fingerless gloves.

'But Jean Brown, it's spring,' she said.

I looked at her blankly.

'Oh. Yeah,' I said. 'But I get cold.'

Ray Charles was singing out of Val's little silver radio.

'That's because you're too thin,' said Val as she showed me to the coats.

She riffled through the small array of knits and jackets. She held up a mauve cardigan with white lace flowers embroidered on it and glass buttons cut like diamonds.

'How about this?' she asked.

I looked at Val and at the glass buttons. That was what Evie was like, I thought. She was like diamonds. The light in her and the way it sparkled and the way she made me feel different.

I had spent the whole afternoon remembering Evie's fingers and how she ran them against my arm in assembly. She pressed them, up and down, on the outside of my jumper, and every time I thought of it I got the shivers.

'That's okay,' I said, and Val went into the back room to sift for gloves.

The view of the street was sliced at an angle by the pole that Fitzy had run into with her car. It had still not been straightened. Ray Charles and Val sang together now, Val warbling high from the back room.

The nativity scene behind the counter bore no dust. Next to it, Val had put together a small shrine. Prayer beads were draped casually next to a cedar crucifix. Two white candles burned, and Val had propped up name cards in front of them, as if they were guests at a dinner party. One name card said *Bart* in Val's wobbly cursive. The other said *Rosie*.

'I've only got these ones with the fingers,' said Val, who had reappeared holding a dreadful pair of black leather ladies gloves.

'That's okay,' I said.

The sun had caught the bent-over pole and reflected silver light at Val's window. Her new display did look very fresh, just as Nan had reported. Val went back to dusting grief off all the hard surfaces. Her phone rang.

I was standing in the doorway when I saw Davo Carlstrom walk out of the Goodwood Police Station and cross the street.

He looked exhausted. His shoulders were slumped. He'd lost weight. His bootlaces strayed behind him. I saw him avert his eyes as he passed Woody's, so he didn't have to see the hole where Rosie should have been. He pushed one hand through his hair to brush it off his face and his eyes were as red as blood. He looked like he'd been crying.

'Oh yes, I'm praying,' Val was saying into the receiver. 'It's everywhere. *Everywhere*. I know you don't like it when I say it, but it feels like the end times.'

It didn't occur to me to wonder what Davo was doing at the police station. It didn't occur to me to think what he might have said, or what he might have done. I was just struck by the sight of him, so shrunken, pushing his hair off his tired face. And his other hand: gripping a little plastic horse and holding on to it for dear life.

•

All up, Mack and Davo had sat in the police station for two hours that afternoon. This, Mack thought, was the best information he'd had so far. This was a picture of Rosie that no one else could draw: a troubled, solitary figure; someone who pushed love away; a girl who was lost at home and all at sea. The whole thing was like an awakening.

Davo didn't know anything about the money. He swore it to Mack and Mack believed him. Davo said, 'What money?' and so Mack told him.

Someone in town, he said—not revealing any names—had found money in the hidey-hole. That someone had left it there, in good faith and honesty. Then that someone had gone back and found the plastic horse. They had left that there too, and eventually come forward with the information.

'You knew about the horse?' asked Davo.

'I was told of its existence,' said Mack.

'Who found it?' Davo asked. He seemed very intent on knowing the answer.

'Just a kid,' said Mack, much to my disappointment.

'I was protecting you, Jean,' he told me a long time later. 'Well you could've protected me with more respect,' I said.

Davo kept on at Mack to tell him, but Mack refused. Davo gave up and trotted the horse along his leg.

'Would Rosie have that kind of money?' asked Mack.

'No,' said Davo. 'How would she? She was always talking about saving up to go, but she wasn't talking about right now. She meant in the future, when she'd saved up enough.'

Mack had talked to Roy Murray. He knew Rosie's wages. He'd spoken to Judy White. He knew Rosie's expenses. The year before, as a graduating present, Rosie had bought herself a stereo with her own money. A Sony CFD-770 Boombox. She loved music. She loved playing it loud. She'd saved up for many months. She also kept herself in cigarettes, beer and clothes. But that was about it and she bought at op shops mainly. Judy White didn't have money. Rosie got the job at

Woody's because there was none. Carl White liked to put it all in the pokies at the Bowlo. There were no nice steak dinners.

Judy White said, 'Rosie didn't have any money. You can check her bank balance I'm sure. But she didn't use the bank. She got paid and she spent it on whatever she needed, just week to week. The last money she actually saved she used to buy the Boombox.'

Mack had checked Rosie's bank balance. She had $7.43. No recent transactions. No credits since February, when she'd deposited a cheque for a hundred dollars that Aunt Alison had sent her on her eighteenth birthday.

'Do you know who might've given her that kind of money?' asked Mack.

'No,' said Davo. 'Do you?'

Mack stared at him, looked away. 'No,' he said. 'I don't know.'

Mack changed tack. 'What about that Corolla that I asked you about a couple of weeks ago? The one that went missing from Bart McDonald's carport?'

Davo leaned back in the cheap vinyl chair and looked at Mack. He almost smiled. 'You think Rosie stole Bart's car?' he asked, incredulous.

Mack looked back at Davo, trying to get a handle on the situation. 'I don't know. What do you think?'

'Are you fucken serious?' asked Davo.

Mack *was* serious, but he quickly felt foolish. 'I'm just pursuing all avenues,' he said.

'Trust me. Rosie would not know how to hot-wire a car,' said Davo. He held on to the horse. 'Carl taught her to drive and all, and she got her licence. But she was pretty wobbly at it. She didn't know shit about cars.'

'It's just that, mate, if she did a runner, how did she run?' asked Mack.

Davo looked at the floor, thinking. There was only a freight train. No passengers, no stop. Mack had checked with the bus lines. He'd spoken to the drivers. No one had seen Rosie.

'I guess she would've hitched,' said Davo after a time. 'Tegan said people hitch up north all the time. Rosie told me. She said Tegan hitched to Byron heaps.' Davo stared off into space. He looked like a man deserted. As if he'd suddenly remembered again that he'd been left.

'And what were you and Lafe fighting about the other day?' asked Mack.

Davo shook his head. He wouldn't look Mack in the eye. He just said quietly, 'I didn't like the way he was talking about her.'

Mack went in fast. What way was that? What did he say? How well did he know Rosie? Why didn't she like him?

Davo put his hand in his hair. He scrunched up his face. He pulled his hand back and hit himself in the forehead, as if to stop his eyes, which had filled with tears. He shook his head, hot, embarrassed, in pain. A sound came from his throat like a yelp, his cheeks flushed with blood. The noise he made was that of an injured animal.

'Fuuuuuck,' he said. He looked at Mack. He was blurry-eyed and ashamed.

'Calm down, mate,' said Mack.

Davo couldn't say any more. He couldn't think any more. He took his horse and pushed the chair back, slamming the little waist-high gate on his way past the counter.

Mack sat back in his chair. He tapped his pen on his pine-wood desk. He stared through the wall opposite. He burnt a hole with his eyes, searching for some kind of vision. Sergeant Simmons came out from the office and said, uncaring: 'Did you get anything? Is that kid a fucker or what?'

All Mack could see was Rosie. He saw her plain as day on a Sunday night in August: black tights, red jumper, standing on the side of the road. Maybe she'd walked just out of town, past the Bowlo. Maybe she'd made it all the way to the highway. She was escaping her difficult life. It was the only way she knew how. Her thumb was out in the cold air. She was hoping for a passing car. She was hoping for anything or anyone who could take her to a faraway and much more interesting world.

24

Nance drove Judy White home from the hospital first thing in the morning. The Goodwood Grocer was supposed to open at eight am, but Nance put a sign on the door that said: *Opening late today—Sorry for inconvenience. I should be back by 10.*

They drove out of Clarke carefully in Nance's silver Laser. Nance wasn't great at manual and she shifted the gears with lots of revs so they left the traffic lights near the Plaza with a little jump. Judy was jumpy enough already. She quivered. The seatbelt hurt her ribs. The seat, even covered in soft sheepskin, hurt her thighs. Nance had insisted. She'd beat Opal Jones to the punch. Judy was relieved it wasn't Opal, but she'd hoped for Mrs Bart.

They drove south out of Clarke through the thick trees and along the straight road. Nance sat at eighty kilometres an hour, even though the speed limit was a hundred. The closer they inched to Goodwood the more Judy's chest collapsed in on itself at the thought of Rosie.

They left the trees, and the lake opened out on their right, massive and brown. Judy thought of the water. Litres, megalitres, gigalitres of water. Nance put her foot down as they went past the browned grass near the boat wharves.

'Gives me the shivers,' Nance said.

They went over the high bridge, where the water was at its deepest. Judy White hadn't known Bart that well. She only knew how he felt about Carl. Why Bart had beat up Carl that day two years ago, Judy didn't know. Carl snarled at her when she'd made the mistake of asking one night after he'd been drinking. Why was she so stupid as to ask him anything when he'd been drinking?

But Bart—he was a good man. He was gentle when he had that heart attack and she tended to him at the hospital. His wife was such a good woman, too. Coming to visit her like that. If she hadn't married Carl White she might've had friends like the McDonalds. But what would she do without Carl? He could still change. And there was no Bart now, in any case. There was only brown water under the high bridge and a gaping gorge of a hole in her heart where Rosie used to be. *My baby, my baby, my baby*, thought Judy White, with her swollen eyes shut tight.

They drove into town past the Bowlo. Nance went around the long way to avoid Woody's. Judy thought only of Rosie as they pulled up outside the empty White house.

Nance walked her to the door and helped her inside. She opened windows and threw out dead flowers. The musty smell of sorrow hung in all the curtains. Nance put the kettle on. Judy said, 'You go open the shop, Nance. I'm fine.'

Nance went reluctantly. She left Judy with bread and eggs and milk in a picnic freezer bag. Judy White sat on her couch and put her large-print puzzle book on her lap like a blanket. A short while later she heard Opal Jones knocking.

'Jude? Knock knock,' said Opal. She kept on banging and yelling—'Yoo hoo, Juu-ude'—for what seemed like ages.

Judy White just sat there on her couch and tears went everywhere on her face and dripped down her blouse and onto her jeans and over her puzzle book and even the floor.

•

That afternoon I went to George's. Backflip and I had walked from our house, along Cedar Street under the mountain, across the train tracks and along the delinquent street, where sinks and whitegoods grew like broken flowers in the weeds. George's house was cold, even in spring. The interior was lino, and fake wood, and cheap venetian blinds that were always tangled. There was a deep crack in the glass coffee table and no art and not many books. Just remote controls and *TV Weeks* and scattered blocks of Lego.

George's oldest brother, Vinnie, was in the backyard with Toby, who was throwing a basketball at a crooked hoop. It was not so much a yard, just a concrete slab with a Hills Hoist in the middle and several struggling pot plants. Vinnie was sitting in a lawn chair, drinking a Carlton Draught.

'Oi, Jean,' he said. 'My little mate.'

Gosh, I loved Vinnie. We all did. I beamed when he greeted me warmly.

Vinnie had been in Rosie's year at Goodwood High. He was a skinny redheaded kid when we were younger, but over the years he'd grown to be six foot tall, which made him comparable to Ethan, if not Big Jim himself—the tallest man in town. Vinnie excelled at Design and Technology. He had giant freckled hands. At school he made pencil boxes and cheese boards and spoons. Now he was making an outdoor table for his new house in Clarke. And before he'd started the table he'd made his own workbench, so he could start the table. He told us all about it proudly from his lawn chair. He did the whole thing with two-by-fours and it had a face vice and a tail vice and joinery that was heaps good. It was so fluky because he got all the wood for free on account of a construction site that ran out of money and a very disgruntled foreman. Vinnie could charm a disgruntled anyone.

Vinnie had enrolled in TAFE over the summer: a certificate in carpentry. He always said he wanted to give it a crack. He'd moved out of home and was studying and living in a share house with two other guys near the Clarke Plaza. George said they'd had a party with a whole keg of beer and the police came. But Vinnie, apart from his drinking, was a good and quiet man. His giant freckled hands were gentle. He could wrap them all the way around Toby's clenched fist, down to the wrist. And he was much stronger than George's dad. He was, at nineteen, the man of the house.

'What the fuck about Rosie?' he asked, drinking. His beer cooler said *Goodwood's Good For Wood*, with the sawmill and the blushing lady.

'She's disappeared,' said George. 'No one knows anything.'

Vinnie looked at the concrete.

'It's so full on,' he said, shaking his head. 'Rosie White.'

Toby got the ball through the slanted hoop. Vinnie leant forward in his flimsy chair.

'This calls for beer, hey,' he said. 'You can get them, Georgie.'

George sprinted off to the fridge and came back with a sixpack, not entirely cold, and we sat on the concrete and drank them while Vinnie spoke of Rosie.

He'd liked her. He had really liked her. She was such a funny girl. Funny weird, not funny ha-ha. Toby, who was half listening, ribbed him. 'She turned you down, but,' he said, passing the ball from one hand to the other.

'She turned you down, too,' said George. She rolled her eyes.

Toby closed his mouth and turned back to the hoop.

Vinnie had asked Rosie out, it was true. She had turned him down though, that was true also. She seemed pretty into Davo Carlstrom. She was such a strange girl but, hey. Hard to figure out. Never really got her. But fully good-looking. Just heaps more interesting than the other girls. Now it's fucken Derek Murray working at Woody's. How fucked is that? No one used to wanna go there if he was hanging around—like a full-on weirdo—and now he's actually making the chips and shit. Cannot handle that guy. He's like a twenty-year-old virgin.

Ha ha ha ha. Toby was laughing.

Vinnie laughed too, a big man's laugh. He made Toby seem so small. The two brothers shared an unkind moment against Derek Murray. Then Vinnie stopped laughing and looked very stern. His expression went stony and he sipped at his beer. Cross-legged on the concrete, we looked up at him.

Vinnie was rueful. 'Fucken Derek,' he said, and stared. 'Get this though, hey.' And then he told us a story we had never heard before.

The previous year, when Derek Murray stole runty Daniel's football and left him with a bloody nose, Daniel came home and told the whole family all about it. He was crying. He was so short. He loved that football. He was only in Year Seven and Derek Murray was six years older and a whole foot taller. It just wasn't cricket.

Vinnie was incensed. He couldn't believe it. What kind of arsehole steals a little kid's football and hits him in the face? Overcome by the injustice of it, he punched the pleather couch cushion. Fred Sharkey told him to leave it. 'Just leave it, Vin. Derek Murray is dumb as a box of hair.'

Vinnie couldn't leave it. Daniel was his little brother and he had to restore his honour. He left on his bike. He rode across the railway tracks and along Cedar Street and down to the Murrays' sunken weatherboard house. Vinnie knocked on the door. No one came. He knocked louder. Soft footsteps sounded from inside. The door finally opened and a face peeked out from behind it. It was Doe Murray.

Doe Murray! A sighting! No one ever saw Doe Murray.

Vinnie asked if Derek was home. Doe looked terribly nervous. She looked out past him and up to the sky, her brow furrowed at the cheerful white clouds. 'He's in his room,' she whispered. Her mind was absent.

Vinnie said, 'I'm a mate—can I say a quick hello?'

Doe Murray opened the door and let him through, ignoring him completely. She stood in the doorway like an unjoined person and looked up to the perfect sky.

Vinnie walked in—he didn't know where he was going—and went down the hall. He saw a closed door. It had a plastic STOP sign on it. He took a punt and opened it to find Derek Murray, sitting in his underwear, playing *Street Fighter*. Derek looked stunned. He said 'Hey. What?'

Vinnie closed the door behind him softly. He got Derek by the neck and pulled him up so he was standing. Derek was an older boy, but not a bigger one. Vinnie punched him in the stomach, hard. Derek went *whoosh* as the wind came out. Vinnie held him by the neck as he wheezed and spluttered. Spittle went down his chin. He was plainly winded. Vinnie stared him in the eyes, very close. He squeezed his neck, tighter and tighter with his giant freckled hand, and Derek coughed and choked and tears came out.

Then Vinnie let go, and Derek fell back on the bed in his briefs. Vinnie stood tall and looked at him, disgusted. Satisfaction was his, but he didn't feel satisfied. He just saw the stains on the carpet, and the dropped joystick, and Derek's wretched pile of pornography.

Then Vinnie let himself out of Derek's room and said a nice goodbye to Doe Murray. She closed the front door behind him and that was that. Vinnie didn't know if anyone in town knew he'd done it. That he'd gone in and winded Derek Murray, choked him in his own house, and left him rasping in his awful bedroom. He had never told a soul.

We looked up at Vinnie like he was the sun.

George beamed and shone in reflected glory.

Toby had stopped playing with his ball and was leaning up by the Hills Hoist listening, visibly impressed. Backflip panted. Vinnie leant back in his chair and rested his empty bottle on the concrete. His hands were freckled and rough with woodwork and big enough to go all the way around a person's neck.

•

I left the Sharkey house with my head full of Vinnie's story. George's street was wide and had overgrown grass in all the cracks in the pavement. Backflip wanted to sniff every one of them. Edna Field was standing in her carport, waiting for an outrage. Emily and Trent Ross's alcoholic father was slumped on a deck chair, asleep on his own shoulder.

As I went past the Carlstroms' front yard, Dennis was walking inside, the screen door shutting behind him. The Torana had its bonnet open. Lafe was leaning up against the crap caravan. His row of empty beer cans had been removed from the fence. There were just a few in the grass now, resting on their sides among the dandelions.

Backflip stopped to sniff and I yanked her lead. She was strong, though, and I was stuck for a moment, right near the Carlstroms' fence. I tried to ignore Lafe, who was leaning just a few metres away. Music was blaring out of their kitchen window. There was no sign of Davo. Lafe's khaki coveralls were unbuttoned just under his navel. There was a gaping hole there, full of darkness. He leant, standing, with his hands behind his head and smiled at me, vacant. He pushed his tongue out of his mouth a fraction. I looked right at him, just for a second. His eyes were like corpses. They had no life in them at all, just blankness, like Carl White feeding money into the pokies and drinking. Lafe leered at me and grinned, his vile tongue moving in and out of his mouth while he thrust his hips forward real easy in one foul motion.

I yanked Backflip's lead hard and walked fast towards the train tracks. My face burnt with humiliation all the way home.

25

The tireless members of the New South Wales Country Women's Association were a unified and resourceful group, and the Goodwood branch was no exception. Due to the unexpected and tragic events that had befallen Mrs Bart, Mary Bell had convened an urgent meeting of branch participants. Good old Mary Bell. First she had been toppled by Mrs Bart in the vote for Secretary; now she had risen—a phoenix in a pleated skirt—and put aside her petty grievances, organising a fundraising dinner in honour of Goodwood's own much-admired Flora McDonald, as well as Goodwood's other, far-less-celebrated woman in mourning, Judy White. Mum and Nan and Fitzy were to attend the dinner together at the Goodwood Community Hall; George and I were to watch videos at my house while they were gone.

Judy White was having a terrible time of it. She had no husband and no daughter and, for the moment, while Terry was still in Ballina, not even a son. Her ribs and thighs and eyes were dented. She had refused to leave the house and didn't like a fuss, but Opal Jones, who Judy had finally let in for a quivering cup of tea, said Jude would gratefully accept anything to help with the bills while she convalesced. Jude was a wreck, said Opal. A remnant of a person. And she was back in that same old dressing-gown, wandering from room to room. Gazing out a window. Hovering near a curtain. How a woman could spend all spring in nothing but terry towelling was beyond anything that Opal Jones could bear to imagine.

Mrs Bart wasn't as much in need of funding, but she was deep as a dell in grieving and had no idea what to do with the business. Her son Joe continued to provide friendly service to the people of Goodwood as the new face of Bart's Meats, but there were murmurs that Joe's wife in Sydney was growing tired of his generosity, mainly since it was taking place somewhere other than their marital home. Nan said Joe would have to go back soon, at which point the future of Bart's Meats was in doubt. Mrs Bart seemed altogether unequipped to take it on by herself—she was no butcher—and her sister Jan, who some suggested might have been a good candidate to move to Goodwood permanently and help out with the chopping and carving, was both squeamish and vegetarian.

Nan dressed up for the dinner and looked a picture in peach when she arrived at our house an hour early on the Saturday evening, so she and Mum could have a glass of wine and a catch-up. Fitzy wasn't invited to the prelude, given her propensity for being annoying, and was picked up after. The three of them went off on foot to the hall.

George and I had long been deemed responsible enough to be left alone. The official plan, as we told Mum, was videos and a sleepover. The actual plan, as organised by George, was that Lucas and Ethan were coming over to drink whisky and Coke in the yard.

Lucas and Ethan arrived at dusk—the same time Kevin Fairley would've been moving his cows from one paddock to the other. Lucas had a bottle of Jim Beam secreted in his backpack. George had bought a two-litre bottle of Coke from the Goodwood Grocer and four bags of salt and vinegar chips. We mixed the Coke and Jim Beam together in Mum's glass tumblers and sat at the outdoor setting drinking.

Lucas was in a particularly confident mood, on account of twenty-five dollars' worth of weed that he'd purchased from Trent Ross earlier that afternoon. Trent and wayward Gary Elver were jamming in the shed behind Elver's Auto and Lucas felt very good about himself for having been with them for fifteen whole minutes; and for smoking a cone there on the shed couch while Lady lay on a dirty bed against his feet. Gary, stoned as a boulder, had demonstrated various types of drum rolls. Trent had sat silently on the concrete floor with a small bowl and a pair of scissors.

George did her best to be unimpressed by Lucas's story, and all she said was, 'Well I hope you brought it with you,' and, right on cue, Lucas triumphantly produced a fat and badly fashioned joint, which was smoked over the course of the evening, compelling George at one point to emit a small vomit under the grevillia.

'I'm fine, it's just like sneezing,', she slurred, returning to the table looking pale and unfazed. Lucas laughed with his head all the way back.

We were all drunk by then. George kept topping up our tumblers with whisky, forgetting to add the Coke. By nine, the outdoor setting was like a ship on a rough sea. We clung to it and it spun and at one point Lucas fell out onto the grass. Backflip was up immediately, licking his face. I shushed everyone in case we woke the magpies, who had taken to viciously swooping the garden during daylight hours and making Backflip's life a misery.

'Magpies don't swoop at night,' said Ethan, with a reassuring tone and a tender look, and George elbowed me under the table.

I was surprised, especially in the rowdiness of our conversation that we managed most of the night without much mention of Rosie or Bart. George talked mostly, and Lucas Karras. Ethan was quieter than usual and appeared to be distant. He was like a cow in a paddock, privately ruminating. He seemed sad somehow, in a way I could not determine; and he sat upright in his chair the whole night, not once reclining back against the frame. He looked poised to fall forward, hunched over like a much older man.

I drank and my eyes became warm in their sockets. The night breeze drew tears from them every so often. I could feel my cheeks were shining. At one point I lay on my back on the grass next to Lucas and Backflip lay her whole furry body across us like we were a raft and I laughed and laughed.

A little later, George and Lucas disappeared inside. Ethan and I heard them giggling. Then we saw the door to the spare room close behind them and I didn't care.

'What's in there?' asked Ethan.

'A daybed. Mum's quilt squares,' I said.

He smiled and shook his head. It was calm and still in the almost-darkness. Backflip wandered out from inside and settled down on her outdoor mat, letting out a tired sigh. And then Ethan got up from his chair and lay down on his side on the grass beside me, shooing away the mosquitoes, saying, 'Oh Jeannie,' as he settled in close by my arm. I remember him putting his hand in my hand and tracing the inside of my palm with his rough fingers. I felt my heart quicken and I knew his intention. Then he looked right in my eyes and put his lips against my neck, and I turned towards him, too, and we lay kissing on the damp grass while he fumbled at my clothes. Before long he was above me, and his dull weight felt nice on my body. He put hot breath in my ear and I liked it when he kissed me. He put his hands in my jeans and I shut my eyes tightly. 'Jeannie,' he said again, all soupy, like he knew me very well; even though I felt more and more—as he moved above me—that I did not know him at all. Regardless, outside of myself, I felt for his long back under his shirt, finding his skin uneven there. I half noticed him wincing. He tasted like whisky and for a short time we moved together in the garden, under the stars and branches, and the cold ground felt damp below me in the warm evening.

But after a while of it, I abandoned the idea of pulling Ethan's shirt off over his head. I shuffled out from under him and sat up.

The night spun. I felt giddy.

Ethan seemed sheepish and quickly deflated. He lay on his side and stared up at me, expectant. I sat next to him and was still. All of a sudden I didn't want to be kissing Ethan West at all.

I wasn't sure what to do next. I didn't know how I was supposed to act in such a moment. Ethan propped himself up on his elbows, looking very disappointed. After a long and awkward silence he sat up and turned towards the back fence, away from me, and fumbled at his shirt, pulling it down where I had lifted it almost off. That was when I saw the dim impression of his welted back in the soft light that spilled out from the living room and onto our patch of grass. His lovely, well-proportioned back—which had thick weals across it, surrounded by deep dark bruises, the colour of oil slicks and mud.

It was the whisky that made me reach out and touch them. I was loose of my inhibitions and my sense of propriety, and I put my fingers right against his injuries tenderly and Ethan flinched and jerked away.

'Don't touch it,' he said.

I drew my hand back and was surprised to have felt it, and horrified at what had been done to him.

'What happened? Who did that?'

He was crouching now. He looked at his knees, holding them with his spear-arms. Backflip, sensing unease, had hopped up and come over to nuzzle him. 'Good dog,' said Ethan. 'Good dog.'

Backflip went around in a circle and butted her head into Ethan's chest, wagging her tail. He held her around her ribs and dug his hands into her fur.

'Who did that?' I asked again.

Ethan seemed full of sorrow. His eyes were so gentle. He wiped at them with the back of his hand, as if there were tears there, and looked ashamed. 'Oh, you know,' he said. 'My dad got heaps pissed off at me.'

The image of old Mal West with his bung leg came into my mind. Old Mal, leaning up against the bar at the Bowlo, looking indignant. Old Mal with his stupid cane, limping along Cedar Street, growling at the concrete, spitting at the birds.

'Constable Mackenzie came over asking about me working for Kevin,' said Ethan to his knees. 'He asked my dad about it. And my dad hates dairies, since his accident, you know. He fucken hates them. Hates the cows and that. He said I was never allowed to do it again. So——I didn't tell him. I asked Kev not to tell, and he swore he wouldn't——but he must have told Constable Mackenzie.'

Ethan's handsome face was hollow. He turned back to look at me. 'That's why I didn't tell anyone——you know——because my dad gets pretty pissed off.'

I felt my cheeks stinging and wondered if Ethan could see me blushing.

I thought about how the wounds had felt under my fingers. They were raised like ridges; the foothills of the mountain. My mind went to Judy White, convalescing in her terry towelling.

Ethan looked at me expectantly. I didn't say one thing. What could I say? I said nothing at all, and Ethan came over with a deep expression that only Lucas Karras could puncture as he came out into the garden looking very happy with himself and slightly dishevelled. George wandered out after, eating salt and vinegar chips. She offered the bag to me, smiling, and I took a handful; and the boys were over by the back fence by then, peeing into the bushes.

'Off you go, Myrtle, do your business,' said Big Jim's gentle voice from over the fence, and the sound of Myrtle rustling in their yard made Backflip wander over and sniff for her under the wooden palings.

'Yeah, do your business,' said Lucas to Ethan from the back of the garden, and the sound of Ethan West trying to laugh made me feel like I might cry.

•

The next day, I spent most of the morning lying on the couch in the living room feeling terrible while Mum fussed about, rearranging furniture, talking on the phone to Tracy, reading aloud particularly humorous sections from a Bill Bryson travel memoir, and complaining about the magpies.

It was two weeks into spring, and a family of birds had taken up roost in the flowering gum. The gum was grand and ancient. Its giant branches offered Backflip shade when it was too hot for her to use her kennel. The rest of the tree hung into Big Jim and Fitzy's yard and offered a little shade for Myrtle, too. But the dogs were to have no peace that spring. None of us were. Within mere days of the roosting, the swooping had begun.

In everyone's memory, that year was particularly brutal. The magpies attacked like guided missiles from the sky. Mum rarely went outdoors. And Fitzy started wearing her bike helmet, decorated with a cluster of brightly coloured cable-ties, every time she gardened, or hung up the washing, or checked the rain gauge. Poor Fitzy, she looked a real sight watering the herbs with her helmet on, and with the neck brace she'd acquired from hitting the pole outside the Vinnies, and her intense prescription.

I had a nap in my room after lunch, and when I came out again I found Mum sitting in the sunroom, her book face down on her knees, watching Fitzy weeding. She was dealing with a bad case of wandering jew, and such a big task clearly demanded further protection. Fitzy had put netting over her Stackhat and coloured prongs, giving her the appearance of a confused space bride.

Mum was silently laughing, with tears coming down her cheeks.

'She looks like she's been let out for the day,' she said.

Fitzy was suffering with the lack of rain. Apart from the two brief showers we'd had during winter, Goodwood was as dry as bones.

'Lake'll drop', said Big Jim, looking up at the empty white clouds. And then, grimly. 'And you know what that means. Fish'll stop biting.'

Fitzy watered and watered. She worried about her family, who were apple farmers in Stanthorpe, Queensland. The drought there had dried them up for the best part of a year. Their apples refused to grow.

Fitzy requested a copy of the government's newly published National Drought Policy. It arrived promptly by mail. She read sections aloud to Big Jim in their garden regarding how farmers should 'increase self-reliance'. How are they supposed to do that? Choreograph their own rain dance?

'Did you know,' she asked Mum, 'that stress from drought can cause a person, and I quote, "disappointment, guilt, shame or *feeling like a failure*"?' Mum did not know that. Fitzy went on, reading from the Lifeline Information Service leaflet that she'd also requested by mail, her head bolt upright atop her neck brace, 'It can also cause "Physical symptoms such as headaches, difficulty sleeping, loss of appetite, aches and pains, muscle tension, weight loss/gain, chest or back pain, diarrhea or constipation, injury or accidents."'

'Accidents? Really?' asked Mum.

'Yes!' Fitzy said, 'It affects everything!'

'I had no idea,' she said to Fitzy. And then later on to me in the kitchen: 'It's obviously the lack of rain that causes Fitzy to crash into things.'

That evening, Sunday, was my night to make dinner. I decided to make it special in an attempt to improve my mood. Mum popped out to visit Denise, and when she got home she found me stirring spaghetti sauce with my bike helmet on.

Mum stood next to the pantry, forced herself to frown, and told me it was uncharitable to make fun of Fitzy.

Then she poured herself a glass of wine and pissed herself laughing. When it was time to eat she put her helmet on, too, and we sat together in front of the television, with the curtains drawn in case Fitzy happened to walk past the back window.

'Oh, Jean,' Mum said, grinning. 'We're awful.'

With our helmets still on, I cleared the plates and filled the sink to wash up. Mum finished her wine and Backflip was fast alseep on the rug. It was warm enough to have the kitchen window open, and crickets sang out in the darkness.

'Dear, oh dear,' said Mum to the television. 'Oh, how awful.'

I walked over to look, with my washing-up gloves and my helmet on.

It was the Prime News. A lady on the edge of a forest holding a microphone. Shots of the forest floor, lots of dry leaves. Police in uniform. Lots of police.

'Where's that?' I asked.

'Belanglo,' said Mum. 'They found two dead bodies in the forest. They think they might be missing backpackers. They were hitchhiking. Two girls.'

I looked at the lady and the police tape and the forest. I took my helmet off and held it against my chest.

I thought straight away of Rosie.

•

Mack and Tracy were home with the news on, too. Tracy had Jasper in the bath with the door open. He splashed around with his plastic tugboats and practised whistling while Tracy sat on a little stool and said, every so often, 'Hoop-la'. Mack was on the couch with a beer.

'What's that they're saying?' asked Tracy.

Mack was quiet, watching. He saw the police. He saw the dead leaves and the news lady with the microphone.

'They found two women at Belanglo,' said Mack, watching.

'Are they okay?' yelled Tracy. She came into the doorway, with one eye on Jasper.

'No. I mean they found bodies,' said Mack.

'Oh, that's horrible,' said Tracy. She went back into the bathroom and then came out again straight away, her eyes wide. 'You don't think?' she said.

Mack was thinking. He had many thoughts. They raced at him from every angle. Rosie. Davo. Carl. Hitchhikers. Bodies in the forest.

He had so many thoughts and he didn't know what to think.

26

The rest of Goodwood could speak of nothing but the bodies at Belanglo. On the way to school on Monday, I bought the *Gather Region Advocate* and the *Sydney Morning Herald* from the newsagent. Helen got a few copies of the *Herald* each day. I bought the last one.

'You shouldn't be reading about it—it's just awful,' said Helen, in a more pronounced version of her panics. The paper quaked in her hand as she gave it to me. She quivered like Judy White. Bill sat next to her on his stool, in front of the cigarette display. A couple on a white horse had big white smiles in an ad for Alpine. A man with a brumby and a rope had a big dirty smile in an ad for Marlboro. Bill had neither. He grimaced at me, like all he ever heard was bad news.

Coral had pulled her trolley up early to buy the papers. She was standing outside Bart's Meats talking to Joe. Poor burly Joe. His dad was yet to be accounted for and already he'd inherited Coral.

'They don't *know* who they are, they just *think* they're the backpacker women,' said Coral, gesticulating. 'So it could be her. It could be. Yes.'

Joe was squinting at Coral like the sun was in his eyes, but he was standing in the shade. Coral just kept looking at him and nodding, *yes*.

At lunch, George and I spread the papers out on the grass and studied them.

'It's not Rosie,' said George. 'How would she've got up to Belanglo?'

'How would she've got anywhere?' I asked.

George looked annoyed.

We read the article under the headline FRENZIED KILLER MARCHED GIRLS TO BUSH GRAVES. It was dreadful. The police had identified one of the women—a missing English tourist. They suspected the other body was that of her friend and travelling companion. They'd been in Australia on holiday.

George winced as she read. 'Ugh,' she said.

'It's not her,' I said, feeling guilty to be so relieved.

'But listen to this,' said George, and read aloud, '"Police have also yet to rule out the possibility that there may be other bodies buried in the forest."'

We sat back on the grassy hill. Toby and his idiot friends were playing basketball on the court. Liz Gordon and Kiralee

Davis were smoking surreptitiously by the fence. Puffs of smoke rose above them while Bec Kelly kept watch for teachers. Ethan and Lucas were just up the hill from us with their football.

George looked very grave. She folded up the newspaper. There was no hint of a joke in her voice.

'Jean, I always felt like something bad happened to her,' she said.

●

That morning, Davo Carlstrom walked back into the Goodwood Police Station in a terrible state. Mack was standing behind his desk, talking on the phone.

Davo paced in front of the pinewood counter, waiting for Mack to hang up. He was clearly agitated, and fighting back tears. The posters for domestic violence hotlines and Neighbourhood Watch looked over him. He paced and stopped pacing and hit his fist on the counter.

'Mate, it's not her,' said Mack calmly as he hung up the phone.

'How do you know?' yelled Davo. 'How do you know?' His voice was crackling.

'They think it's the friend of the first victim. I mean, they're sure. They're sure it's her friend. They just have to do a formal identification before they release it to the media,' said Mack. 'Mate, I'm telling you—it's not Rosie.'

Davo sat down on the bench under the posters and put his lovely olive hands over his lovely sunken face.

•

Mack arrived at our house just before dinner.

'Are you staying?' asked Mum as he came in. She was chopping onions and had a tea towel over her shoulder.

'No, no,' he said. 'Just a beer. I'll get home to Trace.'

Mum opened the fridge and got out two bottles of Reschs. She opened one for herself and one for Mack.

'You poor bugger,' she said, wiping her watery eyes. She popped Mack's beer in a stubby holder that said *Goodwood's Good For Wood* and fitted the Reschs just perfectly.

'What a time,' said Mum, and put her hand on Mack's shoulder. She looked almost disbelieving. 'What a terrible fucking time.'

Mum and Mack were close. After Mack's dad Lang shot himself in the head, cleaning his gun, Mack was catatonic for a fortnight. According to Nan, he rocked himself back and forth on the verandah and could not speak. Mum tended to him. She was only a teenager herself at the time, but she tended to him like a garden, and slowly he stopped rocking, and eventually he was able to sprout words again, and later he even flourished.

I remembered Mack's mum Grace Mackenzie from when I was small. She mustn't have been that old, but her skin looked translucent, like you could see her insides if you held her up to a light. There wasn't much to her, just a thin face atop a thin body. Nan said she died of a broken heart long before her actual death. But she continued to exist, in a half-life, spending most of her later days in a rocking chair, where she stared out the window and quilted. Her view was of the verandah where Lang had ended it all. Nan never knew why she didn't change her position.

Grace Mackenzie died her actual death when I was five. She was sitting in the rocking chair and her heart pulled up to a stop. Mack was the one to find her. Mercifully, ravens did not attend.

Mum tended to Mack again. She held him through Grace's funeral. Mack produced tears, but no sound. Apparently I got uncommonly upset and had to be carried away by Nan, who declared me to be very intuitive for a five-year-old and 'not to be rushed'. I was never sure what she meant by that. Maybe I was not to be rushed into the sad event of a funeral. Or maybe Nan wanted me to stay young and green as long as possible.

'Terrible fucking time is right,' said Mack now, drinking his Reschs. 'I just came from Nan's. She's pretty freaked out.'

He gripped the stubby holder and looked weary. He followed Mum into the living room and they sat on the couch. Paul Simon was singing out of our stereo.

'Ceils, seriously, I haven't seen anything like this in my time on the force,' said Mack. 'The things I'm hearing are just horrible. The injuries.'

I hovered in the big archway that separated our living room from our kitchen. Backflip, who had been outside eating her biscuits, made a dramatic entrance, her toenails scratching across the wooden floorboards as she hurried in.

'Good dog. C'mere, Backflip. Good dog,' said Mack.

Backflip was thrilled. She panted and turned in circles and backed up for a butt scratch. Mack acquiesced. I went into the kitchen and tried to listen and chop the rest of the onions at the same time.

'They've got forty guys searching the forest,' Mack said, scratching Backflip's butt. 'They took a few boys from Clarke. They took Simmons. The base is at Bowral, but they're calling in help from all around.'

Mum sipped her beer. 'Awful.'

'*Everyone* thinks it's Rosie,' said Mack. 'I had *that* many people stop me on Cedar Street today. Fitzy just stopped me on my way in here. But it's not her. It's not her.'

Mum seemed worried and relieved at the same time. I could sense her mind racing.

'I hope she wasn't hitchhiking,' she said. 'If she did leave by choice then I hope that's not how she left.' She raised her voice. 'You are *never* hitchhiking, Jean.'

'I never would,' I said loudly from the kitchen.

Mack studied the rug. 'I'm so tired, Celia, I could fall asleep sitting here.'

Mum rubbed Mack on the shoulder. Mack rubbed Backflip

on the butt. There was a heavy feeling to everything. Dismay had spread from the town and seeped in through our open window. I chopped the onions. Tears ran down my face but I hardly noticed them. I could hear Fitzy calling out, *Myrtle, Myrtle*. Mum and Mack shared a moment of weighty silence. Paul Simon was singing. He said that if he could call us Betty then we could call him Al. The crickets chirped loudly. I was on my way to the pantry for the olive oil when the phone rang.

'I'll get it,' I said, being closest.

It was Tracy on the other end, asking for Mack.

'What did I do now?' he said smiling, getting up. He was always cheered by Tracy. He even whistled just for a moment on his way to the receiver.

'Sweetheart,' he said. And then his voice went dry. 'Who called?' he asked. Then silence. 'He's positive?'

Mum looked up from the couch. Mack was nodding. He made agreement sounds. Listening sounds. Sadness sounds. The noise of crickets drowned most of it out. 'I love you, too,' he said. 'I'll come home.'

He hung up.

I had taken his seat on the couch next to Mum. Backflip stood in the middle of the rug looking at Mack, wagging her tail with her ears back. Paul Simon was singing about Joseph now, and a yellow moon.

Mack stared at us and said, 'Looks like someone found Bart.'

234

27

Paulie Roberts was a tall, straight-shouldered man, with freckles that swarmed like bees across his face, and lips that needed Chapstick. He had a weedy son at our school, Tom Roberts, and a nice wife called June who worked at Harvey World Travel in Clarke. The Roberts had been in Goodwood for four generations. Paulie's grandfather worked at the sawmill when it was still in operation. Paulie Roberts was the proud owner of a handsome cedar dresser, made from a red cedar tree that had grown by our river, crafted with his grandfather's own hands, destined to be handed down in the Roberts family for generations to come.

Paulie Roberts lived for fishing. He and Bart knew each other pretty well from around town. Paulie enjoyed a sausage and fished on Sundays. In fact, Paulie fished as many days as he could manage, after work and on weekends. He'd often see Bart setting off and offer a wave. The two men would share a few beers together at the Wicko if they happened to be there at the same time, having a chat to Smithy at the bar. Paulie held the Biggest Catch record until Roy Murray broke it. He hooked a black bream under the bridge on Grants Lake on an overcast Sunday in '87 and he knew he had a winner. He popped it in his bucket and brought it back to town for weighing and measuring. Carmel Carmichael and Bart presided. Bart described the bream as 'immensely thick and solid' and the *Gather Region Advocate* published that quote, next to a photo of Paul holding the big fish in one hand and a well-earned beer in the other. If you'd looked above the bar at the Bowlo, you'd have seen a golden plaque with Paulie's name on it, the date of his catch, and a drawing of a fish arching upwards, kissing the sky.

Paulie Roberts had gone out to the lake that Monday after a morning at work installing outdoor lighting at the back of the Clarke Hotel, and then a few hours spent at home on the garden. Tom almost accompanied him fishing but changed his mind at the last minute on account of a stomach ache he acquired from eating too many unripe strawberries. Paulie loved green strawberries. Tom told his dad he'd better have a lie down instead of dropping a line that day. Paulie was forever glad that Tom was spared the discovery that lay ahead.

Paulie drove over the high bridge above the deep water. He let the spring wind wrestle his hair through the open window. The boats bobbed to meet him, as if waving. He looked at Bart's ghost boat, as he always did since Bart had disappeared, with grief and a feeling he couldn't describe. Luck? Guilt? Guilt that he felt lucky that it hadn't been him? Lucky that his guilt didn't stop him from fishing? He liked Bart tremendously, but Paulie was so horrified by what had happened that he pushed his feelings into a space the size of his tackle box and shut the lid. It wasn't him. June still had a husband, Tom still had a father, he still had fishing on the big lake. It was Bart. It wasn't Paulie. He shook the whole thing off like Backflip did when she got out of the river.

Paulie Roberts parked his car and carried his gear to his boat. He started up his motor and cut the lake with his wake. The brown water lapped against the fibreglass hull as he curled around the marshes. He didn't usually go left. He usually went to the middle, or close to the bridge, where the water was cold and bottomless and full of opportunities.

But that day he went left. He intended to fish the horseshoe inlet where no cars or feet could get close to by land. The bush was dense and scrubby right up to the edge. But The Horse, as it was known to locals, had its own opportunities: it was deep in the centre, and the flathead and bream and blackfish would not expect him.

His boat was motoring along nicely as he hugged the bank and watched the tiny fish part in the marshes. The wind was high. Clouds flew past the sun above him, and for a moment he closed his eyes to the sky. He saw the inside of his eyelids go dark and light and dark and light and dark again; and when he opened his eyes he saw the clouds pass and pass and pass. He felt happy it was spring.

As he entered The Horse he slowed his boat and took his time around the edges. He could tell the depth from the way the water rested and he smiled at the deep centre. He was just about to make a right turn and head towards it when he saw the log. A big log, stuck fast in the marshes. Maybe there was some discoloured fabric there too—faded greys and browns; he couldn't really tell. It was a heavy-looking log, wedged in and half sunken.

His thoughts went here and there.

Thick log to be floating on the lake. Lots of trees find their end in the marshes. Rotting wood is wasted on the water. The sawmill made beautiful tables and dressers. It's such a shame there's no more cedar. Maybe he could try his hand at furniture.

Paulie got closer.

It wasn't a log.

He looked and saw that, yes, there was fabric. Faded greys and browns and some hint of old yellow. Then matted hair, then bloated skin.

All the blood went from Paulie Roberts's face as he cut his motor and dropped his anchor. He was near it now, just beyond the marshes. He could see it in there, closer to the shore where no cars or feet could enter.

Not a log. A body Or what was left of it. There could be no doubting it, as the clouds went past and past and past.

Paulie felt sick to his stomach as he stood up in his boat, leaning over the edge to get a better look.

He knew what he was seeing. It was Bart McDonald. Or what was left of him. There was no doubt about it.

Paulie Roberts had not been among the people who had searched the lake—the divers, the policemen, the group from town. He'd said to June, 'Why go looking for something you don't want to find?'

'True enough,' said June.

And now, true enough.

He sat down in his boat, queasy, as the breeze came in across the marshes. He looked away from the body. He couldn't bear it. But the smell whooshed up his nostrils. He breathed it in thick and tried to get it out again, quickly. He did it as if blowing his nose and felt like a horse, snorting. 'Uggghh,' was the noise he made, before he vomited half-digested unripe strawberries into the brown water of the lake.

Paulie Roberts went full speed back to his car, pushing his boat to its very limit. Then he pushed his car, over the bridge and along the long road that hugs the mountain. Kevin Fairley's cows were in the north paddock through the trees, which were all a blur, like all the world was at that moment.

He got home and told June. He left his car door wide open in the carport.

'June. June!' He was so nauseous. 'I found Bart McDonald in the lake.'

June sat down on the couch as if someone had pushed her over. Tom set aside his lemon water. His stomach ache came on again like a wave.

Paulie went to the Teledex and moved the white plastic pointer down to M and pressed the button. He found Tracy at the other end of the telephone. He spoke as fast as clouds.

Tracy said, 'Jesus, Paulie, are you all right?'

Paulie swallowed air and pushed down his stomach. 'Yeah. I'll be right. As soon as I get the smell out of my nostrils.'

•

By the time Mack got home it was almost seven. Tracy met him at the door. She put her arms all the way around him and he rested his chin on her shoulder. The two of them stood in the doorway as if stuck in time.

Mack closed his eyes. He'd call Clarke station in just a minute and find out the procedure. It was pitch-black and he had no resources. Clarke station was at half-mast; everyone was searching Belanglo. The darkness might let him wait till morning. Tomorrow for the gruesome business.

When Mack finally slept that night, he dreamt of water. Tonnes and oceans and fields of water, crashing through a dam wall, lying in wait at his ankles, destroying their bedroom furniture.

28

At first light the next morning, the browned grass next to the boat wharves was covered in cars. Some had arrived in darkness. They parked with their headlamps high-beaming on the brown water. Then dawn came and the sky was streaked with pale light. It was yellow and orange and then it was day. Police cars, cars from town, cars that brought the 'authorities'—as Nan called them—or the SES, as they were properly known, and a lone ambulance that couldn't offer much in the way of lifesaving to a month-old, half-decomposed corpse stuck fast in the marshes.

Bart may have gone in whole, but he came out much diminished. The water had been cold that winter, which slowed the rate of decomposition. But there was not much to remember him by after the fish had done their nibbling business. The bream and flathead and blackfish had their way with his skin and tissues. They'd bitten and nipped and pecked him. They'd eaten away at his kind face and extremities, and burrowed passages for bacteria to find his organs. Over the years, Bart had thrown a lot of bait in the big lake, to tempt the fishes into his waiting bucket. But as it turned out, nothing proved as delicious a meal as Bart himself.

Poor Paulie Roberts stood on the bank, mystified.

Why him?

That had been the thing all along. That it *wasn't* him. It was Bart. Paulie had been spared. And he'd been fishing every chance he got since Bart vanished. Why did he turn his boat left?

The log that wasn't. It was a vision he'd never bury; a smell he would never forget. All he could try were topical applications. He bought a Vicks nasal spray from the Grocer in an attempt to clear the smell from his nostrils. Nance had been helpful. 'I have some potpourri that's quite pungent?' But what was Paulie supposed to do? Carry around a little dish of it? He sprayed his Vicks, more times than the packet suggested. But still he was the only one on the bank who could smell it.

'Can you smell it?' he asked. He was standing with Smithy and Carmel Carmichael who, as the proprietors of the only two drinking establishments in town, felt the need to be near the water that day, in honour of their friend, in honour of one of the unofficial leaders of Goodwood, now confirmed dead.

'Smell what?' asked Smithy.

'Bart,' said Paulie.

Smithy looked appalled. Carmel said, 'Oh God, *Paul*.'

Paulie took that as a no.

The three of them stood together. Merv and Big Jim drove out also. Mack told everyone they should go home. There wasn't much to see; and what little there was to see would traumatise even the most hardened member of any authority, let alone Bart's friends. The huddle conferred. Mack turned his back on them and stared at the lake, watching the boats bob. A pelican sat on the water, out towards the middle, oblivious. Mack was glad when, in the interests of their ability to sleep that night and the night after, the group from town decided to leave before the authorities brought Bart to shore.

Mack stood alone then, near the other police and the SES truck and the ambos. The cars from town backed out and departed. If Coral or Nance or Opal had been there, they wouldn't have had a bar of leaving. But Big Jim and Merv, Smithy and Carmel—they had little interest in drama or gossip. They were happiest when others were happy. They were saddest when the town was in mourning. They had loved Bart McDonald, true and honest. They drove away slowly with their eyes cast low to the road.

Mack was standing alone when the authorities eventually trudged out of the marshes with the unspeakable stretcher.

There was no doubt about it: it was the body of Bart McDonald. He was still wearing the windcheater he set off in, though it was no longer intact. The fish had begun it—the unbuilding of Bart—but since he had risen to the surface by the time Paulie found him, others had joined in, too. Flies; a certain type of beetle; several birds. Perhaps there had been ravens. Mack looked out at the pelican and wondered. He looked back at Bart and felt so nauseous. In life, Bart had a red, kind face, but now he was so many colours. He was sodden and dismantled. There was a hint of a boot on the bottom of what was once a strong leg. Mack could discern it only by the trace of laces. The stretcher was put into the van, and the men and women from the authorities spoke in faint voices. Someone even said 'sorry' to Mack, as if it meant anything at all.

Mack would leave the rest to the authorities. There was nothing more he could do there by the marshes. He pulled his police car out onto the road and headed towards the high bridge over the water. He would go to the McDonalds' house, where Mrs Bart and Pearl were taking the saddles off their horses. He would go there right away.

Mack drove as fast as clouds. The bridge felt even higher than usual and he soared. A kangaroo lay flattened on the road just after. Mack sped up towards the group of ravens that were gathered. A sickness like bile rose up from his stomach. The ravens were picking and pecking at innards. And Mack ploughed right through them. *Bam*. He got one. Right under his engine: the bird flapped and crunched and splattered all over the bitumen—a mess of wings and organs—and Mack was not even a tiny bit sorry.

29

With the discovery of Bart, and the morbid details of his condition—which spread from the mouth of Paulie Roberts, through the medium of Opal, who mourned the news by talking about it that Tuesday to anyone who'd listen—Goodwood was absolutely beside itself.

Nance, at the Goodwood Grocer, gave impromptu performances from behind her counter, in which she offered her thoughts on forensics and cause of death. She had read *Postmortem*, *Body of Evidence*, and was halfway through a brand-new hardcover of *All That Remains*. Patricia Cornwell had shed a lot of light on how the authorities dealt with corpses. Medical examiners needed a cast-iron stomach, that was for sure. They were normal enough people, but at the same time, heroes among us. As long as there was death in this world, their work was never done. We could all learn so much from their dedication.

Coral was quite distressed by Nance's uncaring tone and the content of her oral dissertations. She wheeled her tartan trolley out of the Grocer to the bench on the pavement and sat in the sun while tears rolled down her rouged cheeks. 'It's too soon,' she told Mum when Mum was on her way out. Mum had been quite interested in Nance's revelations. For example, some substances fluoresce under certain laser lights; and some bodies that have been exposed to the elements for an extended period make cause of death impossible to determine. In certain cases, a psychic may be consulted.

'He's barely out of the water,' said Coral, and Mum sat with her for a time in the sun, while Backflip sat tied to the pole.

'Nance's just being stoic,' said Mum. 'Everyone grieves in their own way.'

Poor Coral. At eighty-seven, she'd been positively girlish when Bart was alive. She'd blushed and winked and slapped his counter. Now she looked every one of her years, and like a few more had come crashing down upon her from some crack in the sky. She heaved her way through town with enormous effort.

•

Smithy, Big Jim and Merv stood outside the Wicko in the long-sunned afternoon with a handful of Wicko regulars. Val Sparks emerged from the Vinnies and joined them.

246

'How did we miss him?' said Big Jim. 'We did The Horse, me and Merv; I thought we went round every inch of it.'

'We did, BJ,' said Merv. 'Every nook and cranny. If he was in The Horse this morning, well—that's where he was. But I swear blind he wasn't in The Horse when we looked there.'

Irene Oakman arrived, harried and dressed in crushed velvet. She'd rushed straight to the Wicko when she'd heard the news, clutching her house keys.

'He was in The Horse?' she asked, incredulous and out of breath. '*No*. I checked The Horse. Didn't I, Smithy? You went right, around the little inlets, and I went left in the tinny. I checked all over The Horse.'

'Same as us—we checked it a couple of times, I reckon,' said Merv. Big Jim nodded.

Val Sparks prayed silently. She said, 'God taketh away,' and blessed herself. Smithy put his arm around her and she worried she'd be forever infected with sorrow.

They expected to see Roy Murray. Where was Roy Murray, anyway? He and Bart had been good mates, fishing buddies, drinking companions on occasion.

'Where's Roy?' asked Smithy. 'Has someone broken the news?'

'I haven't seen him round a whole lot,' said Big Jim. 'Derek's been working mainly. Since—' everyone looked at their own feet '—since Rosie.'

Irene Oakman looked like she'd recovered a distant memory. 'Oh yeah. Roy. Why didn't he come out and search with us, I wonder?'

'Same reason Paulie and a lot of guys didn't,' said Smithy. 'It wasn't a pretty sight as I understand it. I spoke to Paulie. He said Bart was in a horrible way.' Smithy shook his head and said with intense solemnity to the small gathering: 'God is good, but never dance on a small boat.'

Val Sparks looked set to faint. How the grief and horror encroached upon her. She took herself back inside the Vinnies where she turned up her little silver radio and dusted. Her votive candles burned aimlessly. She fretted as to whether to blow Bart's out.

•

Helen stood in the doorway of the newsagent, talking with Bill while he smoked a cigarette on the pavement—Marlboro Reds, because he fancied himself as similar to the rugged man in the advertisement. He wasn't. A pile of newspapers behind him announced more on the search of the Belanglo State Forest, which Nance thought was certain to hold clues of Rosie. On that point, Coral could agree. What were the odds? they thought, shuddering at the notion. Two girls. A similar age. Belanglo was not so far away. What if there were more in there?

Derek Murray was behind the counter at Woody's. He

looked like a ghost boy, waiting for an order, an unpleasant expression on his face.

It was revealed much later that that day was the worst day of trading Woody's ever had. It was no wonder. The news of a rotted body made no one hungry; and it was later considered ironic that the discovery of Bart turned the whole town off meat for the best part of September.

Three doors up, Bart's Meats was closed. There was no sign on the door and no sign was expected. Burly Joe stayed back at the McDonald house with Mrs Bart and Pearl and Jan, who had extended her visit to be with her sister until news came. Any news. That's what sisters were for.

The only consolation for Pearl was that Bart had been found in The Horse. Of all the alluvial beds and sheltered inlets and boggy corners, her dad had chosen the Horse: the best-named place in all the lake. At that, Pearl looked content for almost a whole moment. Then she cried with difficulty while Oyster, Pears and Apples neighed a dirge in their stables.

•

Meanwhile, Nan was properly teary for the first time since Bart disappeared. Mum and Backflip went over there after the Grocer and dropped off a bag of vegetables for a light spring soup. Pop hid in his shed with his feelings. 'Terrible thing,' was all he could muster. Pop had receded further inwards since Bart had been found. He became quieter and more removed. It had been weeks since he'd asked Nan to dance after dinner.

Nan started chopping. Then she stopped. 'No one will be hungry for this.'

She put the knife down on the board, gripping it still, looking out the little stained-glass window over the sink.

'Mum?' said Mum.

'No, no. I'm all right, Celia,' said Nan, gripping the knife, her fingers going white and red from the pressure where the blood was and wasn't.

Backflip wagged her tail, expecting a liver treat.

Mum stayed quiet while Nan recovered. Nan wasn't one to loosen her grip on her emotions.

After a few minutes, she resumed chopping and fetched the soup pot and put the gas on.

'At least he's been found,' said Mum. 'At least we know what happened.'

Nan turned around. She was blotchy and red and very stern. She said, 'What do we know? That he's been in the lake this whole time? Celia, we have *no idea* what happened.'

•

Mack went back to the station after he'd visited with Mrs Bart and Pearl.

'I'm so sorry, Flora. Pearl,' he had said. 'This is not how we wanted to find him.'

Mrs Bart just stared. While once she had paced, now she stared. She stared holes in the walls, in the carpets, in the bed linen, in the back of the bathroom door. She'd taken to sitting on the toilet, with the lid down, just like it was a good old regular chair. 'Just in case', she said blankly, as if sickness may escape her instantly without her even sensing its approach.

Of course it was too soon for a formal identification. That would probably require dental records at this point. But Mack could be fairly certain—he could be sure—given what he saw, given Bart's windcheater, given Bart's boot. He was sure it was Bart, and the family needed to brace itself for a formal identification stating that fact.

Back behind his pinewood desk, Mack felt helpless. He had Paulie Roberts come in and give a formal statement. Mack took it down longhand and typed it up later on the station's handsome new computer. He noted many details: Paul thought Bart was a log; Paul didn't disturb the log/body in any way; no one else was present at the time of the discovery; the smell lingered.

Paulie proved nauseous throughout his delivery. He stopped now and again to breathe out like the old bellows that Lang Mackenzie had used to stoke the fire when Mack was small. Paulie swallowed air in big gulps and saliva flooded his mouth. He turned his head to the side, searching for relief.

Mack emptied his metal rubbish bin and set it down next to Paulie's chair. 'Just in case,' he said.

Paulie thanked him greenly and seemed happy when the whole thing was over.

'Why me? I don't know. Just bad luck I guess,' he said, on the other side of the counter now, heading for the door.

'Worse luck for Bart,' said Mack.

•

At school, George and I sat on the grassy hill in the sun and pondered the universe in the gravest tones we had ever used. We spoke as deep as the lake, and as wide as our seventeen-year-old horizons could fathom. I'd never seen George so serious.

Death.

It was our first experience of it as almost-adults. George and I were five when Grace Mackenzie shed her translucent skin and escaped her sadness. We were eight when George's elderly dog, Digger, dug his last hole and lay down inside it. We hadn't had a death since. And Goodwood had not lost a man of such note—a man so revered—ever.

The news was filtering in to school slowly. Some parents had heard it early on Cedar Street and spoken it to their children. Some teachers had gleaned it from classroom chatter, or had stopped by Nance's on the way to school and been given an unexpected lesson in forensics. By that stage it was conjecture and rumour for some, and dire certainty for others. Who else could it be? said the believers. Paulie

Roberts saw him good and proper. Was sick down the side of his boat. It was no log, June told us.

The doubters were less vocal. Maybe it was someone else? We heard Jackson Harrington say that as he passed us. And Mr Berg was always quick to dissent. What if it was Rosie? If he or she—if the *body*—if it was so sick-making, then it can't have looked like Bart. Bart had such a kind face. It was too soon to jump to conclusions.

But it wasn't too soon, because the majority of the town had already bent its legs, readied itself and confidently jumped there, and in this instance the majority was right.

'Pearl would be glad at least that he was in The Horse,' I said to George, just before the bell rang.

'How could she be glad of anything?' asked George.

I shifted uncomfortably. 'I just mean, it's nice that it's called after a horseshoe. Nan told me Pearl collects horseshoes.'

'I guess,' said George. 'Didn't turn out to be a lucky one though.' George frowned. She was not her usual self. She didn't talk as fast and incessant. She made few jokes. She'd become so serious, much like the rest of the town. It was almost holidays. Ordinarily the whole school would be abuzz with excitement. But instead there was a heavy feeling to everything—a communal gloom—and no one knew how to shake it.

'I feel sick,' she said. 'Do you want my sandwich?'

'I feel sick too,' I said, and we left our lunches sitting on the hill between us.

30

The authorities were having a difficult time with Bart.

The fish had nibbled him, and the water had wrested the skin from his limbs, and bloated his trunk, and sunk his organs like tiny ships. In fact, the log-body of Bart McDonald had been through so much since anyone last saw him, that any messages it now tried to transmit—even to the most skilled medical examiner—were very hard to decipher.

Bart travelled all the way to the Institute of Forensic Medicine in Sydney, where he lay on a silver slab while a forensic pathologist did the best he could. But, as far as Mack could understand, the answers Goodwood longed for were to be confusing at best.

The merciful thing, which happened by Wednesday, was the relief of a formal identification. No matter how big a lake fish gets, lake fish don't eat teeth, and as much as Bart was diminished, his teeth were still intact. The forensic pathologist in Sydney declared the teeth to be, without a doubt, the teeth of Bart McDonald.

Mack knocked on Mrs Bart's door and found it opened by Jan. Mrs Bart was busy, staring at the bathroom door from her seat on the toilet. Jan went to tell her sister while Mack waited in the hallway. There came no answer.

Jan said blankly, through the wooden door: 'Flor. Mack's here. He's spoken to the doctors. It's him, Flor. It's Bart. They know for sure.'

All Mack heard was the sound of staring.

The rest of Goodwood, though, breathed a sigh of relief. The town could not take much more uncertainty. People were desperate. They were hopeless for some answers. No one could tolerate the question marks left by the missing.

'God bless,' said Val Sparks to an impromptu gathering at the Vinnies counter, gently illuminated by her votive candles. 'A conclusion.'

And yet there was still very little to conclude. As Nance had cleverly foretold from behind her all-seeing counter, the state of Bart's body meant that there was certain to be a problem. And, as Nance had suspected all along, that problem was cause of death.

•

Mack received the preliminary autopsy report on Thursday afternoon. It spilled out of the station's fax machine and landed in a mess on the carpet. Mack spread it over his pinewood desk and read with his head propped up on one arm.

The medical terminology caused him a slight pain to the temples. First, the autopsy disclosed 'minor degrees of pulmonary congestion and oedema'. Mack leaned back in his chair and puffed out some air. 'Water on the lungs' was how it was explained to him later. Mack read the report from beginning to end and then called the forensic pathologist himself for an explanation.

Water on the lungs.

The lake was in Bart's chest.

A drowning.

That much Mack could gather.

But, as the pathologist explained, it was slightly more complicated than that. The lake shared Bart's chest with Bart's heart. And Bart's heart had not been a healthy organ.

Mack read on. 'Severe coronary artery atherosclerosis with posterior wall myocardial fibrosis.' That sounded bad. It *was* bad. Bart was a heart attack waiting to happen, and it seemed that a heart attack had waited until just that moment—when Bart was on his boat, blissfully fishing.

Mack felt his own heart thumping. The voice of the pathologist was slow and muffled. Mack saw Bart in a quick vision, grabbing at his burning chest like he was patting out a fire. Old Lang Mackenzie was there too, stoking with his bellows, his beetroot head and a lonesome raven. Mack closed his eyes and waited for it all to pass.

The pathologist had three theories.

The first one sounded simple enough: Bart had a heart attack on his boat. He'd felt the thrust inside him, assailing him from within, and must've been in a precarious position—like near the edge, sitting or standing—and he'd been so overcome by the pain and the shock of it that he went over into the water, where he swallowed a chest full of brown liquid, until he spasmed, and frothed, and wilted, and drowned.

Death by drowning. That's what everyone had thought.

But the pathologist had a second line of thinking: that Bart did not 'drown' at all. He had a heart attack on his boat. He felt it take him from within, in an instant. And it *took* him, just like that—so sudden. Bart died standing; or he died sitting. And *then* he went over, from his precarious position—graveyard dead—and hit the lake as cold as the water was. The forensic pathologist assured Mack that even then, in the instance of Bart not inhaling, the lake would still find his lungs. From all the time he'd spent sunken, aimlessly caressing the silty floor, the water would've seeped in and kept on seeping. The pathologist assured Mack of that. 'That's what water does,' he said down the line. *That's what water does*, thought Mack for a long time after.

257

None of this was a shock to Mack. Everyone knew about the heart attack Bart had had on the riding trail with Pearl.

But then there was option number three: that somehow, at some time, Bart fell into the lake. That before the heart attack had even considered its move, Bart suffered some form of misadventure. Did he trip? Was he pushed? How could anyone be sure? But whatever it was, it caused Bart to take leave from his own boat and wind up in the water. Then, overcome with the stress of it, or the cold, and coupled with his already developed condition, *then* Bart had a heart attack and drowned. And the water seeped in, regardless of the order. The water seeped and seeped, because that's what water does.

Mack leant back in his chair and stretched his arms back over his head like he used to before a game of football.

He got to the end of the report. The blessed conclusion. The forensic pathologist had hedged his bets and sat on the fence. His preliminary findings—which would be passed on to the coroner—posited death by 'atherosclerotic coronary artery disease with a contributory effect of drowning'—in which the drowning part either happened before, or after, or not at all.

Mack felt deflated. He chewed the inside of his mouth.

A coronial inquest had been ordered. The question marks were bound to hover. It could take months for the authorities to determine how Bart had died—and when.

And, in any case, where had Bart been this whole time?

The first thing Mack had been quick to note was that Bart was not wearing his life jacket. They'd found two on his ghost boat when they searched it, and Mack had asked Mrs Bart if Bart had owned another. 'I have no idea,' said Mrs Bart, who had no taste for fishing. So he asked Irene Oakman and Roy Murray the same question, but they didn't know either. For certain he had two, because they'd both worn a second one. But they couldn't be sure if he had more. And whether he did or didn't, Bart had not been wearing a life jacket when Paulie Roberts made his terrible discovery.

The authorities had their opinions. The lake was cold that winter. Cold water stops a body from coming up again once it goes down. Mack had asked a lot of questions. Does a body always go down? The answer was yes, it does. A body always goes down. But then Mack heard words like 'bacteria' and 'gas' and 'distension' and he shut his mind to the black thoughts the whole thing gave him. He thought of Belanglo and the inevitable ravens. He was verging on hallucinations. Mack closed his eyes again and waited for the dark clouds to pass and pass.

The undisputed facts were that Bart had died and sunk to the bottom. Then perhaps he'd floated along it, but no one knew for how long or for how far. Currents at the bottom were different to currents at the top, and no one had been down there taking notes. Bart bore no concrete signs of pre-death injury, like a person hitting him over the head or engaging him in a scuffle; but then again it was very hard to tell. Water does all kinds of things that make 'post-mortem' and 'ante-mortem' just approximate phrases. Water smudges and mystifies. It seeps in and destroys. It dampens a for-certain diagnosis. Mack hadn't known this about water, but now he did: *that's what water does*. So Bart had injuries, yes, the pathologist had said. He had gouges as big as valleys. He had cuts and abrasions and lacerations. But they were just as likely acquired by him making acquaintance with 'obstructions' at the bottom of the lake. Sunken branches, the hulls of old boats, the wings of missing planes.

So Bart had sunk. Then the bacteria and gas and distention had caused him to rise, like the Second Coming, and that's when Paulie found him in the marshes of the Horse.

There was some question as to whether water levels may also have contributed. Bart was, after all, quite wedged. And with the lack of rain the lake was lower. So he may have risen earlier, got stuck just below the surface in the quagmire, only to be revealed as the water level in the lake slowly waned.

Really, though, what did it matter? Bart McDonald was dead and would soon be buried. He had a heart attack and drowned. Or he had a heart attack and didn't. Or he kind of did both at the same time.

Mack folded the fax paper and rested it inside his manila folder. He looked at the framed photo of Tracy and Jasper that he kept next to his stapler. They always cheered him. He was a good husband and father. He wanted a nice time with his family now the warmer months had started. This was barbeque weather, he thought, and almost time for swimming in the river. The fish would be biting and he wished he wanted to catch them. Mack closed the folder and set it aside and longed to stop thinking about it every single waking minute.

31

The news about the discovery of Bart's body had taken up the entire front page of the *Gather Region Advocate*. It also warranted a paragraph in the News in Brief section of the *Sydney Morning Herald*, on account of Bart being notable, and the fact that he'd been missing for so long. It described Bart as a 'local member of council and a much-admired figure in the community'.

Everyone in Goodwood agreed.

I cut out both articles, one big and one small, and slid them into my blue notebook, next to the articles I'd saved about the bodies in the Belanglo State Forest, and the few local articles on Bart and Rosie's disappearance. Rosie's MISSING sign was curled up all along the edges. I couldn't even bring myself to unfold it. I couldn't bear to look at her black-and-white inscrutable face.

Big Jim was devastated. When he pulled up his ute of an evening he'd sit for a while after he'd turned off the engine. I'd see him out of my bedroom window, sitting in the dark driveway, the whites of his eyes illuminated by the moon. Tears spilled out sometimes, and he'd stare through them for several minutes before pulling himself out the door and trudging into the trenches of his house.

All week poor old Fitzy forced a smile as she watered the back yard in her bike helmet, fretting about the lack of rain. She'd shed her neck brace but could only turn her head with limited mobility. Even Fitzy, who didn't like to dwell on sadness, was overcome by the news. Her helmet hung lower, resting on her giant glasses, making her face seem put upon by above. She cowered under the swooping magpies and her giant eyes blinked and welled in the fine dry day.

On the Wednesday after Bart's log-body had surfaced, Mum began complaining of pains in the chest. She said, 'I don't want to alarm you, it's probably nothing,' and stood slightly bent over, holding her heart and breathing deeply.

'Are you having a heart attack?' I asked.

Irritated breathing noises emanated.

'No, no. I don't think so.' She winced.

She had finished organising the sunroom. The space she had made was just waiting for us to get a desk, and when we got a desk it would be just waiting for us to get a computer. But there was no point pushing it. Mum had been too busy being busy. She'd weeded. She'd alphabetised her keeping pile of secondary books. She'd troubled herself for hours with difficult knitting. She'd dragged the vacuum into the garden on the end of our longest extension cord and cleaned out Backflip's kennel, awkwardly holding an umbrella to protect herself from the magpies. Then she O'Cedar-polished the dining table, pruned the houseplants, and took two garbage bags of our old clothes to Val at the Vinnies. Mum had nothing left to rearrange. She just held her chest and appeared afflicted.

Nan said it was psychosomatic. 'Celia, for God's sake, your heart's fine,' and Mum bent upwards so she was straight again and looked genuinely confused.

'But I'm not even thinking about Bart!' Maybe it's indigestion. I'll have a Rennie.'

She had a Rennie. She avoided chocolate, citrus and spices for the rest of the week.

Nan told me not to worry. 'Everyone grieves in their own way,' said Nan. 'The body is very much at the will of the mind.'

•

On Wednesday night, Mum said 'The funeral's on Friday' and it was agreed that we would both attend. It was scheduled for the afternoon, on the last day of school before the holidays: four pm, at the Anglican Parish of Goodwood. If Mrs Bart had

had her way, it would have been sooner, but the autopsy had to be finished before Bart could be sent back to Goodwood. Given the reports from Paulie Roberts, there was no question around the issue of an open casket.

Meanwhile, to the north, the search continued in Belanglo State Forest. No other bodies were recovered. Nance, like an amateur detective, scoured the newspapers for new information daily. So did George and I, every lunchtime. We spread the grass with newsprint, wondering if they might find some hint or clue of Rosie. They didn't.

I grilled Mack for more information when he came over on Thursday morning before school to check in on Mum's heart. He was little help. All he could tell me was that the search was winding up. There was no suggestion of Rosie in the forest and he didn't think I should expect one. 'It's a different case altogether. They haven't found anyone else in there, just those two backpackers.' He shook his head. 'Those poor women.'

I shared this news with George at lunchtime and she, like me, was both deflated and relieved.

Mack said, '*That* many people have asked me if it's Rosie in the forest. I tell you, if one more person on Cedar Street stops me . . .' He trailed off. Then he told me and Mum that the specially trained cadaver dogs who searched the forest wore little booties to protect their paws from the rough terrain.

•

If Judy White had wondered whether Rosie was in the forest, she never said. The backpacker murders were all over the news. Belanglo was not that far by car. If Judy White considered it, as she convalesced in her dressing-gown, leaving the house only a handful of times to go to the Goodwood Grocer, she never once let on.

We did know that Judy quivered at the news of Bart when Nance told her. He was such a terrific guy. A good, honest man with a kind face. She shuddered at the thought of it. He'd been in the lake this whole time? While she had driven past and past? Just the thought of it—oh!—it made her quiver so. She wished she had checked in on his condition. On his worn, unhealthy heart. She should've suggested he get an echocardiogram, or an MRI. She should've asked after his stress levels and his blood pressure on one of her frequent trips to Bart's Meats. She should've done a lot of things.

She would check in on Mrs Bart soon. On *Flora*. God, she should have done so many things—and held on to her daughter. At every moment, as Nance observed, Judy quaked with the hole left by Rosie. *My baby, my baby, my baby.*

•

On Thursday night—the night before the funeral—I rubbed Backflip's rough paws and lay down next to her on her bed.

She went to sleep presently and breathed slowly and every now and again her face twitched and she bared her teeth and fluttered her brown legs in a dream. I lay there for a long time and thought about Bart with his tired, sickly heart. I thought about Rosie, too, even though as the weeks went on I tried my hardest not to. She was a ghost now, only there to haunt me. I wanted to think of anything but Bart, and anything but hearts, and anything but Rosie White in the black-and-white, pulsating dark.

So I thought about Evie, and I admired her bravery. I quaked at her arm against my arm in assembly. By that time, well into spring, I had realised that I loved to think of her. It was so diverting, to visit her in my mind. I conjured her face and was overcome with calmness, like sinking into sand. *If only*, I thought. But if only what? I wasn't sure. I wasn't sure about anything at all, just: *if only, if only, if only.*

32

Bart's funeral was awfully sad and memories of it differed depending on who you spoke to. Smithy was the most lyrical in his recollections and he shared them from behind the bar with anyone who'd listen.

He said that back in Ireland a woman was expected to be keening. 'Wailing over her beloved is keening,' he said. 'She'd keen for an age until it felt righter and then she'd shush up and the town would drink stout.'

Mal West and Dennis Carlstrom listened, while they drank stout.

'But this one was eerie quiet. I could nearly hear the teardrops.'

•

Pearl had attended the funeral on horseback. She rode in and stood Oyster in the small grassed yard next to the church.

He wore new shoes for the occasion and clopped them down Cedar Street, the first time his hooves had ever walked on a properly paved road. Coral said, 'A horse! What a spectacle. It's just what Bart deserved'; and Kevin Fairley, who had left his cows in the south paddock, stood with Pearl and mooed to Oyster, patting the horse's powerful neck while Oyster nickered.

Mrs Bart and Jan drove down in the Mazda. They didn't want a part of any hearse, horse or procession. It was a simple affair, with a veneered rosewood coffin and a service led by Archdeacon Desmond 'Dezza' Barnes, who was succinct and, in accordance with Mrs Bart's wishes, didn't bang on too much about heaven.

Pearl and Mrs Bart and Jan sat in the front row, and the backs of their heads offered little insight into their emotions. I noted Pearl wore black from head to toe, like a raven, but Mrs Bart interrupted her dress with a lovely floral scarf, with high blues and gentle yellows, which seemed to hint ever so slightly towards a better future. A set of original-issue, first-generation My Little Ponies sat proudly on Bart's modest coffin.

Some said the service ran an hour. Others said half that, and their friends said double. I didn't wear a watch and couldn't tell. Some of Bart's comrades from council attended, as did the Mayor, who I'd only ever seen in photos, and who shook hands firmly with many men near the picket fence while

Oyster looked on. Burly Joe's wife came down from Sydney, and Bart's cousins from Wollongong and Bowral. Fishermen who didn't even know him and the owner of Noble Meats in Clarke came to pay their hushed respects.

Opal and Ken Jones sat with Denise and Brian. Mum and I sat with Nan and Pop and Mack and Tracy. Jasper stayed back with Tracy's mum, because Nan advised he 'shouldn't be rushed'. Big Jim and Fitzy sat with Merv. Val Sparks crossed herself and sat with Nance and Helen and Bill and Faye Hayne and Robin Clunes and Smithy, forming a consortium of shop-keepers. Cedar Street pretty well shut for the afternoon, save for the Wicko, which Smithy left staffed more than usual—he put on everyone on the roster—in preparation for the wake after.

The speeches blurred into one speech, in which everyone said the same things of Bart, and the same things were reflected in the eyes of all those who gathered—for everyone saw Bart in the same way, and enjoyed being reminded of their rightness of vision. Loss is like a magnifying glass. It enlarges people. It enlarged Bart until he towered above us like the mountain.

He'd've given the shirt off his back, that handsome Bart McDonald. Bart had time for everyone. If someone was in trouble they didn't have a better friend. He was a true local hero; so giving, so noble. He'd never expect a repayment. He'd buy a round and then another. Pride in his civic duty was his reward, pride in his family. Those fish didn't know what hit them. *Ha ha ha*, he was a bloody good fisherman. Loved a beer and a beef sandwich; loved a coffee scroll. Always had a nice smile and a bit of good advice. He was the best of men, Bart McDonald, and now the town must find a way to carry on without him. May these venerations secure his place on the clear blue lakes of heaven.

Val Sparks nodded vigorously. Mrs Bart frowned. Nan, the atheist, forced herself to smile.

Noises arose at the very back of the church after the service had started, and I turned around to see Roy Murray creeping in with Doe. Roy was holding her around the middle and helping her along as if she was infirm or giddy or had a hard time with gravity. Mum later raised the possibility of an inner-ear infection. Roy led Doe to the back row and they sat as close to the doors as possible, presumably so Doe could make a quick escape in the event of a roof collapse. Doe Murray! A sighting! I don't think anyone thought to appreciate the significance.

I turned around too many times to look at them. Doe was wearing a navy trench coat and a worried face. Mum said, *'Jean. Don't be a creep. Look to the front,'* and I reluctantly obeyed. Then Roy and Doe ducked out just as soon as the congregation was rising and were not seen again. If it seemed curious after, it didn't so much at the time. Everyone went straight across the road and around the corner to the Wicko. 'May the road

rise up to meet you,' said Smithy to the arriving crowd, out
of breath after dashing from the church, full of purpose.

Mum said, 'I'll see you at home after,' and she and Mack
and Tracy went inside.

I walked home past the seven bottlebrush trees on our
street and opened the back door for Backflip. She went around
in circles, wagging her tail, and cried with excitement.

I had no idea what to do with myself. I had told Mum that
I didn't want to attend the wake. Nan was pleased, because
if I was in any way hesitant then I shouldn't be rushed. George
was taking the opportunity to drink cask wine at Lucas's
house with him and Ethan. 'You should come, Jean,' she said.
'Ethan wants you to.' But I didn't want to. I felt like walking
and sitting alone.

I decided I would go the clearing. I took off the dress I'd
worn to the funeral and put on my overalls. I attached Backflip
to her lead and we went out into the absurd afternoon. We
walked through the ghost town, where all the shops were
shut, and headed towards the river.

It was on the way there that I encountered Evie. Of
all the days, it was that day—the day of Bart's awfully sad
funeral—that we had our first conversation.

•

It was almost dusk at the far end of Cedar Street near the
entrance to the oval. The sky was pink across the middle and

small grey clouds hung low over the treetops and high white clouds hung high near heaven and singular birds cut across it, their bodies made black by the sinking sun.

Signs hung up in most shop windows, announcing their afternoon closure. Only Val Sparks gave an explanation: *I am shut, due to the funeral. God bless*, in ink pen and capital letters that all slanted sadly forward.

When Backflip and I went past the Wicko, the beer garden was heaving with mourners. People spilled out onto the street, with schooner glasses. Fitzy hovered near the bent pole that she'd hit with her car, looking apologetic and thankfully relieved of her helmet. I could see my Pop and Merv, deep in conversation with the Mayor. Dezza Barnes, the Archdeacon, was holding court with a group that included Coral and Val Sparks and several of Goodwood's Anglican congregation. I could see my Nan nestled in the corner with Celeste Munch, the potter, who had presented Mrs Bart with a ceramic urn that would soon hold Bart's ashes. And there was Mrs Bart herself, heaving with condolences, holding her head as high as she could manage in the crowd. Her lovely face looked on the very brink of breaking; and Pearl was nowhere to be seen.

I first saw Evie as we turned off next to the Grocer towards the oval. She was sitting in the very last of the light on the hill, reading a book, leaning back on her elbows, with her legs stretched out and no expression. She had headphones on as big as earmuffs.

I stopped and let Backflip off the lead and she bolted across the grass, zigzagging, interrupting tiny flowers.

Evie hadn't seen us. She was facing the river, angled towards the paddocks and the clearing.

I did not hesitate to walk towards her. The strange afternoon glowed with the pink and yellow sky. I felt exhilarated just at the sight of her.

Backflip got to Evie first. She galloped over and Evie was roused from her book. She sat up and ruffled Backflip's ears, and Backflip was briefly elated before running off again, her nose to the ground.

Then Evie saw me. She looked me dead in the eyes and I felt like I had fallen off the deep green mountain. Spirals of air and flapping birds twisted in my chest.

'Hi,' she said, pulling off her headphones and letting them hang around her neck. The noise of drums and cymbals bled out into the air.

Here was Evie: the prettiest girl I had ever seen in real life.

And here was I: standing, looking down at her, and feeling suddenly foolish.

'Hi,' I said back.

My mind went to nothing. She didn't say a word. We were just there together on the hill, her sitting and me standing. I wondered if it was my turn to talk again, even though it wasn't. She pushed a button on her Walkman and it made a sharp stopping sound. The drums halted and her earmuffs hung quiet. She looked up at me, expectantly. Bravely. The colour of her hair was almost white at the ends, like the high clouds near heaven.

'I'm Jean,' I said.

'Hi Jean,' she said. 'I'm Evie.'

I wanted to pass strands of grass through the gap between her teeth.

'Have you just been to that funeral?' she asked.

I told her I had.

'Was it awful?'

I told her it was.

Then she moved forward and put her book down on the grass.

'Do you want to sit down?' she asked.

And so I did.

I lost track of Backflip and what she was doing. I didn't know if she was rolling in mud or eating rubbish. I was wholly diverted. I sat with Evie on the damp grass on the hill and we had our first conversation, in which I asked too many questions, and she seemed affronted and only half answered; and the mystery of her unfolded itself ever so slightly, but then I left wondering if I knew anything about her at all.

Evie and her parents had just moved into the green and red house on Sooning Street and a lot of their stuff was still in boxes. They hadn't been in town much and still felt like strangers. They'd been staying a lot in Cedar Valley where

Evie's grandmother lived and was ailing. It was breast cancer. The old lady was unable to perform simple tasks and required constant assistance. Evie's mum had always wanted to move away from the city and now they were compelled to, by this sad occurrence. They had chosen Goodwood, because it was close to Cedar Valley, and Evie's mum was a dear old friend of Arden Cleary, the novelist who lived on the mountain and wrote naturalist fiction.

Sooning Street, I had nodded, I knew the house she meant. It was the colour of a forest on one side and red on the other. A lady called Grace used to live there with her husband, Teddy, and Teddy was an eccentric who liked to paint things different colours. Grace didn't mind and after Teddy died she left it the same because it evoked his memory. Then after Grace died the house was left empty; and now it was home to Evie and her parents.

They had come from Melbourne. *Melbourne*. I was embarrassed that I'd never been and decided right away not to tell her, but then she asked, 'Have you ever been?' and I was forced to say that no, I hadn't.

'But I want to soon,' I said, and just the thought of it, as we sat on the old familiar oval in Goodwood, with the goal posts set for a weekend game of football, seemed ridiculous.

Evie answered my myriad questions like it was odd that I was asking. Was this something that people from small towns did? Asked about your family? I wasn't sure if it was or wasn't; I just knew I wanted to know everything about her, and I couldn't think of another way to find out than to ask.

After a time, Evie pulled her big headphones off from around her neck and packed them into her cloth bag. As we talked, she fidgeted with the clover. She stared off towards the river and then she'd smile with half her mouth. When I asked her things she was bashful. When she asked me things she was pointed. It felt like my Nan and Pop, dancing, and how they would take it in turns to lead.

As the sun went slowly under, the hill got darker. Backflip finished exploring and sat down near us on the grass.

'Did you know the girl who's missing?' asked Evie.

'Rosie? Yeah,' I said. 'But not that well. She's a year older.'

'A whole year?'

She was mocking me, just gently. Then she seemed to remember herself, realising that it wasn't right to make jokes in close proximity to the missing.

'It's really sad,' she said, shaking her head so her hair moved around her shoulders. 'We just moved here a few days before it happened, and now my dad's all worried it's the Belanglo Forest guy. He doesn't want me walking around by myself. But I like walking around by myself.'

She looked at me again, right into my eyes. I felt things inside me that were too strong for my chest, deep in the parts of me where there was no language. I thought: I love walking around by myself, too. But Rosie, always Rosie——her black-and-white face hung fixed before me. What was Rosie like? Evie asked, and I didn't know what to say. How was I to describe her? She was inscrutable. She was unapproachable. She was inexplicable. It seemed like nobody knew her at all.

And then, before I knew what was happening, our conversation was over. Evie was getting up and putting her cloth bag over her shoulder without making any excuses for leaving.

She stared down at me with no expression. 'Is that tall guy at school your boyfriend?' she asked. The words came out deliberately, abruptly.

'No?' I said. I felt suddenly embarrassed. 'I mean, he took me to look at cows.'

Evie watched me for a second to see if I was kidding, but I wasn't kidding and she laughed. She cracked up there on the hill, shaking her head.

'Wow,' she said. 'It's different here.'

I wanted to say: *No, it's all the same here. It's always the same! You're the thing that's different.*

'Do you have a boyfriend?' I asked her back.

Evie smiled and showed the gap in her teeth. She was mocking me again, just gently. I could feel it. It was like there was a joke that I didn't get.

'No,' she said. 'I do not.'

She was still smiling when she turned around and walked off without saying anything except, 'Bye, Jean,' which came out so casually that I rushed to say, 'Oh, goodbye,' too quickly, and I felt foolish again.

I couldn't understand the electricity she emitted. She was like a substation, hushed and full of currents. There are lamps and streetlights and candles and suns that give off less light than Evie did. She was incandescent in the dusk as she ambled off towards town.

Backflip and I sat on the hill a little longer. The rest of Goodwood was busy keening, and growing quickly darker. My mind finally went still for a moment. It slowed like a wheel and then it halted. What a strange person she was, this Evie. She made me feel like I was changing. Right then in that instant: I was bursting and changing. I was old and brave and free as the air went cool and the birds and crickets cawed in the trees a night song.

33

After Bart's funeral, the rain did not come.

Fitzy watered, with her helmet on and her stiff neck, and Big Jim said things like, 'You get a rain gauge and it doesn't rain. Maybe we should take it down, hon. What if we've gone and jinxed the weather?'

Fitzy watered, in the allowed hours, before nine and after four. She ducked the magpies, who skimmed her helmet prongs, and Myrtle yelped upwards at the sky. Fitzy frowned and accused Big Jim of magical thinking and went inside to have a short, timed shower.

Poor Fitzy. She was dwelling on sadness. She was stuck on the feeling of failure; on the terrible effects of drought; and her family of parched apple farmers in Stanthorpe, Queensland.

Big Jim stood uphill of the rain gauge with his hands on his hips, looking at the perfect blue sky while the magpies scuffed his head. The big man did not flinch.

'Bugger,' he said to the sunny day.

But whatever Big Jim said, it made no matter. The rain did not come.

The earth around our dismal herb garden dried and fossilised. The basil wilted and its leaves browned. The hydrangea slumped. The mint shrivelled. Mum moisturised with great fervour. I was restricted to washing myself in shallow baths. Backflip panted and sought refuge in the kitchen. It was the hottest spring I could remember.

As bad timing would have it, the Fishing's The Funnest parade was scheduled to take place the weekend after Bart's funeral. That was the date that had been nominated by Bart himself, as co-president of the Goodwood Progress Association, back in November 1991, after the great success of the last parade, and amid giddy plans to make the next one even better.

'Next year the fish'll be *this* big,' said Bart with a laugh, holding his hands about three feet apart at the Community Hall while Mum took minutes.

Now, no one knew what to do.

The students at Goodwood Primary had been preparing for a month. The parade was administered by the Goodwood Progress Association, and generally took place at the start of school holidays, but it would surely not have existed without the school itself, and especially the teachers and members of the P&C who undertook production and costuming with great enthusiasm. The teachers had guided K–6 in costume design and paper fish colourisation. Their direction was: fantastical is fine. Grants Lake may not be the Great Barrier Reef, but there was no need to skimp on colour—especially in times as black as these. So the students, particularly the younger ones, made rainbows of fish. Spectrums of fish. Kaleidoscopes of fish. They were gaudy and wild and brilliant.

On the other side of town, Carmel Carmichael made muted preparations for the Fish Fry which customarily took place at the Bowlo after the parade, even though she keenly felt the impropriety of the whole thing, given Bart's disappearance.

At first it was: how could they celebrate when their best fisherman was unaccounted for? And now that Bart was— grimly—accounted for, how could they celebrate at all?

But not everyone agreed. Val Sparks, for instance, thought that a good fun parade was just the thing Goodwood needed, to try and raise the incessant grief off all the hard surfaces. Goodwood, according to Val, needed to dust off the tragedy. To honour Bart's life by celebrating what he loved. Besides, Bowral is right by the Belanglo State Forest and Bowral had still had their Tulip Time Festival on the 28th. Val had gone up there with her elder sister who loved flowers. There was carnival music and Devonshire tea. It was just lovely, and exactly what the community needed to lift its spirits after the horror in the forest.

She made the sign of the cross, from left to right.

'Don't let your hearts be troubled,' she said 'Trust in God.'

Nan, to whom this was spoken, said that while she herself did not trust in God, she did agree with Val on the subject of the parade. 'Well, what good will come of *not* doing it?' she asked in her infinite wisdom, and one would assume the relentlessly optimistic teachers at Goodwood Primary felt the same.

It wasn't until Mrs Bart weighed in, however, that the matter was settled.

She appeared the Sunday after the funeral—just two days later—which was much sooner than anyone in town expected to see her, given her pacing, and then staring, and then official widowhood. But on Sunday she appeared at the Goodwood Grocer to buy every last bag of oats.

'Can you believe that in all the . . . *everything* . . . we ran clean out of feed for the horses.'

This was technically a question, but Mrs Bart made it a statement.

Nance looked up from her obsessive reading and was so startled to see Mrs Bart in person that she fumbled with her shiny hardcover copy of Patricia Cornwell's *All That Remains* and dropped the book entirely.

'Do you need to pick that up?' said Mrs Bart, with many bags of oats.

'No, no, love,' said Nance. 'It's just a stop for the door if it gets windy.'

Mrs Bart said nothing and stared calmly forward.

Nance, forever more, was mortified at the way she lied. But to discuss forensics in front of Mrs Bart? That would have been quite unsavoury. And to feel, as she did, utterly ashamed to have discussed forensics in front of anyone in the wake of Bart's recovery? Well, that was just occurring to her at that instant.

'Just a silly old book,' she said of the brand new hardcover she'd purchased at the tidy bookstore in the Clarke Plaza.

Mrs Bart paid for the oats, out-insisting Nance's insistence that she should not pay. Then Mrs Bart said—and cleverly, too, because if you wanted all of Goodwood to know something, you either told Coral or Nance, and given Coral didn't run a shop and was thus harder to access, Nance was it: 'I think the kids should have their parade. Bart would've wanted it. He would've wanted everyone to celebrate fishing.'

And so it was.

Nance attended the emergency meeting of the Goodwood Progress Association that was held that night—the emergency being what to do about the parade—and told the gathering of her encounter, minus the part where she lied about the book. A motion was passed and it was settled: Regardless of the death of Cr. Bart McDonald, and any potential perception of bad taste, the Fishing's The Funnest parade, as assisted by the teachers and members of the Parents and Citizen's Association of Goodwood Primary, was to be held the following Saturday, as proposed by Bart McDonald himself in 1991, and endorsed that day by his widow, Mrs Flora McDonald, Secretary of the Goodwood Branch of the Country Women's Association, and set forth in writing by the sitting members of the Goodwood Progress Association, whose numbers where somewhat diminished, but whose intentions remained pure and good.

•

After my first conversation with Evie, I was lost in thoughts of her during much of the next week. School holidays had never passed so slowly, and Evie was sure to be spending them in Cedar Valley with her family. I hung out with George at her house; I walked around the oval with Backflip; I rummaged through the racks at Vinnies; I browsed the dusty aisles at Bookworm. I didn't know what to make of my longing for Evie: to speak with her again; to see her; to perhaps go swimming at the clearing and sit in the tree together or drink whisky in the park by a bin fire. All I knew, in my unknowing way, was that when I thought of her face—when I conjured it, and I held it there for as long a moment as I could just behind my eyelids—a feeling of warmth washed over me, like putting my head under the water in the bath. The feeling was so lovely that I took to having more actual baths, something that annoyed Mum given the lack of rain.

'Jean! Fill it halfway only!' she'd yell when she heard the water running and saw Backflip slink in stealthily to sit on the bathmat.

I sat in the tub for much longer than usual and the water would grow cold before I noticed. My book would lie in a half puddle, unread on the tiles next to Backflip. I could not concentrate on reading. I just stared right through the pink tiles and the bottles of shampoo near my feet and Mum's loofa hanging on the bath tap, and thought about Evie.

'Jeannie, you're taking daydreaming to a whole new level,' said Mum, sticking her head in the bathroom door. 'Can you get out so I can have a shower? My heart's burning.' She went over to the big wooden dresser that we used for a bathroom cabinet and had a shot of Mylanta, swallowing it with her face scrunched up like she was eating a lemon.

'Does that taste gross?' I asked.

'Pleasant mint flavour,' she managed to say—which was what it said on the bottle.

I didn't really worry about Mum's heart. I didn't think there was anything to worry about. Mum had decided it was indigestion. And Nan said that heartburn was caused by anxiety. Of course, it wasn't great to be so anxious, but really, you'd have to have had a heart of ice to not be affected by the unfolding tragedies of Goodwood, and the unceasing sorrow that infected us all.

•

Adding to the general feeling of discontent was the news that Carl White had returned, and was living back in the White residence with Judy, who still walked with difficulty due to the pain in her broken ribs.

Opal Jones told Denise at the library that the whole thing was shameful. How could she take him back? she asked Denise. *How?* The man puts her in hospital and God knows why. Beats her near death with his belt. And why? Do you think it might have something to do with what happened to Rosie? You can't help thinking. And poor Terry. It's hard not to want to call DOCs and get him taken out of there.

Poor Terry. He had returned, too—from Ballina— delivered by car by Aunt Alison, who spared no expense on petrol and took him the long way through Bellingen, because he liked to look at different rivers. They stopped at Thora and spent a whole afternoon trying to make a sighting of the rare Bellinger River freshwater turtle, which Terry had done a project on in Year Eight. Then, hours later, she bought him a schnitzel in Crowdy Head, where they spent the night in a motel, because Terry liked the name of the town and had always wanted to visit a lighthouse.

Unfortunately, it was only when they arrived back in Goodwood that they learnt of the return of Carl White. They pulled into the driveway of the White house and there was

Carl's car, parked darkly under the jacaranda. Opal Jones reported a kerfuffle in the front yard between Alison and Carl, and the term 'fucking mongrel' being used in a shrill voice. Then, after much appeasing by the embattled Judy, who quivered and held Terry to her aching breast, Alison agreed to enter the house and reluctantly stayed for a dinner of defrosted sausages and an uninteresting salad. Opal Jones did everything she could to monitor the proceedings, but there was the entire exterior of a house in the way, so she returned to reading her cookbooks next to Ken, who sat listlessly in a pastel shirt, awaiting wifely instruction.

None of us knew that every day that passed was one day closer to finding Rosie. It's only now, looking back, that I see those days in particular, after Bart's funeral, as a calendar in reverse. I see the squares and the numbered days. I see it all running backwards, square by square, day by day, from the day that Rosie was finally found.

34

On the morning of the parade, Mum was suffering a particularly bad case of heartburn. She'd exhausted her antacids and took to drinking warm milk in an effort to quell the pain. Backflip, who enjoyed milk herself when permitted, sat upright on the floor before her, holding out her paw every so often, in case Mum might like to shake her hand.

George and I decided to meet beforehand at the oval and when I got there she was sitting with Lucas and Ethan, and Lucas was holding a big bottle of Coke like a prize. He handed it to me as I arrived, grinning, and the brown liquid smelt suspicious. He nodded for me to try it and I did. I gulped and tasted the deep fire of whisky mixed within.

Ethan looked at me gently.

Past the oval and up along by the clearing, Kevin Fairley's cows were grazing in the south paddock. Ethan gazed off in their direction and then back at me. I took another sip of the bottle and held it out for his spear of an arm. He took it and drank.

'Pat made the weirdest Lego fish,' George was saying. 'He's been working on it all week. It looks like an aeroplane but he says it's a trout.' She was shaking her head, smiling. She was very fond of Lego Pat. He was her second-favourite brother, after Vinnie. Ethan told us how his little brother, Petey, had been very serious about his contribution too. Their mum was good at craft and had been helping with his props and costume. Petey West would carry the spirit of the ocean with him down Cedar Street.

The children of Goodwood were too young to understand the weight of the troubles. Their small arms could not reach the depths of the town's despair. The Fishing's The Funnest parade was to continue in the face of it all. It was to be a reminder that innocence and joy still resided in darkened, keening Goodwood.

'Unless you have a heart attack and drown, fishing *is* the funnest,' said George, and took a big rebellious swig. Ethan looked horrified. Lucas laughed. George gave me a look. 'Oh, I made *one* joke. It's my first one,' she said, beaming with the notion of being risky. 'Come on, Jeannie,' she said, putting her arm around my shoulder and pulling me into a partial headlock. I pushed her off and laughed. Here was the old George. The hilarious and ridiculous George who was never serious about anything. I had missed her, I thought, as the four of us sat around and made stupid jokes on lighter subjects and took turns with the bottle. I felt older, drinking whisky. I liked the feeling; and we loved parade day, George and I. We loved the colour and the Fish Fry after.

Lucas put his hand on George's knee and she pretended not to notice, but Ethan did and he looked at me, smirking, and then he looked tender. I felt him edge closer as the level of Coke and whisky in the bottle slowly receded. He was subtle about it, much like Backflip when she knew she was supposed to be outside when the back door was open and every time you'd turn around she'd be a tiny bit closer to the soft rug in front of the heater.

Cows bellowed in the faraway paddock—their moos arrived with the breeze—and Ethan turned his head to look at them. They were tiny in the distance, like the little plastic ones from the toyshop in the Clarke Plaza.

Before long Ethan was right up next to me, with his feet touching mine. He was laughing along and pretending not to be there, much like Lucas's hand was pretending not to be moving further and further up George's thigh, and George was pretending not to notice. The four of us sat like that for a long time, radiating with the alcohol and pretending, as the afternoon light cast long tree-shadows on the oval. I didn't mind either way—Ethan being close or not. His skin was warm and his game of footsies was pleasant. I remember feeling not much of anything about the afternoon.

'It's almost four,' said George. She staggered slightly as she got up. Walking back across the oval, Lucas dared an arm over George's shoulder. Ethan left his hands in his pockets but he walked so close that he bumped into me every so often as we came upon the town.

When we got to the main road, the parade was just starting, and already it was clear that Bart McDonald got his wish, albeit posthumously. It *was* even better than last year. The Goodwood Primary P&C had festooned the awnings of Cedar Street with blue and brown streamers and balloons, which flapped lazily in the light wind. Participating shop-keepers, which was everyone apart from Mountain Real Estate ('Spoilsports', said Nan) hung coloured cardboard fish in their windows and Val Sparks had made aquarium-themed bunting for her display at Vinnies. In the shining spring afternoon the cartoon colours were dazzling under an unclouded sky.

George's parents hooted for Lego Pat, who'd made a trout of many coloured blocks, which looked much more like a plane. He held it proudly above his head as he marched. Little Petey West walked barefoot with a bamboo rod and a paper rainbow fish dangling on the end. In his other arm he swung a yellow bucket. There were twenty-three children in the parade in total—Coral counted them—and they all wore either blue or brown, to symbolise the ocean or the river.

Smithy and Nance and Val Sparks stood together, cheering and clapping. Nance's great-niece held a crêpe-paper whale clasped in both hands; and three girls from Year Four, dressed in aqua blue dresses, ran along with green streamers that had shells stuck on them and fluttered along behind them like eels.

'Seaweed,' said George, with a knowing smile.

'Seaweed,' I said back, and we were merry and slightly drunk.

Paulie Roberts attended with his family. He looked noticeably troubled by the seaweed streamers. Later, he covered his eyes when Faye Haynes's grandson, Dan, went by, draped in paper lakeweed like a marsh. Paulie's wife, June, held him around the shoulders and Paulie grimaced.

Mack and Tracy's son, Jasper, was the youngest participant. He was only two and Mack held his hand at the back and he walked on his squat little legs, dressed in browns for the river and dragging a soft toy platypus on a string along the road, like he was walking a little dog.

The sight of that caused the biggest *Aaawwww* from the crowd, which was the biggest crowd I'd seen for the parade, ever. Everyone lining the pavement clapped and whooped. Outside Bookworm, Emily Ross led a woodwind quartet, asthmatically, and they performed a medley of water-themed numbers, including 'Sittin' On The Dock Of The Bay' and 'Take Me To the River'. Fisherdads and fishermums waved and crouched with their cameras, aimed at their adorable children, who were gently corralled by the teachers of Goodwood Primary. Mum, Nan and Pop, Coral, Big Jim and Fitzy were there, and the locals from the Wicko, and even old limping Mal West, who eyed me and Ethan standing together and acted like he didn't know his own son. Mrs Gwen Hughes, resplendent in a blue mirrored shawl, wore extra stones—two topaz bracelets, a shimmering sapphire necklace and huge lapis earrings—to celebrate the oceanic theme.

Everyone was there.

Everyone except Judy and Carl White, any member of the Carlstrom family, and Mrs Bart and Pearl.

Everyone except Rosie White and Bart McDonald.

'They're having a whale of a time,' said Smithy, who was properly smiling for the first time since winter. 'Look at them, happy out, leaping about the place.' His whole face lit up like a lantern.

The people of Goodwood were, for the first time in a long while, happy.

Afterwards, at the Bowlo, Carmel Carmichael had organised three big barbeques in a row along the wall opposite the green. The smell of fish was smoky and everywhere. It was to be fried and served with white bread rolls, tartare sauce and an iceberg lettuce salad.

The turnout for the Fish Fry was, as happened every year, even bigger than the turnout for the parade. The Bowlo never saw a day like it, and all the face-painted kids ran around together on the green while balloons gathered in corners and under the white plastic tables.

George and Lucas and Ethan and I sat in the fading sun near the fence, so no one could smell us drinking. We didn't have much left to drink, but we kept a steady pace and remained warm and, in George's case, slightly slurry. The line at the bar was long all evening. Never had so many kegs been required. I saw Mack and Tracy dancing under coloured lights. Mum and Nan were in a deep literary discussion with Arden Cleary, who wore a checked tweed jacket despite it being spring. Big Jim was belly-laughing with Irene Oakman, both in their best King Gees. The whole thing was triumphant and festive. It was like Goodwood had been granted a reprieve. The whole town was drinking and eating and enjoying the music.

Then the multitude of coloured hanging streamers in the doorway parted to reveal Evie, who was standing there with no expression next to her parents.

My heart wheeled to a stop.

Evie.

I hadn't even considered that I might see her there, but as soon as I did I thought, *of course*. Her parents were new in town. It was a great chance to meet people.

I watched her—Evie—as her parents were introduced to people and her dad shook lots of other men's hands and her mum clinked other ladies' wineglasses with her own.

Evie looked as if she wasn't really there. She was floating like a streamer, hovering in the doorway, looking around for no one, in her faraway world. Then she saw me across the green and she held my gaze for a long moment before turning away.

I felt the electrics in every bulb and cord and socket in the Bowlo rush through me.

The food was served. Smithy and Merv were the main men at the barbeque and the charred white fish, flaked and broken, sat steaming on huge plastic platters, surrounded by wedges of lemon.

It was twilight when the paper plates were set aside, full of scrunched napkins and tiny bones, and more people started dancing.

Evie had been with her parents the whole time, not really eating, not joining in the conversation. I was flushed in my face from the whisky and Lucas started pashing George in front of us, so Ethan lay back on the concrete and closed his eyes and I excused myself to go to the bathroom.

I caught Evie just as she was leaving.

'Are you leaving?' I asked. I could not hide my disappointment.

'Yeah. I'm going home,' she said, looking me right in the eyes.

I had nothing at all to say, so I just looked back until it became uncomfortable, and then I looked at the carpet instead.

'You should come over if you want,' she said.

My face felt hot. I looked back at her blankly.

'You know where my house is,' she said. 'When you're done here, you should come over.'

And just like that she turned and left, and I was standing on the carpet, a little giddy, and Nan and Pop were dancing—him in his good yellow shirt, her in her peach dress. Pop was leading. Nan smiled completely. She gripped his shoulders and closed her eyes. Pop swayed and tilted. He moved his feet back and forward, and back and forward, as they made a slow and gentle circle that went around and around on the floor.

•

I walked towards Evie's house with a flock of birds in my chest. I went along the dark road much faster than usual. I tripped up a gutter and almost fell over. I was full of whisky and everything in the dark world was whirling.

I hadn't said goodbye to George or Ethan. George was pashing Lucas in the shadows, and Ethan had gone off somewhere when I got back to our spot near the fence. George didn't see me, and I turned around and went back across the fairy-lit green.

I told Mum I'd see her at home and she waved, full of wine, and said, 'Jeannie, *honey*. Feed Backflip! I'm gonna have a dance.'

She hardly blinked.

'Celia!' said a woman from the CWA, before they fell into a deep and immediate discussion. Mum didn't seem to have a burning heart that night. The mirror ball spun diamonds of light around the room, and my Nan and Pop swept across the foreground—gliding—and soon I was walking very quickly towards town under a blanket of country stars. I felt like yelling and running. I wanted to be new and different. I was a sparkling fish in a bucket, flipping and beating around on its side.

Evie.

I turned the corner onto the laneway that cuts through to the car park behind Woody's, and down towards Sooning Street. Derek Murray was sitting on the edge of the metal fence, near his filthy Kingswood, smoking a cigarette. He was all by himself. The light bulb shone stark on the wall near the dumpster bins. Derek Murray's face was empty. He blew a line of smoke out and stared. There were two black holes where his eyes should be. He heard me coming and looked over sharply and more smoke came out of his nose, giving him the appearance of a dark dragon. I was startled. I had never seen him look quite so unpleasant. His mouth made a repellent smile and I thought of Lafe and his leering. I walked faster. The laneway felt so narrow and I wanted to be at the end of it. I could feel Derek Murray's eyes on me.

'Nice night for it,' he said, and I skipped into a run and ran the rest of the way to Evie's house.

There it stood: her strange-looking house, red and green. I hovered in front of the gate and tried to collect myself.

The front door was closed. I walked up the steps and stood on the landing. My chest was bursting. I considered turning around again. I took a deep breath and tried to steady myself. And just as I raised my hand up to knock on the door, it came open and, as I breathed all my air out, there was Evie. She had changed out of her jeans. She wore tights and an old green T-shirt with a Dalmatian on it. The cartoon dog, covered in spots, stared out under big white writing that said *Dalmatians Are Spot On!*

'I didn't know if you'd come,' she said.

She looked down shyly, and I did the same. Then she opened the door wider to let me in. 'Would you like a cup of tea?' she asked.

I was drunk. I knew that Evie wasn't. I told her that I would love a cup of tea, even though I didn't, and I soon found myself standing in the kitchen, while Evie put the gas on under the kettle and fetched two teacups from the cupboard.

The kitchen was modest. I imagined old Grace and Teddy would've resided there happily. Teddy, the eccentric, had done a little painting in the interior too. The door of an unknown room along the hall was purple, but the skirting was an unrelated blue. There was a confusing mixture of browns and oranges on various shelves in the pantry. I leaned against the bench as Evie spooned leaves into an old pink teapot.

She asked me if I wanted milk and I said I didn't. She seemed to be smiling, but she was yet to look me properly in the eyes. Some of her braveness was gone, and there were constellations of beauty spots on the skin of her long arms. The cartoon Dalmatian stared out from her shirt, full of innocent joy. Leaning against the bench, I had no idea what to do with my hands, so I folded my arms and looked at the floor mostly, and sometimes up at Evie.

She was so beautiful in her home clothes. She was what Nan would call 'lovely'. The sweet darkness went forever through the gap in her teeth. She took a deep breath, pouring the boiled water into the pot, and finally she fixed her eyes on me and I fell all the way off the deep green mountain. I stood there—stuck in the feeling of falling and not having yet hit the ground.

Then Evie went to get something from the drawer, right next to where I was standing. She fumbled around for the tea strainer with one hand. She was there so suddenly, so close, to one side of me, facing the bench, rummaging around in the utensils.

I wanted to fill the silence. My mind raced around for some piece of conversation. My face felt hot and I was about to speak when Evie turned her head up from the drawer and looked at me, holding the tea strainer. And then she was turning with her whole body, quickly, and then she was kissing me. I turned into her, kissing her, without thinking. I put my hands up to her face, on both sides. I heard the metal strainer fall to the floor as she moved in front of me and pushed me with all her body against the bench.

I felt like a flower, pressed in a book. Her arms, her legs, all parts of her were against me. She moved and moved there, slowly. And in just a small moment I felt her hand go up under my dress, searching, and just like that she found me. It made me breathe in so sharply. She kept her mouth on mine all the while, swallowing my breaths. And soon we tumbled from the kitchen into the hallway, onto the carpeted step, and the birdsong in my chest turned to a heavy fluttering of wings in her fingers, until the walls of the hallway, breathing quickly, brilliantly flickered with lamp and moon and stars, seemed like they went all the way to the sky.

35

The next morning was Sunday and Mack was enjoying a cup of Nescafé when Judy White called the station and asked if he would please withdraw the Apprehended Violence Order he was lodging against Carl—as soon as possible—and that she'd like to drop the assault charges, also.

Mack held the receiver in his hand and wanted to punch a hole in his stupid pinewood desk, but instead he took a pencil in his hand and broke it in two. The lead poked out of one end like a bone, and for a small moment he felt quite good.

'Jude——' he started.

'I've made up my mind, Mack. I know it's hard to understand!' A nervous laugh came down the receiver. '*Ha ha ha!* I know, I know. But he feels *so* awful, Mack. He really does. He's been so good since he got home—very caring, and helping me and stuff. Just *so* much better.'

Mack said, 'I'm coming over,' and hung up before Judy could protest.

When he got to the White house, Carl was gone.

'He's out,' said Judy White, meekly. 'He was already out when I called you. He really had to go out.'

Terry White hovered in the kitchen and gave Mack a look to indicate that this, and everything else, was complete bullshit. Mack gave Terry what he could of a nod without Judy noticing. Terry went on to his room.

'Jude, no part of me wants to do this,' said Mack.

'Yes, well,' said Judy.

They went back and forth for a few minutes, Mack persisting and Judy holding her ground. She really seemed to be digging her heels in, even in her slippers.

Mack said, 'I can still go forward without your cooperation but it'll make it very difficult—if you would just . . .'

Judy cut him off. 'I'm sorry, Mack, but I want him here,' she said. 'He's not forcing me. Terry needs to have his dad around. He should have his dad. After everything. Terry needs him. *I* need him.' She verged on quivering now, her voice wobbled.

Mack stood, because he hadn't been offered a chair. Judy looked like she'd said all she wanted to say.

'At least tell me what the fight was about,' Mack said.

Judy studied the ground like it was suddenly very interesting. She kept her arms crossed, defiant.

Mack raised his police voice. Hands on his hips, his tone almost hostile, he pushed: 'Judy, you tell me what it was all about. It was about Rosie wasn't it? This is serious, Jude. She was . . . She *is* . . .' He shook his head. 'If you know something, you can't protect him.'

'It wasn't *about* Rosie!' said Judy, and tears sprang into her eyes. She made a heaving noise. She breathed in hard, sucking back a sob, and the sound of it was animal.

Mack didn't know what to do. He stood perfectly still.

Another animal sound was emitted, and then another—guttural, primal—and he could not believe she'd produced them.

'Steady on,' he said. 'Steady on.'

'It wasn't *about* Rosie,' heaved Judy. 'It was about *money*.'

An uncomfortable moment followed in which they stood opposite each other and stared.

'Money,' said Mack, deadpan. He did not believe her and Judy could see it. She could see it and what could she say? All she could do was steady herself and explain. It was against her very nature: to explain. She was used to shaking off the intrusions of Opal Jones. She was used to closing her bedroom door and keeping what happened there behind it. But now here was Mack, and how it all looked, and what with *everything*. Judy knew she had no choice but to open herself up and explain that the night Carl had taken to her—the night he had made a sorry sack of her body with his belt, and she

304

had crumbled and broken before him—they had fought, of all the silly mundane things, about money.

Carl had a problem: a big one. The pokies. They were his mistress, and sometimes, when Judy lay awake at night, she wished he had a real mistress instead; instead of those machines that sat and jingled and took everything—took every cent of savings they had; every bit of Carl's self-worth; every bit of everything.

It'd been a problem for a long time and, while no one spoke of it in front of Carl, everyone in the White house knew it. The night in question, Judy had gone to the tin she was keeping up in the top back corner of their built-in wardrobe, behind the suitcases. It was a lovely metal tin with roses on it, and she had bought it at the Sweetmans Park markets when Rosie was just newly born. Judy found a new hiding spot for it every few months. She worried terribly about money, or their lack of it, and she often stashed some away, just in case. And Carl didn't like her doing it. He really, deeply didn't. But she got so anxious and worked up, just quietly to herself, about Terry and Rosie and how she was ever going to help them get along in life. How ever was she? So she popped a few dollars here and there into her tin. She even treated herself now and again, too. Maybe twice a year, she and the other nurses from the hospital would go to the Clarke Plaza and get mani-pedis and, once, a deluxe facial.

But Carl took all the money he could get his hands on. He'd already hocked his fishing gear last summer when he was down on his luck; and he'd hocked the bass guitar that he used to play, when Judy first met him in Cedar Valley, and she'd drink Kahlua and dance while his band played at the Commercial Hotel. Then he'd hocked Terry's old bike, without even asking Terry's permission.

The night in question, Judy had gone to find her tin. She'd opened it up to count the money, because she needed to do *something*. Rosie had been gone for so long she could hardly breathe. She wanted to scream: *my baby*. She felt covered in oil, like a seabird caught in a slick. No matter how much she showered she came out coated with grief. She needed to get out of her dressing-gown and have something done about her hair. Opal had told her: 'You need to let me take you to Clarke and we'll have a nice morning. Just try and forget it all for an hour at the salon. Wouldn't that make you feel—oh, I don't know. But we have to do *something* with you. Get you out of that terry-towelling.'

The tin was empty. Carl had found it and taken every last cent. Judy put it back in its spot and she turned around and there was Carl, taking off his belt. He'd just got home from the Bowlo and was stinking drunk. It was really only when he's stinking drunk. He doesn't even know himself then, and he feels *so* terrible about it after.

'It was stupid of me to do it again,' said Judy, looking genuinely contrite.

'Again?' asked Mack. 'Were there other times?'

'Oh, well,' said Judy. 'I just mean I know he doesn't like it. I know that. And it's not good to have any cash in the house either. Like when Rosie was saving for her boom box, she . . .' Judy trailed off and a tear ran down her pale face and splashed on her folded arm. 'She was saving for that stereo and she said, "Mum, can you hold on to this?" and gave me a hundred dollars that she'd made at Woody's. I said to her, "You just don't wanna spend it all on ciggies!"' Judy cry-laughed and softened. 'I don't know. She asked me to hold it for safekeeping.' The softness went away. 'And he took it.'

Judy was vacant now, gazing deeply into the carpet.

'And Rosie knew?'

'Oh, God, yes! She knew. He'd done it before. Gone into her room and taken money from her drawer when she was at work. It wasn't that much, twenty dollars or whatever. But *her* money. That's why she gave it to me to hold on to. I said I had a good spot. She could hardly get into Clarke to deposit it in the bank, could she? Where else was she gonna hide it?'

'And this most recent time when you brought it up with Carl?'

'Oh, I didn't bring it up. I don't bring it up,' said Judy with a nervous laugh. 'I'm just not supposed to have my money like that. He doesn't like it. He'd rather we keep it in the joint account. That's just the way he is—he can't help it.'

Mack wanted to punch Carl out with his bare fists and keep on punching him until he was smeared into the carpet. Mack thought of the kangaroos that always lay flattened on the road before the high bridge over the lake. He wanted Carl to be just like that—his guts spilt and level with the road—and passing cars bumping over him on their way in and out of town.

'I just worry, but I don't need to, really. He's promised he's going to get some help about his problem. And I think it just makes him feel bad that he can't, you know, *provide*. He was feeling so bad. He feels just awful about himself sometimes.'

In Mack's mind, Bart was there too, and the two of them—Mack and Bart—were laying into Carl, and Carl felt just awful about himself as they kicked the living shit out of him, and squelched him into the very ground.

'Because Bart, well, I don't know—I think Carl had some money trouble with Bart. I mean—not *Bart*, but one of Bart's mates probably. I don't know. Bart was always sticking up for people.' Judy had kept on talking.

'Why do you say that?' asked Mack.

'Because Bart came around here—you know—this was a couple of months ago. I haven't thought about it at all. Isn't that funny?'

Judy looked confused. Lines formed along her brow.

'Because Rosie went missing just after that. I forgot all about it. Isn't that funny? It must've been just a few days before she went. And after that I was just no use to anyone.'

'Bart came here? Why?'

'Well, because of Carl—and money,' said Judy, who suddenly appeared to be doubting what she was saying. Mack could see her mind turning before him, her thoughts going off in different directions.

'I just thought it was about money. Bart said—what did he say?—he said: "Is he here?" And I said no, because Carl was up at the Bowlo. And Bart said something like he was glad he wasn't here. I figured he might want to beat the shit out of him like last time. Then he said . . . that's right, he said: "Jude, I'm going to do what I can to help. Okay? But none of you can live like this." And I said, "Oh, Bart, we'll be right," because it's fine! It'll be fine. He was a terrific guy, wasn't he? Bart. I wish I had checked in on him. I wish I'd asked about his blood pressure and whatnot.'

Mack stared at Judy. 'What if Bart wasn't talking about money?' he asked.

'Oh, but he must've been,' said Jude, who had done what she could to stop her mind wandering. 'I mean, I knew he wouldn't have owed money to Bart, because Bart would never have lent him any! But I just assumed Bart was speaking up for someone else. Didn't you notice how he always stuck up for people? He had time for everyone. I just thought: Carl owes money to someone down the Bowlo because of his problem. That's all. And Bart was always sticking up for people.'

Mack swayed on his feet.

'Carl is really trying to stop it, Mack. He is. He's going to change. He feels *so* awful about what he's done, especially in front of Terry. And with . . . *everything*.'

Judy did not once uncross her arms.

When Mack left Ken Jones was washing his car in the drive.

'Maaate,' said Ken, with a big smile.

'Hey, Kenny,' said Mack, without one, and he didn't even stop for niceties. He just walked out and under the jacaranda and clumps of damp purple flowers stuck themselves to the soles of his boots and Mack almost slipped all the way over on the way to his car.

36

That same morning, Roy Murray drove his Pathfinder out to the lake and set his boat towards the deep water to fish for bream. Derek Murray remained behind his bedroom door with the plastic STOP sign on it, and played *Street Fighter* in his miserable underwear. Since Rosie's disappearance, Woody's was closed on Sundays. It sat behind its roller door in the dark.

But there was another member of the Murray family: one who Goodwood rarely saw. A woman who had long ago lost her mooring and sunk like a ship into her peculiar home. A person who had become more like a rumour than a human being.

Doe Murray.

For more than a decade, Doe Murray had kept herself hidden away. But that morning would be different. That rainless morning, Doe Murray stepped out under the blue sky. Perhaps she looked up and checked it for cracks. Perhaps she walked with her head down to the uneven pavement. But Doe Murray left the low weatherboard house and walked—on her underused feet—up Woodland Street, with its handsome paperbarks; right at Cedar Street, near the Wicko; and along the wide footpath to where the shops were.

Doe crossed the street before the newsagent and walked in the shade of the awnings opposite, turning her head to the windows to find her own hollow reflection. Helen saw her and wondered if she were an apparition. Surely that couldn't be the real Doe Murray. The eyes must be playing tricks. But they were not; and it was. And the real Doe went right past Mountain Real Estate and directly into the Goodwood Police Station, where Mack sat surrounded by pinewood and a pile of useless paperwork concerning the violent deeds of Carl White.

Mack looked up and there was this woman, standing there like an apparition.

'Doe Murray?' he said to her, as if she might not know the answer.

'Mr Mackenzie,' said Doe, because she always got it a bit wrong.

Mack was halfway through the word 'Constable', in an attempt to correct her, but she cut him off midway, only to create an obscenity that he had not intended.

'About the day Bart drowned,' said Doe Murray, or the apparition, without further ado.

Mack was still so surprised. He stood up and went straight to the counter, saying nothing.

Doe looked up at the ceiling, and through it to the sky.

'What about it?' asked Mack, mystified.

'Roy,' said Doe. She was being terribly matter-of-fact.

'What about him?' asked Mack, transfixed by the apparition.

Then the apparition spoke to Mack—in words that made sentences and sentences that began to make sense. Doe Murray told Mack, very slowly, as if Mack were dim, that Roy, too, had set out to the lake on the morning Bart had. Roy, too, had driven his car over the high bridge above the water; along the fast flat road after; and parked on the browned grass near the boat wharves. Roy, too, had planned to spend the day fishing.

'And?' asked Mack.

'And then he came home,' said Doe Murray.

'And?' asked Mack.

Doe Murray's eyes narrowed. 'He was as wet as the lake,' she said, stirring with nerves.

'He was . . .' Mack trailed off.

Here was this woman: this Doe Murray. First time she'd set foot in his station. First time he'd heard her talk since Derek Murray was just a boy; after which she'd receded like water after a flood, and let herself seep into the boards of that weatherboard house, never to be seen or heard from again. Until Bart's funeral the other day—that's right, she had been there, hadn't she? She had; and Mack hadn't thought to appreciate the significance. So up until then—and until now. Here was the apparition that spoke and looked like Doe Murray. Her voice was really quite ordinary. She didn't have much of an accent that he could hear. She was still a good-looking woman, but older in the face. Crows' feet had stepped on the sides of her eyes and left their footprints there. Mack looked at the creases and thought for a moment of crows and then, involuntarily, of their close cousins: ravens. He shuddered at the sick feeling. He closed his eyes and gave a quick shake of his head and opened his eyes to find Doe Murray again, looking at him expectantly.

'He was as wet as the lake, Mr Mackenzie,' she repeated.

Still, Mack said nothing. What was she telling him? That Roy Murray had something to do with Bart and his drowning? That Roy Murray went fishing that day, even though he told Mack he hadn't?

Mack looked at Doe Murray. 'What are you telling me?' he asked. 'What do you think you're telling me, Doe?'

'I'm telling you just that—that Roy was sopping,' she said, annoyed.

'Why don't you come around here and let's have a chat about it,' Mack said, trying to soften his tone and regain his command.

Doe Murray looked up at the roof again, as if she could see the sky right through it. She scanned the ceiling for cracks, appearing apprehensive. The door behind her had swung closed: shutting out the day, shutting in Doe. She was safe and trapped, trapped and safe. She had made it this far. She drew a deep breath and allowed Mack to open the little pinewood gate by the counter and usher her to the black vinyl chair, and she didn't mind the little *whoosh* it made when she sat down, even though it sounded like wind, and winds are made of sky.

Mack sat down at his desk opposite. He got out his statement pad and a pen.

Doe took a little white pill out of her purse and swallowed it without water.

'What's that?' asked Mack.

'That's *my* business,' said Doe.

Mack sat, wordless. So did Doe. She fidgeted with her sleeve and trembled slightly. She flinched at nothing. Then she gathered herself. She dropped her anchor and stabilised. And with the look of a swimmer mounting the starting blocks, she braced for her unburdening, and Mack merely stared as she spoke—an unfettered and unwavering monologue, under an uncracked and invisible sky.

•

Doe Murray had woken on that Sunday in August like she always did: alone. Roy was always up before her, no matter what time her eyes would open. It was as if he knew she was stirring and made sure not to be there when she roused. The same happened at night, when Roy would potter and watch television, or fill out his order books and reconcile the takings or stay out late at the Wicko or the Bowlo, drinking and playing the pokies. Doe went to sleep alone and woke up alone, and it had been that lonely way for years.

Roy had proposed a day at the lake for himself, like he did most Sundays. But that day, and the week preceding, there was something fishy. That was the word Doe used—*fishy*—and Mack stifled a smile when he wrote it down: *Roy—fishing at lake—seemed fishy*.

Roy went off in his Pathfinder, Doe stayed indoors, and Derek spent the day playing his awful video games in his underwear. The boy didn't seem to feel the cold. In fact, Derek didn't seem to feel much of anything, except a rising anger. It came off his unpleasant face like sweat. And if the anger wasn't there, there was just blankness. He was wooden, or stone, with two vacant holes for eyes.

Later on that Sunday afternoon, Roy arrived home and drove his big car all the way into the garage. That, said Doe, wasn't normal. Usually he pulled up in the drive and left it there. She couldn't remember when he'd last used the garage, except for during the big hailstorm we'd had last summer. *Hailstorm.* Doe Murray seemed to find it hard to say the word. What worse phenomenon was there than a hailstorm? Stones of ice flung from cracks in the sky. Only lightning was near as dreadful.

Doe looked as queasy as Paulie Roberts and Mack had to prod her gently. 'Roy put his car in the garage,' he said.

Doe caught up with herself and found her place. 'Yes,' she said, 'very fishy,' and went on.

Roy had closed the garage door behind him and come through the joining door into the landing outside the laundry, where Doe was waiting in the doorway, which is known to be, structurally speaking, the safest part of the house.

She asked him why he was sopping wet.

'Did you fall in the lake?' she asked. 'Was there rain? It's been so dry.'

Roy's eyes were wired like poles. His hair was clumped wet weeds. He had actual droplets on his cheeks: water, or sweat, or tears, or all three.

'I . . .' he said. 'I . . . Doe, angel' he said.

And that was the extent of his explanation.

The two of them stood there on the tiles, and Roy dripped and had no language, and Doe felt safe in the doorway, but also confused by the wet husband before her. But there was nothing really to worry about, was there? So he'd had a little swim. Maybe he was embarrassed because he'd had an accident. Silly old Roy, he could be so clumsy. Even though his face did look awfully strange and his eyes spoke a silent *something* that she had never seen them say.

Roy went to the bathroom and took off his wet clothes and showered. Afterwards, he washed his clothes himself, which was also quite fishy. Much later Doe heard him vacuuming his car. But Doe Murray went to sleep alone that night without thinking more of it. Not until she read the news two days later in the paper. And only then because she had retrieved the paper from the bottom of the bin, where Roy had buried it among the eggshells. There was egg all over the headline on the front page of the *Gather Region Advocate*: POLICE SEARCH FOR LOCAL COUNCILLOR IN GRANTS LAKE. She scraped some yolk off and read. She was horrified. Bart had gone missing on the very same Sunday that her husband had been as wet as the lake.

Mack chewed the inside of his mouth and tapped his pen on his desk.

'And you never asked him more about it?' he asked.

'Yes I did,' said Doe.

'And when was that?'

'A few days after,' she said.

Doe had read the eggy paper and knew that Bart was missing. Of course, she also knew about Rosie, that Rosie was missing—and Roy had been very odd about that as well. He hadn't wanted to discuss it. And that was extremely fishy, since Rosie was the only employee that her wet husband had.

'I may have my problems,' said Doe Murray, 'but I can put two and two together. *Four*. I know how to get to four.'

'And what would you say four was here?' asked Mack.

'Well, four is fishy,' said Doe, and continued.

After Rosie had disappeared, Roy was distressed. Of course he should be; Rosie had been working for him for almost two years. But it was a fishy distressed, not the regular kind. And then there was Derek. Maybe the fishiness lay with him. He skulked around more than usual and he and Roy weren't getting on. Doe asked what was wrong, but Roy wouldn't say. Roy was angrier than she'd ever seen him, and she had not known Roy to be an angry man. Detached, yes. Solitary, unreachable—sure. But not a man of anger. All Roy had said was that Derek was to take over Rosie's shifts whether he liked it or not, and after a long history of defiantly refusing, Derek miraculously agreed.

Doe sat most of her days on their brown couch and observed the comings and goings. Derek hadn't been nice to her for years. Not even civil. As soon as he'd become a boy, rather than a baby, he started asking after his real mother. Roy had always told him the truth: that his real mother was dead. But he also told him a lie: that it had been an accident.

The whole town knew it was no accident. The whole town knew how she'd suffered—the long life of sadness, the postnatal depression—and that she'd taken her life with a whole bottle of sleeping pills while baby Derek slept in his cot in the next room. Poor Derek had to find out at school, from the mouth of an older girl, who said it to him like he should be ashamed of himself; and Derek Murray went home with a stinging face, and was never nice to Doe Murray again.

In the years that followed, Doe Murray sunk like a ship.

She had tried to be a good stepmother. She had wanted so much to have a child of her own, but Roy Murray said he wouldn't have it, not under any circumstances. He said, one night, after a lot to drink, 'I don't want another kid killing my wife,' and Doe had always wondered if Derek had overheard.

•

Mack had been sitting back in his chair while Doe Murray delivered her oration. They had danced around in circles, covering various angles of her story while she sat before him, weighted down by the very air above her. But now Mack leant forward slowly, so as not to alarm the apparition.

'And what did Roy say when you asked him about it? After you read about Bart in the paper?'

'He wouldn't say,' said Doe. 'I said, "What's going on here, Roy? Why were you wet the day Bart went missing? Don't make me start guessing." But he wouldn't say. He just said he ended up in the water. And when I asked him he got very upset. He started to say something. And then he just said, "Derek."'

'He said "Derek"?' asked Mack. He looked squarely at Doe Murray and her strange expression. There was her face, yes—her eyes, mouth, nose—but the combination was almost not a face at all. It was more like an abstract shadow, from so many years without sun, and so many years without having looked upon the faces of others.

'Derek what?' asked Mack.

'Just Derek,' said Doe. 'But I assume he meant Derek Murray? Roy's son?' She looked at Mack like he was dumb as a box of hair.

'Yeah, I know which bloody Derek he meant,' said Mack, who was running short of patience. 'What *about* Derek do you think he meant, Mrs Murray?'

Doe caught his tone and collected herself.

'He said, "Derek," and I said, "Yes?" And he said, "Derek got himself in some trouble." But he couldn't get it out. He said, "I can't say. *I can't say!*" and then he said, "It'll be okay, it'll be fine." And I thought: I don't think it sounds very fine. But that was all he said about it, and I have known better than to mention it since, because he's still acting fishy. I have never known him to be an angry man.'

Sitting forward, Mack hunched his back. His nausea rose and he was glad for his metal rubbish bin, just in case.

Doe Murray waited for a response.

'Doe, do you think Derek did something to Bart?' asked Mack.

'I don't know.'

'Do you think Roy did something to Bart?'

'I don't know. *No.* I don't think Roy's that kind of man. I know he's not.'

'Was Derek home the day Bart went missing?'

'He was when Roy left, but then he went out for a few hours in his Kingswood.'

Mack rubbed his temples. He wanted Doe to know full well that he had a very bad headache coming on.

'What *do* you think?' he asked her, exasperated.

Doe sat back.

When she next spoke, her vague sarcasm was gone. Her narrowed eyes were wide again. She looked, suddenly, genuinely sad. She said, 'Derek's not been good to me. I've tried, but he hasn't. I'm not his mother, and I have my own problems. But Roy is a good man. I don't know what's happened. He's been devastated about Bart. *Devastated.* But Derek . . . I know it sounds awful, but I don't know about Derek. He is not a smart boy. Something's happened. I don't know what, but Roy is angry. Or he is disgusted. He's disgusted at Derek—his only son! He can hardly look at him! And Derek just plays those horrible games in his room.' Doe Murray shook her body, like she was shaking off a disgusted feeling of her own.

Mack heard everything she'd said. He turned it over in his aching head—for his headache had set in like a bad storm by then, and his temples pounded while his sick feeling went up and down like waves, so all he could manage to ask was a question that struck him suddenly from above and didn't matter at all.

'Doe, how did you get here?'

'I walked.'

'How'd you manage that?'

'I've been trying it for twenty-six days,' she said. 'To come here. I didn't want to talk about this on the phone. Twenty-six days of trying and today is the twenty-seventh day and I just *did it*.' She smiled. It was the first smile Mack had seen on her face for a decade. Just like that, her face looked like a face again.

'Good for you,' said Mack, and the two of them sat quietly while Mack wrote down streams of notes on his statement pad.

37

I had got home late after being with Evie, but luckily not quite as late as Mum. Mum had rolled in from the Fish Fry at one, with a *toot toot* from Mack's car. I heard Tracy laughing loudly out the window, and then the sound of Fitzy spilling out also, hooting, drunk as a sailor. 'BJ!' she yelled. 'Come get me!'

Mum had cracked up laughing, yelling 'Jim!'—since Big Jim must've gone home earlier—'Jim! You better get her!' Then the sound of Big Jim opening their door and saying, 'What have you done to yourself?' as warmly as pie.

Mum's keys had gone into the lock just as Backflip had finished eating her biscuits, so I had closed my bedroom door and lay thinking—of every detail I could possibly think about Evie, and her golden skin and her breathing. I lay there smiling, on the edge of almost laughing, until I fell asleep.

On the Sunday morning I slept until ten, which was three hours later than usual. When I woke up I could still taste the whisky and my eyes were stuck together with sleep. It took a moment to remember Evie again, and her twinkled hallway, and later her bedroom, with one low lamp, and a tiny single mattress on the floor with a quilt that we lay on after, with my hand on her stomach and my head tucked into her naked shoulder.

I remembered her quiet lungs after—how they made her body go up and down and my hand went up and down with her. I remembered that we kissed slowly and forever until I put my dress back on and said I had to go home and feed Backflip.

Evie didn't get up. She didn't put her clothes back on. She just got under her quilt and said, 'Goodnight, Jean,' like it was the most normal thing in the world.

●

When Mum finally got up on the Sunday, her heartburn was bad again. On top of that she felt 'a little rusty', as she described it to me while she took Panadol and Berocca and made fried eggs.

Fitzy was a little rusty, too; and so was Big Jim, even though he'd gone home earlier than the ladies. In fact, the day after the Fish Fry was one of Goodwood's rustiest days on record. Never had so many kegs been required, according to Carmel Carmichael. Never had so much wine flowed, as freely as the river.

George phoned as I was eating my toast.

'Where did you go?' she asked, rusty, on the other end of the line.

'Oh. I left,' I said.

My mind went blank wondering what to tell her.

'You went home?'

I paused, and then I said, 'More to the point, is Lucas officially your boyfriend? Because you were not subtle. My mum has already mentioned it.'

It was true, she had. Mum said, 'I think Lucas Karras took George to look at cows last night, if you know what I mean,' and smiled from the couch.

'Oh my god, kill me,' said George down the telephone.

Meanwhile, Mum ate her fried eggs and put her plate down on the coffee table and stood in front of the living room bookshelves, holding her chest.

'We need some medical books,' she said. 'We don't have any medical books.'

•

Nan visited Mrs Bart and Jan that afternoon. None of them were rusty. Nan brought a banana bread for Pearl and a casserole for the ladies. They sat outdoors in the spring sun near the stables and Pearl rode Oyster around the paddock for a while, and then out and off towards the foothills of the mountain.

Jan did most of the talking. There was much to say about burly Joe. He'd be leaving soon—his wife had had enough. And then what would they do with the shop? Goodwood needed Bart's Meats and Mrs Bart didn't want to see it close. Jan was going to stay on longer and see if she couldn't prime herself for some work behind the counter. If they could only hire someone to do the actual butchering, then Jan could certainly stomach the selling. She'd hold her breath and wear plastic gloves so none of the meat would touch her, and then she'd come home at night to a nice vegetarian meal, like always, and everything would be all right.

Mrs Bart stared beyond Nan, over one of Nan's padded shoulders, and said she could quit the Secretary position at the CWA. Everything had carried on well without her since Bart went. If she quit her post, then maybe she could be a butcher. Stranger things had happened, and she wasn't squeamish. There was even this part of her that just *desired* it.

Nan nodded and said maybe one of the young men in town could do the heavy lifting. What about that nice tall Ethan West? Or no, come to think of it, he seems to prefer live cows to dead ones. What about Davo Carlstrom? He seems to be at a bit of a loose end.

'Isn't Davo Carlstrom mixed up in the business with Rosie?' asked Jan.

'They were sweethearts,' said Nan. 'He's terribly upset.'

'Amazing they haven't found a trace of her,' said Jan, and Nan agreed that it was, while Mrs Bart stared—and she didn't mention Bart's missing Corolla, and she didn't mention Mack's questions about how well Bart knew Rosie, and she didn't mention how she'd tried to talk to Bart about her, because surely he would care. Bart cared about everyone. He had time for everyone. What a horrible thing that Rosie went missing. And yet. Bart hadn't wanted to talk about it at all. It was so *odd*, and it had always nagged at her. It was always somewhere in the back of her mind.

•

Doe Murray had hovered in the doorway of the police station for a long time before she left, looking up at the sky.

'Do you need to try twenty-seven times?' asked Mack. 'Because I can go back to my desk and pretend you're not here.'

He had found his discussion with Doe confusing, and illuminating, and frustrating, in equal measure. She had told him her concerns, but she had given him almost nothing he could go on. She said, 'You mustn't tell Roy I've been here. You *mustn't*.' And Mack had opened his drawer to look for Panadol.

'I don't need twenty-seven tries,' said Doe Murray sternly as she stood in the doorway, which was, structurally speaking, the safest place at the station. She held her handbag to her chest with both hands, as if it were a baby, and she rocked back and forth in her comfortable-looking shoes. Mack stood behind her, in case she fell backwards.

Doe rocked. And with each rock she grew stronger, with each rock she grew braver, and on what turned out to be the final rock, she launched herself onto the concrete outside, exposed under the unbroken sky, and Mack watched her walk triumphantly off towards the safety of the awnings on Cedar Street and, ultimately, to her sunken, lonesome home.

●

By nightfall, Mum had dragged out an Encyclopaedia Britannica and had it wide open on the living room rug, studying diagrams of the heart.

'Why would they call this bit the "inferior wall"?' she said to Backflip, pointing at the big heart on the page. 'That is not reassuring.'

A short while later, I heard her on the phone to Denise's husband Brian who, apart from being boring, was also a doctor and had an office in Clarke where I'd been taken for several injections.

'I just worry about an ulcer,' said Mum into the phone. I could only imagine how boring Brian would have been on the other end of the line. 'Okay, sure. Maybe I'll come in later in the week,' said Mum. And then, 'Oh no, I wouldn't worry about that! *Ha ha ha ha*. No, I think that would be a very rare thing, wouldn't it—two heart attacks in the one town.'

Mum asked Brian to give her best to Denise and hung up. Then she cracked two Rennies out of their plastic packet and proceeded to move them around in her mouth. She sat on the rug next to Backflip with the big heavy book, tracing her fingers around the valves and chambers.

38

The news of the bodies in the Belanglo State Forest had disappeared from the newspapers. Two women had been found there—and their families had collected them properly now, and the policemen had continued searching with their soft-booted dogs, but they had found nothing else to speak of. By that month—October—they'd found no other back-packers, no further remains, no men, no women, no killer. And no scent or trail or trace of Rosie.

We didn't know then that it wouldn't be long now. That the calendar was just running backwards from the day when there would be answers. At that time, all there was were questions, which drifted around Goodwood like despair, and propelled Mack into Woody's on Monday morning, first thing—as Roy Murray opened the roller door, his white hair as dry as old bones.

'Morning, Roy,' said Mack.

'Mack,' said Roy.

'How're you travelling?'

'Yeah, fine,' said Roy, who looked tired in the eyes like he had for months now, and who wasn't even making much of an effort to hide it.

'You didn't stay for the wake?'

Roy busied himself with turning on the lights and the grill.

'Nah. Look, I wanted to, but you know Doe. It was such a big deal to get her out of the house. We had to try ten times just to walk out the door. So, you know, I needed to get her home.'

Mack nodded. 'Nice service,' he said. 'Quiet. Nice.'

Roy nodded.

'How's Derek?' asked Mack, changing tack.

Roy flinched. 'He's all right. He's working at least. He's all right.'

Mack stood on the lino floor and looked at the bain-marie and the black grills behind. It was all so quiet when there was no frying; there were no meat smells. There was no Rosie.

'Roy, I heard some things,' he said.

Roy reddened. His entire face—the weathered skin, the swollen nose from drinking, the tiny spider's webs of veins—went red so quickly and so intensely that he looked like he might burst a valve. He began to straighten things on the counter that were already straight. He attempted a surprised chuckle that came out like a cough.

'What kind of things?' he managed to say.

Mack looked at the red man—he looked at his red friend, really, because he would've considered Roy, in a general way, to be a friend—and by the look of his friend Roy's face, he knew he was on to something, and Mack felt almost pitiful to keep on looking, and almost embarrassed that he had to ask.

'You know what I'm talking about,' said Mack, taking a punt on Roy's redness; on his discomfort; and on his looking as sick to the stomach as Paulie Roberts. Mack took a gamble. He took Doe Murray's fishy notions to Woody's that morning, just as he had taken them to bed with him the night before. Mack had lain awake listening to Tracy's sweet breathing—it always cheered him—but that previous night even Tracy could not help. Mack had half-slept and half-dreamt of Roy Murray, wet as the lake, yelling over and over: *Derek! Derek! Derek!* And there was Doe, too—an apparition—somewhere on the shore. She hailed him from near the sunken marshes. *Mister Mackenzie!* she yelled, incorrectly. And then, *Roy! Derek! Bart!* For fuck's sake, so much yelling, thought Mack—who could neither sleep in peace nor wake from his ghastly half-dreams. Mack had taken it all with him to Woody's that morning; and to Roy. And he made a snap decision. Mack—a man who did not gamble—decided to bluff.

'You know exactly what I'm talking about, Roy. And it's time we sat down in that booth back there and you tell me in your own words: *everything*. Because let me tell you, it's not looking good from where I'm standing.'

Roy discoloured further; he headed towards purple now: the doleful shade of a bruise. He gulped air and swallowed and found no crack in Mack's stony expression. If ever there was a face for playing poker. And without arguing he walked to the front of the shop and closed the glass door, leaving the roller shutter up so the daylight still came in, and he and Mack ushered themselves to the back booth, where no one ever sat. White-haired, red-faced Roy Murray looked like he might break down and cry like a big old baby as Mack waited patiently for him to make words.

'Derek,' Roy said finally, his eyes drained of any light.

Derek.

•

Mack sat in the booth and waited. *Derek.* The word hung there between them in the thick air.

Poor Roy Murray's eyes were filled with tears. They were brimming like the lake after rain.

So far, Mack had managed not to mention Doe's visit at all, just as she had requested. He had also managed to get Roy Murray to mention Derek, all of his own accord. Mack just sat still with his poker face and realised that asking questions was not always the most effective way of eliciting information. Perhaps he had been doing it wrong all these years? When presented with a red-faced man in such discomfort as Roy Murray, Mack didn't have to say much of anything. He just suggested, and then he bluffed, and then he waited; and Roy was left to unravel all by himself.

'Bloody Derek', said Roy, putting his head in his hands and covering his exhausted eyes.

'What's happened, Roy?' said Mack. 'I need you to tell me in your own words.'

Roy Murray's tears didn't fall. He just kept on rubbing at his eyes. He put his thumb and finger there and closed them and rubbed them, and made a sound like '*Gaaah*' in an attempt to squash his feelings. The sound was almost as animal as Judy White, almost as primitive. But nothing could be squashed. Nothing could be put out, or ignored, or left unspoken any longer. Roy Murray had been tired in the eyes since winter and the red rims around them puffed with his bad feelings.

'Derek,' said Roy finally, raising his head up to Mack, looking at him squarely. 'Derek hurt Rosie.'

And with that, all the notions and half-dreams and visions that Mack had been carrying—like a wind inside him, blowing in all directions—all of it stopped. It stopped; and the hair on the back of his neck stood upright; and his stomach fell like being pushed off a ledge.

He stared.

'What do you mean?' he said flatly.

'He hurt her, Mack. I saw,' said broken Roy. And he told the rest of it without being able to look Mack in the eye for more than a few moments, and Mack—suddenly still inside—listened.

•

Derek Murray didn't have any luck with girls. That was how Roy prefaced his story. That was all Roy could say in his son's defence. Derek never seemed to have one: a girl. He was going to be twenty-one in November and he didn't know how to talk to them, didn't know how to look at them. He didn't know how to like them either.

Rosie had worked at Woody's for almost two years and Derek would go in and hang around towards the end of her shift sometimes, ordering burgers just so she'd have to make them. Roy knew Rosie didn't like Derek at all. Roy could tell. But Derek couldn't tell. He didn't recognise the signals. Or he did, but he didn't *want* to recognise the signals.

All Roy knew was Derek was up there at Woody's at least three times a week last winter, talking shit to Rosie, trying to impress her, getting pissed off when she wasn't impressed. And Rosie dismissed him with her signals, without being able to dismiss the boss's son with her words. Roy saw now that he should've said something. He should've said, 'Back off, son. She's not keen on you.' But he didn't. He didn't say anything at all.

On the Wednesday before Rosie went missing, she closed as usual and night fell quickly and cold. Roy was sitting at home when he realised he'd left his order book at the shop that morning, and he needed to fill it all out that night, which was one of the many chores he busied himself with after Doe had gone to bed.

The Murrays' sunken house was not a far walk to the shops, but the air was icy so Roy hopped in his car to go get his book. Doe was making dinner and Derek was, well, where was Derek? Roy didn't know. Maybe he was out drinking with one of his stupid mates, or out drinking alone. Roy knew Derek wasn't popular, and Roy knew Derek liked to drink.

Roy pulled into the car park behind Woody's and felt something when he saw Derek's car. It wasn't a terrible feeling exactly; it was more like apprehension. He felt ill at ease. There it was, Derek's filthy Kingswood, pulled up at a hurried angle and parked badly. All the shops in that stretch were closed for the day, and the backs of them, which faced the car park, were all dark—except for the stark light bulb above the back door of Woody's, which burned white and illuminated the dumpster bins and brickwork.

Roy got out of his car and went towards the back door, which was slightly ajar and held fast with the plastic doorstop, like it always was when the shop was open, for extra ventilation so the meat smoke wouldn't stick too much to the lino and the paintwork. Roy thought it strange that Rosie would still be there, but only strange by about half an hour, and maybe she'd been held up with the cleaning and closing up.

When he pushed open the door he heard muffled sounds of grunting. His own son's grunting. And he heard a small cry from a girl—from Rosie—and he saw them in the dim hallway that led back towards the dark shop. And Derek had Rosie's arms pinned hard against the wall behind her, and his jeans were lowered so his underwear was showing, and Rosie was gasping, struggling, clenching her teeth. Just as Roy entered the doorway he heard the sound of spitting, and Rosie spat a spray of spittle across Derek's face as he said, 'You want it, hey, angel?', smiling, in a voice so vile that Roy could not recognise in it the sound of his own son.

Derek didn't notice Roy coming in.

He looked mystified by what had happened to his face and how it came to be crowded with spit, and then he looked enraged.

'You fucken *bitch*,' said Derek, and Rosie lifted her knee and made contact with his groin and Derek went backwards towards the wall close behind him.

'*Fuuuuck*,' Rosie screamed—truly animal—with shudders of crying and shaking, and she looked up to see Roy standing in the doorway with his stupid keys in his hand.

She was clothed. Roy looked to see if she was clothed, and she was clothed. Her eyes were wild and smudged with eyeliner, and her face began to crumple as she looked at Roy, and walked towards Roy, and pushed past Roy, and went into the car park; and the sounds of her crying echoed just slightly around the bitumen and the backs of the buildings; and the sounds of her boots went fast and distant; and she was gone.

Roy stood in the doorway and looked at Derek, who was involuntarily sitting now, doubled over on the tiles against the wall, gasping; and Derek said, 'What a fucken *bitch*,' and spat onto the tiles of the shop that Roy had grown and fostered and loved and dedicated himself to.

Roy looked at his son, Derek, who he had grown and fostered and loved and dedicated himself to. He could smell a brewery in the hallway. Above the meat smoke and fat and onions all he could smell was the beer mats that lay on the counter at the Wicko, and the bottoms of a hundred schooner glasses, and the end of a spent keg.

Derek got up and put himself back in his jeans, and zipped, and smiled at his dad. 'She was into it,' he said, and his teeth looked revolting in his mouth; and the air was filled with his stench; and Roy didn't know who on earth this vile person was that he was looking at.

•

Backflip and I had left the house to walk to the clearing that Monday morning. We walked along Cedar Street in the clear day, right past Woody's, and I saw that the roller door was up but the glass door was closed, which was very unusual. I looked in as we went past and there was white-haired Roy Murray slumped on the back booth table, and Mack looking on at him blankly. I stopped for a moment and gazed in, thought better of myself for prying, and continued on down towards the oval.

When we got to the river, it flowed brown with the silt and white with the sky. The lack of rain had caused it to shrink its sides. Where it once was wide and cavernous, now it was not even enough for Backflip to properly swim, not unless she was all the way in the centre.

It'd been ages since I'd been there. Not since Mack and I had gone looking for the plastic horse and found it to be missing.

Backflip ran ahead towards the willow and up along the alluvial bank to sniff, and to check if there were cows in the paddock to bark at. I stopped dead still when I saw there was someone sitting in the tree.

For a minute, it was Ethan. Tall, blond Ethan, who had come there to look at the cows. He seemed to be sitting in the tree and meditating on them, watching the river run. What would we talk about? We hadn't been alone since the night in my garden.

But as I got closer, it wasn't Ethan. I knew the shape of the shoulders and the colour of the flanno and the rough golden hair. It was Davo Carlstrom sitting up there on the branch, his feet dangling over the water. Even there at the clearing the river was lower than I'd ever seen it. His legs were long and he was nowhere near touching the current. The river itself seemed sunken into the sand, like the earth had opened its thirsty mouth and drunk it.

Unfortunately, Davo was facing my direction. If he'd had his back to me, I could've turned around without him knowing, but he was looking right at me and I was just a solitary figure on a long riverbank and Backflip had started barking at the cows and there was no way around hearing it.

Even from where I stood, far away, I could see his heavy sadness. He was stooped in it with his whole body, like a weeping willow, and just below was the trunk where all the initials were and Rosie had carved hers next to his.

I yelled to Backflip, embarrassed, and she barked and strutted about with her back up, and barked again before galloping towards me looking triumphant.

Davo held up one hand.

The handsome, rebellious, older boy—who I had perhaps not said even one word to in my life—held up his hand to me. I saw that he was holding a brown paper bag with a bottle in it. He held up his hand, with the bottle. So I held up one hand too, and the two of us stood facing each other, a long way apart, with our hands up.

After a while I took mine down, and he took his down, and with an unfamiliar feeling of solidarity I turned and walked back towards town and left him to be by himself in the tree.

39

Mack went straight from Woody's, with Roy, to see Derek Murray. The two men did not speak on the short drive in Mack's police car. They arrived at the weatherboard house where Doe Murray sat on the brown couch and looked like she'd seen two apparitions when the men entered.

Roy said gently, 'Don't worry, angel, Mack's just here to have a chat with Derek,' and Doe Murray did not acknowledge Mack at all as he headed towards the closed door with the plastic STOP sign on it.

Mack knocked. Derek didn't answer. Computerised sounds of kicks and punches came from inside the room. Derek was beating the shit out of someone on his screen and Mack could hear the damp blows over and over again.

He knocked once more. Derek snarled, 'Fuck off, Doe,' and Mack couldn't stop himself from thrusting the door open so hard that it slammed against the wall behind and shook the entire sunken house to its very frame.

Derek went white when he saw Mack, livid, in the doorway and his father, Roy, standing right behind him, as grave as a deep hole. Unlike Roy—who had flushed as red as blood back at Woody's—Derek quickly drained of everything. He was all milk in his snowy Y-fronts. A ghost boy, blank and unpleasant.

Derek shot up from his swivel chair and then popped back down again on the edge of his bed, trying to appear unmoved. Mack stared at him. He put on his poker face. He narrowed his eyes and tried the same technique as he had with Roy. But unlike Roy, Derek didn't have a heavy conscience. There was no burden of guilt on his sloped and pallid shoulders.

Mack sat down on the swivel chair and requested that Derek cover up his chalky body in more than just under-wear. Derek pulled on a T-shirt and dusty jeans.

He was uncooperative at first. Unresponsive. He looked at the ground and smiled. He ran his tongue slowly along his top teeth. Derek insisted he'd done nothing wrong. He said his dad had seen two people who were totally into it. He said Rosie looked at him just right.

Mack, for the first time since winter, finally broke. He slammed his fist down on Derek's desk so hard that the joystick fell off and hung by its cord and a mug of water hit the carpet and made a slow dark impression shaped like a rain cloud. He slammed his fist down again and it made a small trough and the wood splintered. The underside of Mack's hand was nicked with blood. Derek's eyes went wide and his smile went away.

Through clenched teeth, Mack said, 'Roy, would you leave us alone?'

Roy, who looked disgusted, complied. He closed the door and his footsteps bled away in the hall.

Derek became cooperative and scared. Rosie was a tease, though, Mack had to understand that. What did she expect? She didn't *say* no and she teased him, like, all the time. It wasn't even that serious what happened. But yeah, okay—okay, maybe he'd tried his luck a bit too hard. But she was not *not* into it, hey.

'A bit too hard?' Mack repeated, incredulous.

A bit too hard.

Mack never went into more detail of his long conversation with Derek Murray. His expression was always too disgusted, and his skin looked fit to crawl right off. When it came to Rosie, Mack could hardly bear it. And he could not bear the pitiful excuse for a young man that Derek was, and his view of the world, which Mack found to be both belligerent and grotesque.

He couldn't even be bothered to take him to the station. He knew he couldn't charge him—not yet. Derek swore blind he didn't know where Rosie was; and he swore blind he didn't assault her. He certainly didn't rape her, because he hadn't got to have her that way anyhow. He'd just tried his luck a bit too hard maybe, that's all. It was just Roy's word against Derek's. And after it all happened, Derek hadn't set foot in the shop again until after Rosie went missing. And now Rosie *was* missing, and Mack couldn't ask her a thing about it. It was Roy's word against Derek's unpleasant face; and Roy had said, right opposite Mack in the booth that morning, that he couldn't testify against his own and only son.

'Rosie left town anyway, Mack,' said Roy. 'Can't we just move on? Please?'

Mack sat in Derek's sweaty swivel chair and wondered what to do as Derek stared at the wet carpet, tonguing his teeth. Mack had grilled and pushed and bored holes with his questions, and Derek just kept on swearing, as if his hand were on a Bible, and as if a Bible would mean anything in his sodden, godless world. He didn't know where Rosie was, and he was home all night when she went missing. Roy said that was true, as far as he could tell. Roy saw Derek go to bed. Derek's window didn't open wide enough for the cat to crawl out. Roy was up late in the lounge room, busying himself while Doe slept. Derek hadn't come out. Mack just shuddered at all of it.

'So you didn't see her again even one time after you assaulted her?'

'I didn't fucken *assault* her,' said Derek, again.

Mack had to stop himself from erupting entirely and putting damp kicks and punches into Derek's pasty frame, over and over, until he seeped into the carpet and down into the depths of the sunken house.

Mack took a deep breath and continued, with his calm police voice. 'You didn't see her again, not one time?'

'Nah. Or yeah—I saw her one time,' said Derek. His bottom lip trembled.

'When was that?' asked Mack.

'The next night.'

Mack waited. Derek licked at his teeth, and then his mouth curled inwards and unexpected whimpers came from somewhere in his throat.

'I seen her out the back of Woody's from my car. I just went to, like, I dunno, I was just there in my car. And I seen her. She was smoking out the back on that folding chair there. But Bart was with her.'

'Bart was there?' asked Mack.

'Yeah, he was there. She was talking to him, all upset,' said Derek, who was properly crying now, grizzly and pathetic.

'Bart was there listening to her?' asked Mack. 'What, was he consoling her?'

'Yeah,' said Derek, sobbing, wiping his eyes with his forearm. 'He was standing there with her. Consoling her, I guess, yeah.'

•

As I walked back along the riverbank, away from Davo, the rain started. It came in fast and hard. The sky had been blue when I left home. I hadn't considered my raincoat. But as I had neared the riverbank a mass of darkness appeared low beyond the mountain. And then the wind picked up as I turned from Davo and it licked the top of the river like teeth. Choppy waves sprang up as flowers do. Branches flapped like the wings of giant birds. The wall of inky cloud from beyond the mountain coloured the whole sky and covered the sun; and the oval glowed ahead, luminous white. It was the swiftest storm Goodwood had seen in many months.

Backflip and I started running up the bank as hailstones began to fall: handfuls of them thrown across the water. The rain was spliced among it—sharp stinging lines—but mostly it was hail. It bounced off the metal fence of the oval as we ran through the gate. It bleached the grass and gathered in the gutters of the toilet block. I thought of Mrs Gwen Hughes and her myriad crystals as the frozen ice fell and fell, and made a brief glacier of our town.

Backflip and I waited it out under the edge of the toilet block. I wondered about Davo Carlstrom. I imagined him sitting in the branch still, welcoming the flood, turning his face up to the deluge. I imagined he wouldn't mind if it pelted and stung him. *Do your worst*, he would have said to the opened sky.

And then it was over.

Just as quickly as it had come in, the dark mass rolled away, and steam rose off the concrete. The ice pellets lay scattered widely, spent and defrosting. The heavens broke with light again; the beams and rays were brilliant from behind the receding clouds. Backflip stood next to me, wet and panting. I sat down against the toilet block wall and turned my face up to the sun. Then I sat and admired the field of thick hailstones for as long as it took for the sound of sirens to arrive from somewhere in the distance.

It was not often that we heard sirens. Goodwood was not much of a place for an emergency. I listened to them and wondered what kind they were: police car, fire truck, ambulance. I put Backflip on her lead and we walked back towards town, slowly and then faster as the noise got louder.

We rounded the Goodwood Grocer and went along Cedar Street. The sirens bent in pitch as they neared us. I couldn't tell which direction they were coming from—for a minute it was back beyond the oval, and then it was straight ahead near the Wicko, and after it was left towards the train tracks and the school. Backflip pulled on the lead, excited.

There was Helen, up ahead, standing outside the news-agent, trying to work out the direction of the noise. She kept turning back and yelling at a person inside who I guessed was

Bill, because it was always Bill: 'No, I said *not* fire! I think it's the ambulance!'

And there was Bill as I walked past the door, hovering on the landing with his arms folded and his head down, shaking it as if disagreeing with the universe in general. Burly Joe was peering out from the doorway of Bart's Meats. Robin Clunes was standing just inside Bookworm, paralysed. Goodwood couldn't take another tragedy. It wasn't ready for the sound of sirens—of fire, or sickness, or crime. Not with *everything*.

Helen looked at me with her mouth closed as I rushed past.

'I think it's the ambulance,' she said.

I started to worry, too, as I got closer to our street, and the sirens stopped at what sounded like a close distance. When I rounded our corner past the Wicko, Val Sparks was standing in the doorway of the Vinnies, crossing herself, and Smithy had his hands on his hips next to Costa Karras and Mal West, who were all looking down our street. I saw the flashing lights. Blue and red. They were spinning off the houses around our house, but mostly off our house, which the ambulance was parked directly in front of.

My heart: it pounded.

Mum.

Her heart.

I started running, and Backflip, thinking it was a game, took the lead in her mouth and pulled sideways and forward with her ears back, gleefully. I felt sick in my stomach as

I approached the handful of people gathered near our front fence.

Mum was nowhere.

There was just Con and Althea, and Frankie Dodds from across the road, and Coral, who was clutching Myrtle.

Backflip took one look at Myrtle and jumped up to lick her face and Myrtle was absolutely delighted to see Backflip and made a whinny like a tiny horse. Coral squealed and turned her back on us, and I yanked Backflip down to the ground, apologising, and forgetting everything for a second. Forgetting where Mum was, or wasn't, and why our front door was still closed and it appeared so quiet.

I couldn't see Mum lying prone through the windows. I couldn't hear anyone yelling 'Clear!' before applying a defibrillator to her silent chest. Squinting, I could not make out the outline of a respirator lying useless on our living room carpet.

Then Big Jim came out from his house and the ambulance men followed, carrying a stretcher.

That's when I saw that Big Jim's ute was parked outside their house, since he'd been using his carport to build a new wooden compost box. That was why the ambulance had had to park outside our house. And Mum's car wasn't anywhere, come to think of it, except that it was, just at that moment, coming down the street with Mum in it, rolling down her window as she approached with a look of true terror on her face—terror which turned to relief when she saw me and

Backflip standing there safely, watching Fitzy on the stretcher, crumpled and blood-soaked.

Fitzy.

Big Jim was sallow. His eyes shone with fear. There were sweat beads on his upper lip and forehead and a mess of blood smeared all over his singlet and King Gees. One of the paramedics was making hand gestures to Big Jim, as if arguing, as he closed the ambulance doors with Fitzy tucked inside. But Big Jim wasn't going to have a bar of following in his ute, because a moment later the paramedic relented and opened the doors and Big Jim hopped in, taking Fitzy's hand in his own, and drawing it up to his mouth, kissing the back of it, as he crouched beside her gurney.

That was my enduring image of the two of them—with Fitzy's aliveness in doubt—as the doors closed again and the ambulance departed, lights flashing. It went around the corner, and a few moments later the siren went on again and warbled off into the distance towards Clarke.

Mum had parked facing the wrong way. She got out of the car and rushed towards us, taking me in a desperate hug, saying, 'Jeannie, what happened? Was that Fitzy?'

I told her that, yes, it was Fitzy.

'Oh God, Jean. For a minute I thought it was you. Is she okay?' The last bit she addressed not so much to me but to the gathered crowd.

Coral, by this time, had raised her voice above the murmurings and, with damp Myrtle still grasped against her daffodil cardigan, assured us that Fitzy was, at least, alive.

'She's alive. She left here alive.'

It was declared as if at royal court.

She was alive. Good old Fitzy.

Backflip panted, oblivious, smiling lovingly at Myrtle.

Mum—who had just popped up to the Bowlo to pick up a cardigan she'd left behind at the Fish Fry—held me in an awkward bear hug out on the street for a long time.

'Can you let go?' I said.

'Don't rush me,' she said. 'I'm not to be rushed.'

40

As it turned out, Fitzy had been taking measurements from the rain gauge. As soon as the storm had passed she couldn't contain herself. It was mostly hail, but there was rain, too. Sharp stinging drops of it. It was the only precipitation Goodwood had had in weeks. What would the rain gauge say?

At the store in Clarke, when they'd bought the thing, they'd had the choice of perspex or glass and Big Jim chose glass. It looked better, and had the feel of the beakers in science class when he was a boy.

He and Fitzy had mounted their rain gauge—a cylindrical glass tube with a glass funnel at the top that directed precipitation into a smaller central tube—on a small post at the back corner of their yard.

That afternoon, when the skies had cleared after the short storm, Fitzy trudged across the sodden grass and Myrtle followed delicately, as if not wanting to get her paws wet. So excited was she by the sudden advent of rain, and the prospect of a measurement, Fitzy forgot her helmet.

She approached the rain gauge and crouched down with her little writing pad in one hand and pencil in the other. She took her time and took her measurement—0 mm—and then, devastated, stood up to go back inside. But Fitzy stood up too fast, and a galaxy of silver stars swam in front of her eyes, as if someone had thrown a handful of sparkly sand at her face in slow motion. According to Coral, who dined out on the story, being the only one apart from Big Jim to hear the screams, Fitzy was head-spun and dazed when the birds swooped, one from each direction, the bigger magpie clipping her ear as she screamed and put her hands over her head in her own defence. Unbalanced, she fell, and there was momentary silence, and then the sound of breaking glass and Myrtle barking.

The magpies settled, one on the fence, and the other on the tree, and Fitzy, who had fallen against the rain gauge and knocked it off its post, continued to fall on top of it thoroughly, smashing the outer tube against the inner tube and conjuring a particularly sharp, knife-like shard from within which—as Fitzy's lower body landed—triumphed upwards into her popliteal artery.

Then came the screaming.

Big Jim, just home and enjoying a Toohey's New in front of *Wheel of Fortune*, ran out to find Fitzy in a soggy pool of blood and rain, and Myrtle yapping with terror.

Coral, who loved a drama much more than a calm day, heard the screams from her couch, where she was also watching *Wheel of Fortune*, and dialled 000.

Fitzy went as white as hail and responded with whimpers to the makeshift tourniquet Big Jim fashioned from his work shirt.

The magpies continued to swoop as he held her damply.

●

That night was dinner at Nan and Pop's, with us, Mack and Tracy and Jasper, and Nan's friend Shirl, who had been having a hard time with her loneliness and closed-angle glaucoma.

Nan roasted a chicken because no one wanted red meat since the discovery of Bart, and Nan thought everyone would be sick of fish. Mack, who had spent much of the day with Roy and Derek Murray, didn't mention any of it at the time. I recall him sitting next to Tracy and appearing lost in thought every so often, but no one was the wiser on any new developments, and everyone was beside themselves with what had happened to Fitzy.

By dinnertime, Fitzy was at Clarke Base Hospital and was—according to the latest update from Big Jim, who had called Mum—receiving a much-needed blood transfusion.

'Big Jim says she's O positive, which is the common one,' said Mum.

'That's very fortunate,' said Nan.

'Unbelievable,' said Mack. 'The woman's a walking time bomb.'

'And she has far too much hair for one person,' said Pop.

There followed a brief and comic history of Fitzy's numerous misadventures, including the flattening of the guardrail next to the bridge and the toppling of the pole outside the Vinnies as the most recent and dramatic examples.

Poor Fitzy. All she wanted was a bit of rain.

Talk moved along to the Fishing's The Funnest parade and everyone agreed it was the best one yet, and the best Fish Fry, too. Tracy said Jasper had not stopped parading around the house, and every time she asked him to stop—to rest or eat—he protested that he 'wasn't finished yet', and marched on in circles around the living room, dragging his toy platypus and requesting applause.

'Everyone needs a little applause on occasion,' said Nan, and proceeded to tell us of her visit to Mrs Bart, and how she and Jan were thinking of keeping the shop open and becoming butchers.

'Good on her,' said Mum, and Shirl whooped like it was the craziest thing anyone had ever heard.

'She could just put a "Mrs" in front of the sign and they wouldn't really have to change anything,' said Mum.

'I think she should call it "Flora's"', said Nan.

There were murmurs of agreement, which gave way to murmurs of resignation, and then Nan looked sad. Mack didn't say a thing about it. He ate his chicken and potatoes and drank more than he usually did in Reschs Pilsener.

'It's her birthday tomorrow,' said Nan. 'It's Mrs Bart's fiftieth.'

No one spoke, and the air felt uncomfortable and blue.

'And the awful thing is that she's terrified something's going to arrive for her—like a big present—from Bart. Or that she's going to find something if she looks around properly in the cupboards. She thinks he might've organised something for her. You know, *before*.'

'How awful,' said Mum.

'From beyond the grave,' said Shirl, quite spookily, like the host of a haunted house.

Mack looked up at Nan, curious.

'Why does she think he organised something?' he asked.

'Well, for her forty-fifth he had that wonderful piano delivered—right on the day. It came all the way from Victoria on a truck. And then there was the rose garden. He was so good at presents. And Mrs Bart's been going through the books and she says there's money missing from the takings tin in the office. Bart kept a good log of it and her and Jan are going through everything. There was five hundred dollars taken out a week or so before he drowned, and Bart had written "gift" in the ledger.'

'Oh, the dear sweet man,' said Shirl.

I looked at my plate.

'Five hundred dollars?' asked Mack.

I couldn't tell if he was looking at me or not. I didn't meet his eyes.

'He was such a generous man,' said Nan.

'Oh wow,' said Mum, 'that's very hard.'

'He had time for everyone,' said Shirl.

41

Mum and I went home that night and I wrote down in my blue notebook everything Nan had said at dinner. If Mack had said something pertinent I would've written that down, too. But he hadn't. And some things I didn't know until much later. He didn't mention Doe Murray and her trembling visit. He didn't mention Judy White, and the fight about money. None of us knew until much later that Terry White, on his way to Ballina, where he eventually moved, buried the metal tin with roses on it near the banks of the Bellinger River and left in it a photo of Rosie and a fistful of petals.

Mack didn't mention Roy or Derek Murray either. He didn't say how Derek had wept like a dreadful child. He didn't say how Roy had gone as red as blood and unburdened himself of everything he had been holding in since winter. And he didn't say how, without even having to think much about it, as Roy talked and talked in the back booth of Woody's, all of it made terrible and unnecessary sense to Mack as soon as he heard it.

Roy was as wet as the lake. He admitted it. He said, 'Bart knew,' and Mack asked, 'Knew what? About what Derek did to Rosie?' And Roy nodded. 'He knew.'

•

It had been the Friday before Rosie went missing; two days after Roy had found Derek forcing himself against her like a hungry animal. Roy had been up at the Bowlo, playing the pokies with Carl White and Mal West. He went up to the bar to get a round.

Bart was at the bar drinking and talking to Carmel Carmichael, who stood under the Biggest Catch plaque that celebrated Paulie Roberts.

Bart said, 'G'day, Roy.'

And Roy said, 'G'day, mate.'

And then, when Carmel Carmichael was filling the schooners and out of earshot, Bart turned to Roy and his amiable smile fell away.

'I saw Rosie White last night out the back of the shop,' he said. Roy went red. Bart lowered his head and crossed his arms. 'I can see you know what I'm talking about. I don't know what to do here, Roy. She's your employee, I understand you'd be concerned.'

Roy coughed and said, 'Of course.'

Then Bart looked away and said, 'I'm going to do what I can to help. I've just been to see Jude and I told her that. Now I'm thinking maybe you better talk to him before I do. And before I talk to Mack. I don't trust myself not to beat the living shit out of him, so I feel pretty stuck here, Roy. Rosie's a sweet kid and she hardly said anything at all. But I've seen some things before and I can read between the lines.'

Roy had never seen Bart look so serious. Then Carmel Carmichael set the beers down on the bar mat and continued talking, oblivious, 'It's mainly people trying to get their twenty-cent hook back that kills them. I tell them: if they're undersize and they're not hooked around the mouth, just snip the line and let them swim away.'

'Yeah, that's a tough call, isn't it?' Bart had said, taking a sip of his fresh beer.

Roy gathered his round, shaken, and went back to pushing his coins into the slot next to Carl White, thinking only of his awful only son.

•

'He knew,' Roy had said when they were in the booth. 'She didn't even have to tell him; he just knew.'

And Mack had looked across at Roy and said, 'And then you saw Bart at the lake?'

Roy didn't even protest. He didn't ask, 'How the hell did you know?' He didn't have anything left to hold back with.

It was true. Roy went fishing that Sunday, the same day as Bart did. He left early and went first to Clarke Bait & Tackle to buy a new rod. He pulled up on the browned grass near the boat wharves and was surprised that there was just one car there, and he was horrified when he realised that the car was Bart's. There he was, Bart McDonald, on his half-cabin cruiser only a hundred metres from the shore.

What was Roy thinking, coming to the lake on a Sunday? He'd been trying to avoid Bart, and Bart always fished on Sundays. Roy had been dodging him all week, ever since he'd had the word in his ear at the Bowlo. Roy had tried talking to Derek, just as Bart had asked him to, but Derek just drove off in his Kingswood. Roy was a failure as a father, as a man. Where had he misplaced his morals?

All he knew to do was to keep his head down and hope that the whole thing would disappear—just like Rosie had. Thank God she'd left. Good for her. But then it was just a hole where she used to be, and Derek's holes for eyes staring there, into nothingness. He had seen with his own eyes that his only son was going to rape Rosie White, right there in the dark shop. Roy could hardly utter the words, even to himself. He couldn't get the picture of it out of his mind. He was disgusted with his son and disgusted with himself.

Unfortunately, Bart was facing Roy's direction. If he'd had his back to him, Roy could've reversed out without him knowing. But Bart had just cut his engine and was standing on his boat, grimacing, and looking directly at Roy Murray.

Christ, thought Roy. What can I possibly say to this man? My friend. What can I possibly say? Roy went red and started sweating as he got out of his car and raised one hand in the air at Bart.

Bart was raising one hand too, but something about his face wasn't right, and with the other hand he was taking off his life jacket, like it was strangling him. He tore at it, and wrenched it off, as if the thing was made of fire and burning his chest. Roy kept his hand in the air and kept looking. He just looked, not really knowing what he was seeing.

Bart grappled with his life jacket and wrestled it off and it dropped down out of view. Then his knees went out from under him and landed on the edge of his boat. At the same time, his hand went to his chest in a fist and he beat himself there; and then the other hand went to the fist and held it. Roy, on the shore, was far away. But not so far that he couldn't see it. He saw Bart's face turn violently in on itself, and he saw Bart kneeling for a moment on the edge of his boat, as if in prayer, and then he saw Bart's hands, which didn't move from his heart as he went forward and over into the water.

For a moment, Roy froze. His hand stayed in the air. He was appalled at himself, and paralysed. Sweat covered his brow. Then he collected himself.

'Bart!' he yelled, and got no reply from the impression in the brown water that Bart had made when he went under.

Bubbles came up, and then more bubbles. Bart's boat rocked roughly in the water.

Roy went in.

He waded quickly, in his boots and his jeans and his jacket. The feel of the water was enough to cut his breathing and his lower half was arrested with cold. Ice seemed to drag his old legs down as he dived into the brown water. But Roy swam, thrashing. He propelled himself forward, out towards Bart's boat, which was already ghostly in its bobbing. It rose back and forth and made silver waves. By the time Roy reached it, all the bubbles were gone.

Roy duck-dived, down and under the water. He opened his eyes to see murky nothing. He closed them again, and almost swallowed water. His hands reached around, clawing for anything.

But Roy found nothing. He felt nothing. There was no arm or leg or log of Bart. There were no feelings left in his own body. Roy just went around in thrashing circles, gulping air and diving, rummaging about in the water, coming up for air, and eventually he was crying, and then he was sobbing, and then he was holding the edge of Bart's boat, shivering and wailing, the closest a live man had ever felt to drowning.

•

Mack sighed a big sigh as he sat there in the booth and the sun came in and lit up a big square of the lino.

'Why, Roy? *Why* didn't you say something? The whole town has been through hell wondering where he was, and you knew he was in the lake the whole time.' He was exasperated, drained.

Roy, who was weeping now, said, '*Derek*,' and then, between sobs, 'How would it've looked? I went back to the shore and I admit it: I sat down and I cried and cried. He was gone. There was no way he was coming up alive, by the time I'd've got to a phone to call anyone. But how would it've looked? He'd spoken to Jude. I didn't know if he'd told Mrs Bart, too, or you. I didn't know how many people he'd told about what Derek did.' Roy sobbed. 'And I was the only one out there. When he just fell off his boat and drowned. What would you have thought? That I was trying to protect my son. You would've thought that, wouldn't you? You would've thought that I'd gone there and done it to him. To protect my son.'

Mack stared off into space. He didn't know what he was supposed to say. He didn't know what he would've thought if Roy had turned up on that day back in August, with his awful story, as wet as the lake. He didn't tell Roy either way. And he didn't tell Roy that, as far as Mack could figure, Bart hadn't known anything about Derek at all.

As far as Mack could see, Bart had gone to Judy White and said, 'You better talk to your husband.' That was Carl White. Then Bart had stopped Roy Murray, when he was with Carl at the Bowlo, and said, 'You better talk to him first.'

Him.

Carl White.

All of it made complete and unnecessary sense to Mack as soon as he heard it. Bart hated Carl. He had seen things before, just like he told Roy at the Bowlo. He had seen the bruises on Judy White's thighs, years back in the hospital. He knew of the drunken carnality that Carl had subjected his darling Flora to, when he groped her near the bathrooms like some kind of animal. Bart knew that Carl White was unchecked and hideous. Who knew how far his foul hands had wandered?

And then Bart finds Carl's stepdaughter, Rosie White, distressed. She had always seemed dark and troubled, and why was that? He comes across her, upset, and she hardly says anything at all. Maybe she merely hints at something untoward. He reads between the lines. He puts two and two together and arrives at five.

Rosie just wants to *go*, so he says he'll help her with some money. He honours her by not telling anyone. She didn't want it spoken of. Rosie was not a talker. She was inscrutable and proud and brave. And Bart was so generous. He had time for everyone.

Mack didn't have the heart to tell Roy that, if Mack were a betting man, he would bet that Bart hadn't known anything at all about Derek Murray. Mack would've put five hundred dollars on the fact that Bart assumed that whatever was done to Rosie White was done to her by Carl. And those weeks—all the long weeks that Bart lay in the lake, dusting the silty floor, loosened of his own skin, devoured slowly by the fishes, while Goodwood, desperate for answers, sunk into itself like wet sand—all of it could've been avoided. All the while, Roy Murray could have given Goodwood the gift of a swift and merciful conclusion.

In the booth, Roy had looked back at Mack through smeared tears and said, 'Do you believe me?'

42

Fitzy got home from the hospital the following Thursday and spent her time convalescing in their back sunroom, with a view of where the rain gauge once stood.

'Val said she'd pray for me,' she said to Nan, chuckling, when Nan dropped off a batch of chicken soup. 'I said, "Val, don't pray for me, pray for rain!"' And then Fitzy gave Nan an update on the Commonwealth Government's drought assistance programs and read aloud from her printed material on the *Farm Household Support Act 1992*, expounding on how it would help her family of desiccated apple farmers in south east Queensland.

'The lake's never been so low,' said Fitzy. 'I was shocked to see it like that on the way back into town. Shocked!'

Fitzy was right. With the lack of rain, Grants Lake was at its lowest level on record: thirty-two per cent and dropping. Big Jim complained that he and Merv were having trouble reaching some of their favourite inlets, due to the bottom of the lake being too close to the bottom of their boat.

'The lower the water, the less the fishes,' said Big Jim.

'You'd think the less water there was, the easier it'd be to catch them,' I said. 'You know, because they have less room to hide.'

'You'd think, Jeannie. But you'd be wrong about that.'

Fish or not, on Friday I decided it was time for my first swim of the season at the river. I put on my striped swimmers and shorts and got my towel and phoned George, who was not home but out with Lucas Karras. So Backflip and I went alone, along Cedar Street where burly Joe was still doing his duty at Bart's Meats, and Roy Murray was behind the counter at Woody's. I was pleased not to see Derek there, but I didn't know the truly horrible things about Derek then, I just had my wary instincts about him. Roy Murray was standing in a puff of meat smoke as I walked past.

•

Backflip and I got to the corner near the oval in the high sun around the same time that Kevin Fairley left his north paddock and headed off with his dog, Remington, for a walk to the lake.

The cows mooed behind him, and Kevin mooed back. He felt better now that he'd been taking these long walks. He'd been having troubles with some off-flavours in his milk. It was a tasting a little cowy and a tad barny. He walked, lost in deep thoughts, trying to figure out a solution to the problem, and Remington trotted in the tall grasses and Paterson's curse, that terrible weed that grew outside the paddock fences and all the way to the water.

•

Backflip and I turned the corner at the Grocer and the oval fell out before us. On the grassy hill, near the gate towards the clearing, with a skip of my heart I saw someone sitting.

I let Backflip off the lead. She ran off in a sideways gallop with her nose down.

The figure on the hill was facing the other direction. I saw the golden hair and, as I got closer, the headphones as big as earmuffs.

Evie.

•

Kevin Fairley got to the edge of the tall grasses and let himself over the low wire fence, and Remington let himself under it. They walked along the side of the road that hugs the base of the mountain. They'd popped out near the rest stop, not far from the bridge. Not far from the lake.

Up ahead, ravens pecked at the ground where the kangaroos lay flattened. There was a small group of them, clawing the bitumen. But Remington was an old dog and not one for playing chasings. Kevin didn't worry about him plodding along without being on the lead. He was a good old faithful cattle dog.

•

Evie and I walked from the oval along the side of the river without much talking. She looked at me sideways and smiled and looked down again and I looked at her sideways and smiled and was nervous.

Backflip ran ahead to see the cows, and the birds were louder than ever overhead, alive with spring, alive with the bright day.

We got to the clearing and Backflip rolled around on her back, having found no cows, and Evie traced her fingers around the initials on the trunk of the willow, and I lay my towel down beside it, in the shade. Finally we both sat down next to each other and I felt like all the birds in the trees were in my chest: fluttering and beating and singing.

•

Kevin saw up ahead, on the side of the bridge, two men looking over into the water. They'd pulled their ute up on the shoulder on the other side of the road. The tray was full of fishing gear: rods and buckets and a big blue esky. One man was pointing and the other man had his hands on his hips, and then he moved them up to the back of his head. They didn't see Kevin as he came up behind them; and the ravens didn't move from their pecking and scraping at the innards on the road.

'What's up, fellas?' said Kevin, and the two men turned around. They appeared out of breath. They had no reason to be breathless. Their car was just across the road, so they hadn't come far. But they were very excited by something, and not making much sense.

'It's a car!' said one man.

'What car?' asked Kevin.

'In the lake,' said the other man.

Kevin Fairley looked down to where they were pointing. Into the brown water.

It was the back of a car. Its front end was submerged completely; there was no bonnet or front doors or back doors to see. There was only an exhaust pipe, and a number plate, and a bumper. It was all bronzed and silty. Except it hadn't been brown to begin with. In some places an off-white paint colour came through, and Kevin thought of the off-flavour in his milk.

He looked back at where the car would've come from. Goodwood.

Then he looked at the place where the guardrail should've been, before poor old Fitzy had knocked it over. There was nothing there to stop a car from flying over into the lake. How was anyone ever going to have the heart to tell Fitzy?

The ravens *caaaw*ed at Remington, who watched them from his sedentary position with elderly bemusement. The two men were beside themselves.

'It's a fucken car!' the first man kept saying. 'There must be someone in there! What should we do? Where's a phone?'

Kevin Fairley looked at the ravens and imagined the kangaroos that always pronked out of the bush there and scared the daylights out of passing cars. He thought of a car swerving to miss one, and how that might turn out. Looking down at the back of the car in the lake, he could see how that had turned out.

'I don't think there's any hurry, boys,' he said to the two men. 'That car's been there a long time.'

One of the men started striding back to the ute.

'Let's find a phone,' he said to his friend, and the other man followed. He yelled back at Kevin, almost hysterical, 'We're gonna find a phone!' And they sped off towards Goodwood.

Kevin stood and Remington sat and they looked down at the brown water, which was lower than it had ever been in all the records. Low enough to reveal this car, which had swerved and flown and crashed and sunk. Kevin felt a misery rising from the very depths of him. He couldn't help but think of his dear Susan, ailing and passing; and of Bart, coughed up by the marshes. And of Bart's missing Corolla, which he could see now, sticking out of the low water.

•

By the time the sun had set that night, the authorities had pulled the Corolla out of the lake and found Rosie inside it. They didn't know it was Rosie right away, but Mack did. She had to travel all the way to the city and spend a day with the forensic pathologist before she was formally declared as herself.

When the authorities went through the car they found a few things, sodden. What was left of Rosie's bag, what was left of Rosie's army coat, which had slithered off her and seemed by then to be made of green pulp. In her disposal store backpack was a plastic zipped compartment—and in that, drowned and decomposing, was five hundred dollars.

Ballina was generally agreed to be Rosie's planned destination. There were not many diverging theories on that. The contention was that Rosie was heading towards her cousin Tegan, who she was so fond of. She could've got a job under the Big Prawn, far away from the Derek Murrays and Carl Whites that repulsed her.

By nightfall, Mrs Bart understood why Bart had lied to her about the Corolla. Mack went around expressly to tell her. Pearl was watering the horses and Mrs Bart sat down and stared and Jan said, 'God. *Bart*. He really was something, wasn't he, Flora? Imagine! And *that's* why he said the car would probably turn up again. He probably just loaned it to her so she could leave, and then—oh, goodness me. That poor girl.'

Mrs Bart—Flora—just stared. She didn't seem pleased or displeased. She didn't seem surprised or unsurprised. She just said blankly, 'I need to see Judy White. I feel compelled.'

Flora reversed the Mazda out of the drive and Mack reversed the police car and followed her for a part of the way down the hill. Then he pulled over and stopped on the side of the road. The mountain towered above him and he felt hot and sick. He rolled down his window and the blessed breeze flowed in, like water. It was almost as if he had been in the lake this whole time himself. He felt drenched and boggy and gulped at the air with his lungs. Then he opened the door of the police car and vomited a river into the loose gravel.

•

I didn't know any of it yet, when I was sitting on my beach towel next to Evie. I didn't know that the next morning I would be sitting on my bed, holding Rosie's MISSING sign for most of the day, and on many other days after. Her inscrutable face: black and white, and stuck in time. *Please help us find Rosie*, said Terry's sign, next to the relevant phone numbers that nobody ever called. I did not know all the things I would feel, or all the feelings Goodwood would endure, or how the brown water would've felt to Rosie as it seeped in through the seals of the Corolla and into her hollow lungs. On the beach towel, with Evie, there was just the sound of the river, running ceaselessly towards the lake, and the silty earth in it, along with the fish; and the birds above us, all singing.

Evie reached out her arm and put her hand on the top of my knee.

I breathed in and looked at her, so relieved that she was touching me.

She looked back at me and I died.

I put my hand on top of her hand.

Evie paused and seemed to think for a moment, and then, without any expression, she drew me forward, and lay back as she did. I was above her. And without thinking, I did what I wanted. I kissed her. On her mouth, and her neck—and when I kissed her neck she shivered and smiled.

I thought of diamonds as I took off her clothes. In the dappled shade, I thought of the little lamp twinkling in her hallway and the mirror ball at the Bowlo, spinning slow stars around the walls.

Evie unbuttoned her jeans and pulled her old T-shirt over her head. The skin at the top of her leg had goosebumps when I kissed her there, and more when I put my mouth higher. Later, when I found her with my fingers, and felt all there was of her, I was full in my chest with a luminous light; and it swelled with the birds and the wings and the heat at the top of my throat and down to my lungs in a blaze. And Evie—in front of all the trees and all the day—buried her face in my neck and breathed loud and heavy against my ear, and I closed my eyes and moved with her, and behind my eyelids was a single flash, glowing, and everything else in the whole world fell quiet for her breathing.

Acknowledgements

T hank you to Annette Barlow, Siobhán Cantrill, Ali Lavau, Andy Palmer—and to all the good people at Allen & Unwin who worked so hard and well at bringing this book into the world.

Thank you to my mum and my amazingly supportive friends. For some particular inspiration on the subject of adoption, I thank Elizabeth Elliott; and for some particular inspiration on dogs, I thank my dog, Jones.

Thank you to Zoë Bell.

Most of all I give thanks to Richard Walsh—for friendship, guidance, and the gift of encouragement.